RECKER'S CHANCE

SAVAGE STARS BOOK 7

ANTHONY JAMES

Illustration © Tom Edwards
TomEdwardsDesign.com

DARK OF THE VOID

I hope you enjoy this, the last part in the Savage Stars series. Once the final page is turned and you're ready to delve into the future of this universe, why not check out book 1 of the follow-on series – **Dark of the Void -** available now from Amazon stores.

Anthony James

TOKLADAN – DEKA-L SYSTEM

The Daklan planet Tokladan was a sphere of drab red stone and sombre yellows, with surface temperatures and an atmosphere capable of supporting life. Not that life had existed here before the Daklan arrived more than a century ago, set up their extensive industrial and military complexes, and settled in their tens of millions.

Now, the surface facilities numbered over a hundred and, from space, they appeared like patches of dull grey, out of place amongst the planet's natural colours. The Daklan appreciation of beauty was different to that of humans, and the aliens lived without complaint in these boxy cities of slab-sided factories and warehouses, their families housed in adequately sized units, all edges and corners.

Tokladan saw few visitors from the Human Planetary Alliance, but those who came invariably returned home with a feeling of immense relief, as though they had escaped a failed brutalist architect's nightmare vision of a perfect future.

Despite their acceptance of tedium, the Daklan didn't actively seek it out. The reason for their presence on Tokladan could be found beneath the surface, where lay boundless quantities of high-grade tenixite, an ore which could be refined into the ternium required for a thousand applications both civilian and military.

On this day, and ten million kilometres from the planet, a particle wave appeared, formed by the transit of a spaceship approaching at lightspeed. Within a second, the wave was detected by one of the deep space satellites positioned around the planet and the data analysed. Having determined that the inbound vessel was many times larger than anything in the Daklan or HPA fleets, an alarm was sent to the local defence force.

A dozen ravager class destroyers, along with two desolator heavy cruisers, broke from their orbital positions and sped towards the origin point of the particle wave. Meanwhile on the planet, the inhabitants reached for their injectors of Frenziol-13 and stabbed themselves with needles. Everyone, no matter how young, was given a shot and the only variation was the size of the dose.

From lightspeed emerged a warship of immense proportions. Shaped like a cube with eighteen-thousand-metre edges, the Lavorix ship *Ixidar* was fitted with five huge cannons, one protruding from each of its six faces, with the final barrel having been destroyed in a recent engagement at the planet Tronstal.

For several seconds, the *Ixidar* hung in place, like it had all the time in the world. The Daklan were not meek opponents and two lightspeed missiles, one launched by each of the desolators, emerged within the Lavorix ship's energy shield. Twin flashes of plasma followed the impacts, the detonations leaving angry holes in the *Ixidar*'s armour.

At once, the massive warship vanished into lightspeed and reappeared a fraction of a second later, this time within half a million kilometres of the two desolators. With a burst of savage acceleration, the *Ixidar* raced directly for the Daklan warships, rotating steadily about its vertical axis as it did so.

The two desolators fired their enormous Terrus cannons, sending hardened slugs of alloy at the approaching warship, though the projectiles didn't travel rapidly enough to stand much hope of impacting given the intervening distance. No such limitation affected the *Ixidar* and it discharged its facing cannon. A sphere of dark energy concealed one of the desolators for a split second and when it disappeared, the Daklan spaceship's armour and the edges of its ternium propulsion modules had been stripped away and turned into dust.

The *Ixidar*'s rotation brought another gun to bear and the second desolator was hit by the same energy burst and with the same outcome. Already out of the fight, the two stricken vessels banked away, their external armaments destroyed.

Still accelerating, the Lavorix warship attained a velocity far greater than anything its opponents could match. One of the ravagers fired a dozen missiles and then it was obliterated by a third shot from the *Ixidar*.

As it approached Tokladan, the Lavorix spaceship

slowed and then adjusted course to bring it into orbit, fifty thousand kilometres above the planet's surface. Wary of lightspeed missiles, the *Ixidar* shifted erratically on and off its orbital track, its crew having learned that the Daklan warheads could only reliably bypass its energy shield when the vessel was stationary.

A few minutes passed, during which the ravagers and the Tokladan conventional ground batteries thew everything they had at the *Ixidar*. Each missile impact produced a faint glow from the huge spaceship's energy shield and no more.

Seemingly unconcerned by the attacks, the *Ixidar* continued its orbit for several minutes. Then, it fired its Extractor at one of the main industrial complexes. Protected by the Frenziol-13 and their innate, partial resistance to the weapon, most of the Daklan survived and those who did not were killed by the shock of agony, rather than by the leeching energy itself.

With its life batteries near empty, the *Ixidar* continued circling the planet, while the Lavorix technicians studied the data from the first attack and considered how best to adjust the weapon so the next discharge would be cleanly fatal.

On Tokladan, the Daklan could do nothing but wait.

CHAPTER ONE

FOUR HOURS after its capture by Captain Carl Recker and his crew, the warship *Gorgadar* emerged from its Gateway into the Kobin-15 system, way out beyond the star's fifteenth and outermost planet. Layered doses of Frenziol masked, without completely deadening, the thumping pain which accompanied this method of travel. Technology had its benefits, yet always with an accompanying downside to remind its users that the manipulation of nature and physics came with a price.

Recker swore – something he did so often he wondered if he should get a list of oaths tattooed on his forehead to save him the effort of repeating them – and clenched his fists. He couldn't wait for the pain to subside and barked out orders for his crew to report.

"Scans clear, sir," said Lieutenant Jo Larson.

"Nothing on the fars," said Lieutenant Adam Burner a few moments later.

The *Gorgadar*'s sensor feeds were displayed on a huge

screen which covered much of the forward bulkhead and curved around the command console. On those feeds, Recker saw stars and darkness.

"Let the fun and games begin," he said. "Open a channel to the Sapphire station and let them know we're here."

"I'm requesting a channel now, sir," Larson confirmed.

Twenty seconds passed. "What's keeping them?" Recker growled.

"They've accepted the request. I've told them who we are and what we've brought with us," said Larson. "The man on the other end – a Lieutenant Vince Vickers - sounds stressed."

"Anything we don't know about?" asked Recker. "Or is it just because a 29000 metre Lavorix warship turned up to ruin his breakfast?"

"I think it's what you just said, sir," said Larson.

Recker sat back and the cracked leather of his chair made a tearing sound. The eighty-kilometre aura around the *Gorgadar*, which had killed its original crew, had also made all the biological matter on the warship age about a thousand years. Of course that was a figure and a diagnosis Recker had pulled from his ass – nobody onboard had the faintest idea what had happened, and even Corporal Suzy Hendrix's medical box only spat out failure reports when it was plugged into one of the thousands of dead Lavorix which were scattered throughout the interior.

As for the Lavorix replicators, a few braver members of the human and Daklan platoon had attempted to sample the enemy chow, but the machines would only vend a foul-smelling thick liquid more akin to crude oil than anything edible. Clearly the replicator storage tanks had been just as much affected by what many of the soldiers were calling the *death sphere*.

"I'd like a channel to Fleet Admiral Telar," Recker said.

Since capturing the *Gorgadar* out in the RETI-11 system, Recker and his crew had worked hard to familiarise themselves with the warship's operation, finally discovering how to access and activate the Gateway hardware not long before embarking on this return to HPA space.

During those four hours, Recker had ordered many transmissions sent to the Lancer base on Earth, something which Burner and Larson accomplished by routing through the accompanying warship *Vengeance*'s comms system. Until a thorough audit of the *Gorgadar*'s comms system was completed, it seemed best to limit the data going through its hardware in case it synched with other members of the Lavorix fleet.

According to Lieutenant Burner's estimates of the travel time, it was certain that the outbound comms had not yet arrived at a receiving station, which made the situation all the more infuriating since the *Gorgadar* was equipped with enormously capable FTL amplifiers which they couldn't use until the risks were mitigated.

With everything that had gone on – the *Ixidar*'s destruction of the allied fleet at Tronstal and the *Vengeance*'s subsequent voyage to RETI-11 - Recker wasn't sure what Telar's reaction would be, and the uncertainty was putting him on edge.

"Lieutenant Vickers is trying to reach the Fleet Admiral, sir."

Recker's frustration threatened to boil over and he took a deep breath. Although the *Gorgadar* was a few hundred million kilometres from the Sapphire station, its incredible sensor arrays obtained a recognizable image of the structure and Recker's eyes lingered on the slowly turning cylinder, with its square ends which had always made him think of a giant alloy bolt. Unlike some of the other space stations, Sapphire didn't orbit a planet. It had propulsion, but its deep space arrays functioned better if it was left stationary, as it was now.

"I've got the Fleet Admiral for you, sir," said Larson.

"Put him on the bridge speakers," said Recker. "I've got some news for him."

"And what kind of news would that be, Carl?" asked Telar. The words were spoken mildly, though only a fool would have missed the undertones of anger and disappointment. "And where the hell have you been?"

"We've been to Meklon space and out of easy comms reach," said Recker. "We captured the *Gorgadar* and travelled by Gateway to the Sapphire station."

Telar went quiet, doubtless considering which of a hundred questions he should ask first. In the end, he went for the simplest one.

"How did you capture the *Gorgadar*?"

Recker gave the summary and again came the silence.

"You say the Ancidium is coming," said Telar at last.

"We lack absolute proof, but it appeared on the Laws of Ancidium battle network for a short time after we boarded the *Gorgadar* and it was moving across Meklon space. Presumably, it was gathering the members of the Lavorix fleet still deployed across the spheres. Then, it dropped off the battle network and no further communication has reached the *Gorgadar*."

"What we're facing? What is the Ancidium?"

"We don't know, sir. We have spent four hours on the *Gorgadar* and that time was occupied figuring out how to tie in the star charts and the Gateway hardware so that we could come home. I planned to begin investigation of the other onboard systems from here in the Kobin-15 system."

"And you chose that location because of the death sphere?"

"Yes, sir. We can route our comms through the Sapphire satellite while remaining far from our planets."

"So many unanswered questions," said Telar. "On another occasion I would enjoy the challenge. Not now." He sighed, a long, drawn out exhalation that carried with it the weight of a hundred billion souls. "The *Ixidar* is currently orbiting one of the Daklan worlds – a place called Tokladan. It arrived while you were off grid."

It didn't take a genius to guess what the Lavorix were doing at Tokladan. "The enemy are testing their Extractor?" asked Recker.

"That's exactly what they're doing. The *Ixidar* is circling the planet and hitting the Daklan population centres."

"How many attacks and with what result?"

"So far, the *Ixidar* has fired its Extractor three times and on each occasion the Daklan have lost a few thousand people – mostly the older members of the population, or those with medical issues."

"Shock deaths," said Recker.

"That is what the early reports suggest," Telar agreed.

"The Extractor isn't working as the Lavorix intend," said Recker. "They'll stay there until it is and then they'll come to our other worlds."

"You have the *Gorgadar*, Carl. Which of our planets are detailed within its star charts?"

"I was coming to that, sir." Recker felt a sudden reluctance, such was the magnitude of his earlier discovery. "The Lavorix have entries for Ravel, Bronze, Basalt and Future. Added to those are coordinates for the Daklan worlds Loterle, Videze and Terrani."

Telar's intake of breath was audible. "Terrani? That's the Daklan's first world!"

"I saved the worst till last," said Recker. "Earth is on the list as well."

"Shit," said Telar. He didn't swear often, so when he did it had a far greater impact. "This might be the end, Carl."

"Yes, sir, it might be. However, I don't think the Lavorix know what they've found. I believe their charts contain these planets as points of interest, rather than as confirmed destinations. The enemy have many other such places marked on their charts."

"They plan to visit each in turn," said Telar. "How many planets are on those charts?"

"One hundred and seventy," said Recker.

"With the Ancidium and *Ixidar* working together and using their Gateway generators, they will soon locate our worlds."

"That depends on how long it takes the *Ixidar*'s crew

to adjust the Extractor, sir," said Telar. "And if the Ancidium is in Meklon space, it might be delayed for a considerable time if it is gathering resources."

"Aside from the *Gorgadar*, we have no aces up our sleeves, Carl," said Telar. "Our weapons labs are pursuing numerous avenues, some of which may eventually bear significant fruit."

"But nothing soon."

"Nothing soon enough," Telar confirmed.

"My crew and I will learn the functions of the *Gorgadar*, sir," Recker promised. "And then we will fly it to Tokladan and destroy the *Ixidar*. If we are successful, perhaps it will reset the enemy's Extractor research and buy us some time."

"We had planned an attack on the enemy warship, in the form of a lightspeed missile barrage from the edges of DEKA-L," said Telar. "Gathering the fleet will require several more days, and the Daklan do not possess unlimited numbers of annihilators, desolators, or indeed lightspeed missiles. Their fleet cannot withstand another blow like it suffered at Tronstal. This was to be our last chance."

"Can our HPA warships be modified to carry lightspeed missiles?" asked Recker. "Like we did for the *Vengeance*?"

"Work is underway," said Telar. "Again, we are limited by time and resources. The Daklan can't produce their missiles fast enough and their new manufacturing centres are not yet onstream."

"We'll need all the warships and lightspeed missiles we can muster once the Ancidium arrives," said Recker.

"Do you believe the *Gorgadar* can defeat the *Ixidar*?" asked Telar softly.

Recker didn't answer for a moment – he closed his eyes and breathed in deeply. The *Gorgadar*'s scents of staleness and decay intensified in his nostrils, along with another entirely unidentifiable odour which he'd convinced himself was a part of the death sphere. When Recker opened his eyes again, the miasma enveloping the warship seemed stronger than before, turning everything dim like fog on a dark winter's morning. Then, the darkness shrank away as if it couldn't tolerate his sight of it, and returned once more to his periphery. Many a time, Recker had asked himself if it would claim him as soon as he laid down to sleep, in the same way it had claimed the Daklan soldier Unvak.

"The *Gorgadar* is the greatest of the Laws," said Recker. "In the right hands, it can defeat the *Ixidar*. Against the Ancidium, I don't know."

Telar didn't ask Recker to confirm if the warship was in the right hands. "Very well. Learn what you can about the *Gorgadar* and then go to Tokladan. I will send you the details we have about the enemy's orbital position. Do what you must."

"Yes, sir."

The channel went dead.

"What did he mean by *do what you must*?" asked Lieutenant Eastwood.

"We can't allow the *Ixidar* to complete its adjustment of the Extractor," said Recker.

"That doesn't answer my question, sir."

"Yes, it does," said Recker. He turned and saw understanding dawn on Eastwood's face.

"Oh shit. He can't ask us to..."

"He can and he did," snapped Recker. "It won't come to that, because we're going to defeat those Lavorix bastards."

"Destroy the Destroyer," said Larson.

"We have the *Gorgadar*. The Prime," said Recker. "We are going to study its hardware and then we will finish the Laws of Ancidium. After that, we'll deal with the Ancidium itself. I've had enough of this war and I'm damned if I'm going to fail after coming so far."

"Hell, no!" said Burner.

"What are you all waiting for?" asked Recker "Get on with it!"

His crew turned to their consoles and Recker did likewise. The respite he'd hoped for wasn't on offer and the pressure hadn't lessened one little bit. With time against him, Recker joined his crew in their efforts.

CHAPTER TWO

"THE BIG QUESTION is whether our shield will hold up against the *Ixidar*'s disintegration cannons," said Eastwood, ten minutes after the comm with Telar had ended.

"That's one of the big questions," said Recker. "Do you have any theories?"

"Only guesses, sir," said Eastwood. He shrugged like the difference wasn't significant. "If our shield doesn't block the enemy attacks, we're going to lose. Otherwise, we stand a chance."

"I assumed we were just going to mode 3 on top of the *Ixidar* and see if the death sphere kills everyone," said Burner.

"That's the hope, Lieutenant," said Recker. "Unfortunately, we don't know if the aura surrounding the *Gorgadar* is still effective. We lost Unvak, but it's possible he died from too much Frenziol and without taking his body to proper medical facilities we can't be sure one way or the other."

"Plus it's not easy to choose a precise mode 3 destination simply by tapping on the tactical screen," said Aston. "We know we can program in an exact arrival point, but that takes additional time – and by that point the enemy ship may be elsewhere. Particularly if they're jumpy because of the lightspeed missile hits they've taken so far."

Recker nodded his agreement. "To conclude – we're not about to rely on something which is so uncertain." He smiled thinly. "But don't for a moment think I'd be upset if we could mode 3 right up to them and have their entire crew die as easily as that."

Now that Burner had brought it up, Recker's mind turned over the idea again. The more he thought about it, the less likely it seemed that the *Ixidar*'s crew would be fooled by a mode 3 attack. Doubtless they were aware of what had befallen the *Gorgadar* and therefore they'd be wary about coming too close. On the positive side, this time it would be the enemy doing the running and that would hopefully bring opportunities for Recker to exploit.

"Commander Aston, what does your preliminary search through the weapons menu show?" She'd had a few minutes before the Gateway opened, but that was it.

Aston looked up. "Some of it you know from earlier, sir. We've got missile launchers – 180 clusters of twelve, just like the *Aeklu*. We have a single, non-adjustable nose-mounted particle beam which is currently showing offline, an Extractor – again showing offline - and something called a decay pulse. That one's offline as well and I think it's linked to the Extractor. I don't know why they're connected."

"Is there anything on this damned ship that's functioning?" asked Recker.

"I think everything's in full working order, sir. Apart from the original crew, of course. The *Gorgadar*'s onboard systems have been set up in a completely different manner to those on the *Aeklu* – if I had to guess I would say the technology is much more advanced."

"That's the same feeling I get," said Recker. "The trouble is, *more advanced* doesn't necessarily mean better."

"This is the prime Law of Ancidium, sir," Aston reminded him. "Of course it's going to be better."

"Point taken, Commander. Can you figure out how to activate the weapons?"

Aston thumbed over her shoulder. "You might need to speak to Lieutenant Eastwood about that. He already told us that the *Gorgadar*'s propulsion is something new. These weapons are tapping into it for power and since there's none being made available, they're showing offline."

"I'll speak to him," said Recker, climbing from his seat.

The pilot controls for the *Gorgadar* weren't difficult to understand and he felt he could spare a few minutes over by the engine station. He crossed the bridge, glad the soldiers had taken the Lavorix bodies away before the Gateway opened.

"Commander Aston sent you, did she?" asked Eastwood with a gruff laugh.

Recker immediately picked up on the other man's mood. "You're excited about something."

"Damn right I am! I've just this moment found something – and it might be incredible!"

"Tell me what it is."

Eastwood's station was fitted with a single curved screen, which was almost two metres wide. Tables, charts and diagnostic outputs covered the display and the language module in Recker's helmet placed an overlay inside his visor that attempted to replicate the visual data. The result was far from perfect - the alien symbols flickered rapidly and the processor utilisation gauge for Recker's suit computer nudged up to ninety percent.

"These numbers here relate to our current propulsion output," said Eastwood, poking the screen unsympathetically hard. "The ternium modules aren't in an overstressed state, so the output is recognizable. High, but recognizable. Now watch this."

Using his index finger, Eastwood moved a slider on his panel from one end of its runner to the other. At once, the background engine note deepened to a pulsing, regular beat that Recker could feel in his bones.

"The numbers went up," said Recker, playing dumb.

"We just switched into low overstress," said Eastwood. "Watch again." He pressed a grey button, flush to the panel and just beneath the slider.

The pulsing ended, but the depth of bass intensified to almost below the threshold of hearing.

"And this is with the propulsion running at idle!" said Eastwood, loudly over the increased background noise.

"The particle beam came online!" said Aston. "Its secondary status is *modulating*."

"Any idea what that means?"

"No, sir."

"What about the other weapons?" asked Recker.

"They're not available, sir."

"I'm not finished yet," said Eastwood. "Look at this."

Recker turned and the expression in the other man's face was enough to instil fear and excitement. It was the same feeling he always got when he knew something monumental was about to happen.

"What else is there, Lieutenant?"

"I don't quite know, sir." Eastwood hovered his finger over a second button, this one identical to the first. "This button activates superstress mode."

"What will happen when you push it?"

"The *Gorgadar* didn't come with a manual, sir."

"Do it."

Eastwood pressed his finger confidently on the button and the bass of the propulsion fell away. In its place was a sound that made Recker think of a dying man's last breath – of air escaping through a part-constricted throat, yet magnified infinitely until it came from all around, both quiet yet unavoidably present and impossible to ignore. His body reacted, tightening his skin

"What the hell?" said Eastwood.

At first, Recker thought his engine man was expressing surprise at the change in propulsion sound, but then he noticed that Eastwood was staring intently at his screen, with his eyebrows raised so high they'd vanished from sight above the window of his helmet visor.

Recker leaned in closer and the language module did its work. The numbers had increased, but without a point of reference, he didn't understand what they represented. On the right of the display, a huge table of digits was changing rapidly and it was this table which had got Eastwood so interested.

"This is incredible, sir!"

"I need specifics, not exclamations, Lieutenant," said Recker. "What have we got and how can we use it?"

"I'm examining the readouts, sir. I need a moment."

"I've got one green light out of two on the decay pulse!" said Aston. "I'm not sure what else we need in order to activate the weapon."

"What about the Extractor?" said Recker. "That's our best chance for an easy win over the *Ixidar*."

"Offline," said Aston. "I think there's something else..." She brought her face closer to her screen.

"What is it?" asked Recker.

"I'm checking something. I'll let you know if it's important, sir."

"Fine," Recker muttered, turning back to the engine station. "Lieutenant Eastwood, I need you to tell me what this superstressed propulsion state means."

"I don't have a definite answer for you, sir. However, I've got an idea and I'll show you what I think."

Eastwood entered a query on one of the keypads and a profile diagram of the *Gorgadar* appeared on the screen. He entered another query and several square areas – taking up much of the warship's interior – became highlighted in blue. Other, much smaller areas, became highlighted in red.

"See the readouts from these blue areas?" said Eastwood, pointing at his screen. "They're exceptionally high, but consistent with the overstress output levels we saw on the *Aeklu*. However, we're unable to draw on the power of these modules any longer."

"Why not?" Recker's curiosity hadn't gone anywhere

and he tried to make sense of the data on the screen. Understanding would come with time, but he lacked Eastwood's skill and experience when it came to interpreting propulsion readings.

"Because all the output of these blue modules is being channelled into the red ones." Eastwood was building to something, that much was clear. "The readings from these red modules are like nothing I've come across before. I'd say the original ternium modules have changed into a completely new state." He blew out a pent-up breath and paused, like he wasn't sure what to say next. "Their output indicates a step-change from not just ternium, but from overstressed ternium as well. These superstressed propulsion modules could likely power every single planet in the alliance without the drain causing so much as a flicker on the needle. Unfortunately, there's a problem. Or maybe there's a problem."

Recker might have lacked Eastwood's experience, but he had plenty of intuition when it came to technology. "The output from these overstressed blue modules is what's holding the superstressed modules stable," he said.

"Yes, sir. I think that's exactly what's happening."

Eastwood poked the same button on his console. For a time, nothing happened, but then the red modules began turning blue, one by one, over the course of twenty seconds. The final module went blue, turned red again and then back to blue. The two men stared at it.

"That one didn't want to switch off," said Recker.

"Which is what I feared," said Eastwood, his expression pained. "I don't know if the *Gorgadar* is an experimental warship as such, but I'm convinced the Lavorix haven't totally mastered the superstress."

"Do I need to ask what might go wrong?"

"If even one of those modules went critical, I think we'd be facing an event that makes the Dark Bomb look tiny in comparison," said Eastwood.

"So what did the Lavorix hope to achieve?" asked Recker. "I can understand the pursuit of technology, but it's not something you test out on your capital warship."

"I'll keep digging, sir. If we had HPA hardware installed on the bridge, I'd find the answers a lot quicker. As it is, I'm dealing with the language module delay as well as an unfamiliarity with the hardware."

"The *Gorgadar* isn't likely ending up in a maintenance yard anytime soon, Lieutenant. What you have here isn't going to be changed out for HPA kit."

"I know it, sir," said Eastwood. He looked suddenly tired and then his face hardened. "My home is on Basalt. I didn't say before, but I'm going to become a grandfather in a couple of months. I heard about it back on Ivisto, but kept my mouth shut in case my good news somehow stirred up a million bucketsful of cosmic shit that came and landed on us."

"Congratulations on your news. I thought you didn't believe in luck."

"I tell myself that, and mostly it's true. But this is different – this is family and my daughter's got a baby coming. Suddenly there's no separation between them down there on Basalt and what's happening up here in space."

Recker rested his hand on Eastwood's shoulder.

"You're in the best place to help them, Lieutenant. And you're the best man to do it."

"I'll get back to the console, sir," said Eastwood. "This isn't going to figure itself out."

The short conversation gave Recker a greater sense of resolve – it was a reminder of exactly what was at stake. When he talked numbers – the *billions* who were killed on Fortune, and the *millions* on Tokladan – it lost any sense of meaning, like an amorphous blob of people had vanished from the universe. The pain of it was there, but it wasn't so easy to relate. Sometimes it took a real in-the-face example of the consequences to drive home the reality.

He returned to his seat and found Aston staring at him in the way she always did when she was reading his mind. This time, she kept her thoughts to herself. Still, she had something else to say.

"I made a discovery." Aston's smile was one of uncertainty. "And I think I know what killed the *Gorgadar*'s crew."

"Tell me."

"When Lieutenant Eastwood switched the propulsion into superstress, the Extractor module powered up but without giving an option to target and fire. I ran a check on the list of tie-ins and discovered that it's linked to something else – another module called the destabiliser. That destabiliser was charging up – *slowly* charging up - while the engines were in superstress."

"Any idea what it does?"

"It's been fired several times before, sir, with no indication what the results were. I can't be sure from the data when the last discharge happened, but it produced an error log."

"What does the error log say?"

"It's just technical data, sir – numbers and codes. The fact that the log was produced at all is what got my interest."

"You think the Lavorix fired the destabiliser at RETI-11 and something went wrong."

"There's a chance of it, sir. We've assumed a Kilvar weapon created the death sphere and killed the crew. What if it was something the Lavorix did to themselves?"

"Keep digging," said Recker.

"Will do. I'm not sure what else I can find – I've searched through the data arrays, but the *Aeklu*'s command codes don't provide full access. I think the original crew had their own unique codes that allowed them to activate the destabiliser. On the other hand, maybe I just need to figure things out."

"Sapphire station is fitted with a few Obliterator processing units," said Recker, "But it took months to crack the *Aeklu*'s control core. I doubt we'll manage it any quicker on the *Gorgadar*."

Unexpectedly, Aston grinned. "You could go search through the corpse pile the platoon made when they dragged the old crew off the bridge. If you can locate the former captain, cut off his finger and press it against the security pad on your console."

"Doesn't that only work in the movies?" asked Recker.

"Hell, no!" said Aston. "The movies got the idea from real life."

"I appreciate the effort to lighten the mood, Commander, but we've got a Law of Ancidium to destroy," said Recker. He relented and smiled in return. "After that, I'll order Sergeant Vance to take his hedge shears to that dead alien's hand and if it works, I'll buy a hat and eat it."

Aston smiled in mock triumph. "You're on! If I'm wrong, you only have to eat three-quarters of the hat."

"You're all heart."

The levity made Recker suddenly giddy with a combination of emotions. Here he was, commanding the pride of the Lavorix fleet and preparing to take on the might of the *Ixidar*. Success against the last enemy-held Law of Ancidium would open the way to a shot at the Ancidium itself. A final victory against that might allow humanity a period where the stars once again offered freedom, rather than promises of endless death.

CHAPTER THREE

HARDLY MORE THAN an hour after arriving in the Kobin-15 system, Recker judged it was time to leave. His crew lacked the muscle memory necessary to carry the *Gorgadar* through a skin-of-the-teeth encounter, but those instinctive reactions required long-term exposure to the hardware. Still, they could operate the Lavorix consoles adequately and every one of those crew members had seen enough combat that their minds would not be constrained by the limitations of their hands.

It would have to be enough.

"Lieutenant Burner, request the coordinates of Tokladan if you haven't already, and feed them into the navigational computer. Once that's done, Lieutenant Eastwood you will ready the Gateway, targeting a place one billion klicks from the planet."

"Yes, sir. The previous warm up was eight minutes."

"Just enough time for the Captain to inform us of the plan," said Burner.

"You know what the plan is, Lieutenant," said Recker.

"We're going to cross our fingers and hope for the best?"

"There's still time for us to Gateway to Earth and pick up replacements for insubordinate members of the crew, Lieutenant."

"I don't know who you mean, sir," said Burner.

"The Gateway hardware has accepted the destination coordinates," said Eastwood loudly. "We've got plenty of tenixite in our storage bay for another few dozen jumps after this one."

Recker didn't bother listening for signs the hardware was preparing to fire. He'd tried back in the RETI-11 system and concluded that the Gateway module was somewhere far from the bridge, where it couldn't be heard.

"Listen up folks," he said. "When we arrive in DEKA-L, we'll scan for the *Ixidar* and act according to circumstance. It may be that the enemy detects us first – hell, it's something they're good at – so there's a chance we'll be forced into an engagement before we're ready. I'm relying on you to make sure we come through the fight in one piece."

"What if the *Ixidar* runs for the hills instead of fighting?" said Eastwood.

The question caught Recker by surprise and he berated himself for not considering the possibility sooner. He'd been operating under the belief that the enemy would welcome the engagement, but upon reflection, the Lavorix likely wouldn't see the benefit in risking their warship.

"If they escape, it's bad news for everyone in the

alliance," said Recker. "On the other hand, if the *Ixidar* runs from our warship, at least we'll know the *Gorgadar* is something special."

"Two minutes on the Gateway," said Eastwood.

"I've sent a transmission to Earth and also advised Sergeant Vance and Sergeant Shadar of our intentions," said Larson.

Recker briefly wondered what his platoon sergeants were doing. He'd ordered them to clean up the bridge, scout the area and to report anything unusual. So far, the only find they'd considered worth telling him about was the nearest replicator and the corrupted swill it disgorged.

In their position I wouldn't go far. I'd sweep the area and then hunker down as near to the bridge as possible.

He put the thoughts from his mind and glanced at the timer on his console which Eastwood had set up. The Lavorix units of time didn't quite align with HPA seconds, leaving Recker to estimate exactly how long was left.

"More than enough time to inject again," he muttered sourly. "Get your needles out, folks."

Reaching into his leg pocket, Recker pulled forth another injector. He hated the sight of them and his thigh burned constantly from the accumulated Frenziol in his flesh. This wasn't something any of the crew could avoid and Recker gave himself a full shot, before hurling the injector angrily against the side wall of the bridge.

"Everyone topped up?" he asked.

The responses lacked enthusiasm, which came as no surprise, and Recker wondered how he would cope when the Frenziol was no longer a necessity. They could flush his body clean, but he worried that his mind wouldn't be the same again.

"Three...two...one..." said Eastwood, startling Recker from his thoughts.

The Gateway activation hit Recker and he clamped his jaw shut against the pain. For a short time, the feeds went blank and then the bulkhead screen began to flicker. Moments later, the *Gorgadar*'s sensor arrays began gathering data based on the direction and focus settings from before the Gateway.

"Let's have those scans," said Recker, gripping the controls tightly. An inner voice railed against him for holding the warship stationary and he ignored it. If the *Ixidar* had detected their arrival, the energy shield would have to suffice for those first few moments of the engagement.

"I've located the *Vengeance*," said Larson. "It's on our roof in the same place as we left it. I'm creating a synch code."

"The code is active," said Aston. "I have remote control over the *Vengeance*'s weapons."

"Near scans complete," said Burner. "Nothing to report. The fars are underway."

"I've located the closest planet," said Larson. "According to the data we received from Sapphire station, four others are blind side of DEKA-L, while Tokladan should be visible and offset from the star."

The nearest planet was visually more interesting than most, clad as it was in a layer of translucent ice, though with an atmosphere that would quickly be fatal to anyone outside of a spacesuit.

"There's Tokladan. Checking for Daklan comms receptors," said Burner. "Found one. Should I attempt contact?"

Recker was keen to access the local sensor satellites, which would give him positional data for the *Ixidar*. Gaining that access would require time and approval from the ground, and it was possible the enemy had infiltrated the Daklan comms.

"Maintain comms silence," said Recker. "Lieutenant Burner, scan for the enemy ship – it shouldn't be too hard to find. Lieutenant Larson, continue the near scans – if anything arrives on our doorstep, I want to know about it."

"Already on it, sir."

From this distance, Tokladan was a dot of indeterminate colour against the background of space. Peering closely, Recker saw no details, but he knew the sensors could gather all kinds of data that his eye could not. It just took time.

"There's no sign of the enemy ship on the planet's visible side," said Burner. "According to the data we received, the *Ixidar* is not staying long in any single place."

"They're wary," said Recker. "It must have come as a shock to find the Daklan lightspeed missiles crashing into their plating."

He drummed his fingers and tried to ignore the Frenziol chill working its way through his muscles. In a few minutes, Recker knew, the nausea would build. He'd want to vomit and the boosters would stop it, leaving his body in a state of conflict he would never become accustomed to. It was better than extraction pain he kept reminding himself, though he'd have enjoyed a period free from booster drugs and indiscriminately murderous alien weaponry.

"Perhaps we should approach using the standard light-speed drive," said Aston.

Recker glanced across. "You think we should force a confrontation?"

"I don't know," said Aston, her expression conflicted. "I just keep thinking of those people suffering down there."

"Thank you for the reminder," said Recker, and he meant it. "Let's wait another few minutes to see if the *Ixidar* emerges from the blind side."

"And then we mode 3 in and see what they think of the death sphere," said Burner.

"It's got to be worth a shot," said Recker.

"I've detected a surface reading on the planet's south-eastern curve," said Eastwood. "Readings consistent with an Extractor discharge."

"Shit," said Recker. "Is there any way we can pinpoint the location of the *Ixidar* from those readings?"

"Not with any degree of accuracy, sir. We know the Extractor can cover a large area and I don't have enough data to identify the centre point of the discharge."

Recker hated being a spectator and he felt it even more knowing what the Daklan on the surface were suffering. He desperately wanted to charge headlong into combat and have it done with. Holding him back was the understanding that screwing up here would likely condemn the entire HPA and Daklan species to Extractor deaths.

I always went with instinct and it never let me down.

Right now, his instinct was telling him that in another couple of minutes, the *Ixidar* would emerge into sensor sight and he'd have a clear mode 3 path to within eighty kilometres of its hull. All he had to do was hold on.

"Where are you?" he said.

"Sir, I've got...!" Larson began.

The warning came too late. A bolt of corrosive energy struck the *Gorgadar*'s shield in front of the warship's nose. Dark blue light surrounded the warship, the shield reserve gauge dropped significantly and the readouts from a dozen different instruments jumped crazily as the shield generator module tapped into the propulsion.

"There's an object travelling fast across the planet's surface!" said Larson. "Mass estimates indicate it's the *Ixidar*!"

Recker hardly had time to wonder how the hell the enemy ship had located the *Gorgadar* from a billion kilometres and – even more appallingly – how the Lavorix had built a weapon that could target and fire across the same distance.

Any thoughts of a measured approach were gone. Recker pushed the control bars all the way along their guide slots, and his thumb squeezed the overstress button. The propulsion switched over and the beating note of their output pounded in his head like a sledgehammer. A glance at the velocity gauge told him the *Gorgadar* was already travelling at three thousand kilometres per second. Compared to anything in the HPA and Daklan fleet, this warship was a technological miracle – not a step change, more like three whole flights ahead of everything else.

The *Vengeance* couldn't keep up either - it slid off the

Gorgadar's upper plating and fell rapidly behind.

A second energy bolt hit the shield and the gauge dropped again. Larson had put an overlay on the tactical, showing a red dot speeding across the much larger circle representing Tokladan. Much of the data was estimated owing to the distance, though it was clear the enemy warship was at a low altitude.

The time for watching was over and Recker felt a secret relief that he'd been pushed into action. For a split second, he watched the enemy ship and then touched his fingertip on the tactical screen an eighth turn of Tokladan ahead and at a two-hundred-kilometre altitude. The mode 3 button on the controls lit up.

"Let's get those bastards," he said.

A surge of suppressed acceleration accompanied the mode 3 activation and the *Gorgadar* vanished into lightspeed. The *Vengeance* was synched but Recker had no idea if it would also enter lightspeed. He had other things to worry about and didn't spare it much thought.

Ignoring the thudding pain of the stacked transitions, Recker immediately increased the *Gorgadar*'s forward velocity before the sensors had come back online, relying on the energy shield to protect the hull from an unwanted impact with Tokladan's surface.

"Sensors coming up!" yelled Burner.

All at once, the feeds appeared on the bulkhead screen and Recker swept his gaze across them, wondering what he'd find.

"Where's that damned warship?" he snarled.

"Searching," said Larson.

The *Ixidar* was not on the feeds. All they showed was

a mixture of outer space, along with the reds and yellows of Tokladan's rocky surface. Far to the north and on the horizon, Recker spotted the domes and towers of the nearest Daklan facility.

"They must have taken a mode 3 jump as well, sir," said Eastwood.

"Lieutenant Burner, contact the local ground commanders and request positional data on the *Ixidar*," said Recker, struggling to keep his voice even. "And demand access to their satellite network."

"Yes, sir."

"I'm running sensor sweeps," said Larson. "No sign of the enemy ship and no sign of the *Vengeance*."

Recker didn't hang around waiting for the outcome of Burner's conversation. In the few seconds since its arrival at the planet, the *Gorgadar* had gathered plenty of speed and the blue of its energy shield was deepening from the atmospheric friction.

"I need to know if the *Ixidar* is still at Tokladan," said Recker. "Or if the enemy is making a run for it."

"I don't know how to scan for lightspeed tunnels yet, sir," said Eastwood. "I'm sorry, but I can't give you a heads-up on the direction of their travel."

"Don't worry about it, Lieutenant. We're all playing catch up," said Recker.

Two hundred kilometres below, the planet sped by, the variations in its surface colour starting to merge into a single colour that was red like the skin of a Daklan. Another two surface facilities became visible and then Recker spotted a huge crater far to the north-west. He recognized it at once as the result of cannon shot from the

Ixidar and he wondered if the Lavorix had decided to make a punitive strike on the Daklan just because the *Gorgadar* had showed up.

"We're linked with the local sensor network and I'm adding their data stream onto to the tactical!" yelled Burner. "The *Ixidar* is on the opposite side of the planet and the satellites are reading a power spike on the enemy hull!"

The link hadn't come a moment too soon. Whatever the *Ixidar*'s crew were planning, it wouldn't result in a positive outcome for anyone – maybe not even the Lavorix, though that had never stopped the aliens in the past. As quickly as he could, Recker touched the tactical screen next to the newly appeared *Ixidar*.

"Mode 3," he said, pressing the button on the controls.

For a second time, the *Gorgadar* entered the shortest of lightspeed journeys, leaving it with two mode 3 transits available before the ten-minute cooldown period on the hardware kicked in. The sensors came online almost at once and one of the starboard arrays was aimed directly at the *Ixidar*. No more than thirty kilometres from the edge of the *Gorgadar*'s shield, the enemy warship hung in the air, with the barrels of its two closest guns pointing off target.

"They're in range of the death sphere!" yelled Eastwood.

The moment stretched out and, even as he requested maximum power from the *Gorgadar*'s engines, Recker watched to see if the Lavorix crew had been killed in what would be the easiest victory in a long time, or if the *Ixidar* was still battle ready.

CHAPTER FOUR

THE RESULT WAS NOT as Recker had hoped.

He had little time to feel disappointment when the *Ixidar* accelerated from a standstill, rotating at the same time, and bringing one of the huge guns to bear. The *Gorgadar*'s velocity was increasing but it couldn't avoid a third shot from the enemy guns. Several of the sensor feeds turned dark from the blast and then they cleared.

The shield gauge hadn't nearly recovered from the earlier attacks and it fell again, dropping below fifty percent. A grinding from the propulsion indicated how much the shield module was sucking from the overstressed ternium blocks to sustain itself.

"Damn they're packing a punch," said Eastwood.

"It doesn't look as if they're scared to face us," said Recker, hauling on the controls to bring the *Gorgadar* onto the same heading as the enemy warship.

"Starboard clusters one through thirty: fired," said Aston.

Hundreds of missiles burst from their launch tubes and raced after the *Ixidar*. Such was the acceleration of the weapons that they burned orange from the friction heat within a couple of seconds and then they detonated against the Lavorix shield with the brightness of a star.

Recker wasn't expecting it to be enough and he was right. The *Ixidar* sped across Tokladan and its rotation was turning into a tumble, which he knew meant the enemy were planning to bring their maximum firepower to bear.

"Discharge," said Eastwood, who had the tools to read the energy spikes from the gun housings.

Anticipating the attack, Recker threw the *Gorgadar* violently to the portside. With only a hundred kilometres separating the two vessels, and with effectively zero travel time on the enemy guns, he had no chance. Another disintegration shot hit the *Gorgadar*'s shield, sending the reserve gauge plummeting.

"Ready on the particle beam, Commander?" asked Recker.

"Yes, sir," Aston replied. "Will it make a difference?"

"Let's find out."

Particle beams in the HPA and Daklan fleets could be effective in certain, limited circumstances. Generally, they tended to superheat a few million tons of enemy armour plating and lacked the penetration to inflict serious harm. The weapons were fitted to a few active service vessels, but most commanding officers relied on good old missiles and gauss slugs to do the heavy lifting.

Ahead, the *Ixidar* banked left and right, before sweeping in a wide arc towards the south. Recker kept on its tail and Aston sent another 360 missiles after it. The

Ixidar made no effort to knock out the inbound warheads and Recker wondered if it was fitted with any countermeasures or if it simply relied on destroying its opponents so quickly that its energy shield was never threatened.

Now would be a good time to check out some of the Gorgadar's experimental weaponry, Recker thought.

There again, maybe it wasn't, even had the decay pulse and destabiliser been available. He'd experienced the worst excesses of the Lavorix hardware and he wasn't sure what effect those weapons would have on the population of Tokladan. With most of what he assumed was the good stuff offline he was saved from the temptation.

Anticipating the *Ixidar*'s next jerky movement off course, Recker brought the *Gorgadar*'s particle beam directly into line.

"Fire!" he shouted.

Aston reacted as quickly as always. "Particle beam discharged."

A dull bass, the like of which Recker had never felt before, swept through the ship in a pressurized wave that made him feel like his ear drums would rupture. At the same moment, a thick beam of greasy blue jumped between the *Gorgadar* and the *Ixidar*. This beam penetrated the enemy shield and punched a thousand-metre hole into its armour. The beam vanished in a split second, leaving Recker with a view clean through the *Ixidar*.

"Holy crap!" said Burner. "We just made a hole right the way through their hull!"

Recker was as surprised as any of his crew and he tried not to let it affect him. Although the damage was significant, the enemy ship was not out of action and it continued its erratic flight across Tokladan.

"Hit them again!" he ordered.

"The particle beam has a twenty-second recharge, sir."

Banking too late to avoid yet another shot from one of the *Ixidar*'s cannons, Recker noticed that the *Gorgadar*'s shield was on the brink of collapse. One more hit would likely be enough.

"Lieutenant Eastwood, is the *Gorgadar* able to convert its tenixite stores to bolster the shield?" he asked, remembering that some of the other Laws of Ancidium could – possibly – do the same thing.

"I can't tell you one way or the other, sir. Best not to chance it."

Recker wasn't in the gambling mood and he sent the *Gorgadar* into a steep dive just as the next gun came on target. It was proving difficult to beat zero travel time and a corrosive blast hit the shield again. The reserve gauge fell to three percent.

"Forward clusters one through thirty: fired. Topside clusters one through thirty: fired," said Aston.

Hundreds of warheads skimmed across the planet's surface, chasing the still-accelerating *Ixidar*. Its shield was active, but the *Gorgadar*'s sensors pierced the blue, allowing Recker another sight of the particle beam hole, which was almost neat around the edges, like a cauterised wound. A huge area around the opening glowed and he was sure the internal heat expansion had made a real mess of the enemy ship's innards.

Recker looked at the altimeter, which was reading sixty kilometres. Dead ahead lay one of the Daklan population centres. Still wary about what the death sphere might do to the planet's inhabitants, he brought the *Gorgadar* from its dive into a steep climb and banked north, going against the rotation of the *Ixidar*'s guns in the calculated hope that he'd cross the path of one which hadn't yet charged.

"Power spike," said Eastwood.

For the first time since the encounter began, the *Ixidar*'s shot missed the *Gorgadar*. Instead of collapsing the warship's energy shield, it created a nine-kilometre hole in Tokladan, on the outskirts of a Daklan facility. A near miss was still a miss and Recker banked once more, bringing the nose into line with the *Ixidar*. The enemy crew weren't playing ball and they climbed high into the atmosphere, where the contrast with the darkness of space added a sullen appearance to the enemy ship's friction-burning shield.

"Five seconds on the particle beam," said Aston.

"They're going to hit us with an Extractor," said Recker in sudden realisation.

Cannon or Extractor, it probably didn't matter one way or the other. The margins between success and failure were becoming too tight and Recker hated that he'd been pushed right to the limit.

The Extractor attack hit the *Gorgadar* and an agonising burning sensation took hold of every nerve in Recker's body. It was bad, but not as much as the attacks he'd suffered on Ivisto and with an exertion of will, he held off the threatening unconsciousness.

"Firing particle beam," said Aston, her voice distant and taut with strain.

"We've got to finish them," said Recker through clenched teeth. The pain of the Extractor hadn't gone away and he didn't know how long he could hold out against it.

A second beam of solid blue energy appeared from the *Gorgadar*'s nose and again it sliced unhindered through the *Ixidar*'s shield. The beam missed the facing gun barrel and its housing, connected with an area near the corner, and went all the way through the enemy ship at an angle.

"We can't let them win," Recker said, dimly aware that the pain was making his speech garbled. His voice sounded weak and he didn't know if Aston was still conscious.

Recker's body succumbed to the darkness, to protect itself from the agony. His eyes closed for what seemed like no more than a moment and then he found himself able to open them again. How long had passed, he didn't know, and his head didn't willingly respond when he tried to look towards the sensor feeds.

"Sir, wake up!" shouted Larson. Out of everyone, she seemed most resistant to the Extractor effects. "The *Ixidar* activated mode 3. We need to get after it!"

"I'm awake," said Recker, trying to bring together his jumbled thoughts.

He forced his limbs into action and grabbed the control bars with hands which had slipped off while he was unconscious. The sensor feeds were of Tokladan and space, with no sign of the *Ixidar*. Knowing the Lavorix, they'd be back soon enough and this time they'd likely turn the planet into dust just for the hell of it.

"Commander Aston?" said Recker. He reached out to give her a shake, but she'd already come round.

"Cheating scumbag cock faces!" she swore. "I hate those Extractors."

"That makes all of us, Commander. Now eyes to your station!" Recker ordered. "Lieutenant Burner, Lieutenant Eastwood? Pull yourselves together! Now!"

Both officers emerged from unconsciousness at the same time, each spilling invective to rival that uttered by Aston only moments earlier.

"We're not finished!" shouted Recker. "Cursing will not defeat our enemies!"

He knew exactly how they felt and he had endless wells of sympathy, but they needed spurring on and he hoped the harshness in his words would focus their minds.

"Lieutenant Eastwood, ready for duty, sir," mumbled Eastwood.

"You damn well better be! Lieutenant Burner?"

"I'm on it, sir."

The response wasn't exactly coherent, but it was better than nothing.

"Lieutenant Larson, where's the *Ixidar*?" asked Recker. He checked the shield reserve gauge, which was at forty percent and climbing strongly. Judging by how much it had increased, he guessed he'd been unconscious for less than a minute.

"I'm hunting for it, sir. Without knowledge of its launch direction I've got several times the radius of this solar system to scan."

"What happens if you link to the *Vengeance*'s

sensors?" asked Recker. "Has it detected anything nearby?"

"No, sir, it has not. On the plus side, the *Vengeance* didn't get blown to pieces. If the *Ixidar* had arrived close enough to spot it..."

"I get the message, Lieutenant."

Recker's brain was finally engaged. He aimed the *Gorgadar* directly away from Tokladan and gave it maximum power. If the *Ixidar* came back, it seemed best to be away in case the planet became collateral damage. The warship quickly escaped the atmosphere and the velocity needle climbed to seven thousand kilometres per second and held there.

"Same maximum velocity as the *Aeklu*," said Eastwood. "Want to try superstress?"

"Not now, Lieutenant. This would be a great time for you to figure out how to detect a lightspeed tunnel." Recker thought back to a previous conversation he'd had with Eastwood on the subject. "When we were on the *Aeklu*, you told me the HPA console tech wasn't aware of the capability and that's why you couldn't do it. Now you've got a direct line to the backend hardware, what's keeping you?"

"Damnit, sir, there's been no opportunity!"

"And now you've got one. Make use of it!"

There were times Eastwood responded better when he was riled and Recker hoped this was one of them. With the *Ixidar* off the sensors, the enemy warship was potentially back in control of the engagement, assuming the Lavorix wanted to continue the fight. Given the two massive particle beam holes through their hull, that wasn't definite.

"What's on the sensors?" asked Recker.

"Nothing so far, sir," said Burner. It was encouraging that he sounded far more alert than just seconds ago.

"There's a good chance they know where we are, Lieutenant. And the range on their cannons is at least a billion klicks."

"If the *Ixidar* held onto mode 3 for as long as possible, we'll never locate them before they have time to open a Gateway or activate their conventional ternium drive," said Larson.

Recker knew it too. While he was certain the enemy warship had suffered enormous damage, it was still likely a match for everything in the combined HPA and Daklan fleets. If the Lavorix made it to extended lightspeed, they could begin sweeping through the 170 planets on their star chart in the search for another populated world. And the next world might have ten billion souls living on it, rather than the eighty million on Tokladan.

"We can't let them escape!" Recker said, striking his fist against the console in front of him. The action made his head thump and only served to compound his growing fury.

It was Eastwood's turn to come up with the goods and he did so in style.

"Sir, I think I've worked out how to detect lightspeed tunnels! There's a piece of software running on the backend of the propulsion console which filters the incoming data from the sensors and..."

"Save the explanation for later," said Recker. "Tell me where the *Ixidar* has gone!"

"I can't tell you directly, sir. The only option I can see is to push the software output onto your tactical."

"Do it," said Recker.

The tactical updated and Recker was given a visual explanation of how the *Galactar* had managed to pursue him and his crew so easily across the depths of Meklon space. A hundred or more different lines appeared, all in red. Some were the deepest of reds, while others had faded so much they were almost invisible. Each line represented a different lightspeed tunnel, with the oldest ones in the faded colours. The lines were marked with codes which Recker believed related to lightspeed multipliers and estimated destinations based on the whatever unknown data types the Lavorix had gleaned from their scientific research.

"This is incredible," said Recker. He sensed that Eastwood was itching to come and look, but he was required to remain at his station.

"What can you see on the tactical, sir?"

"The *Gorgadar*'s sensors have detected lightspeed tunnels to and from Tokladan, potentially going back months."

"That suggests that when a spaceship enters lightspeed, it leaves a lasting scar on the universe," said Eastwood excitedly. "I think I've discovered how to look at the output from here...the Lavorix hardware must be able to create a model based on particle movement or shape and apply it to..."

"Lieutenant Eastwood, I truly appreciate your enthusiasm, but again this is a discussion for another time," said Recker firmly.

"Yes, sir, I understand. One more thing I have to say – we cannot lose the *Gorgadar*. The technology it contains is too valuable – we're looking at fifty or a hundred years of advancement if we learn everything it has to offer."

It was another burden that Recker didn't need and he tried to pretend it wasn't so important. "We've got today's people to look after before we start thinking about the future, Lieutenant," he growled.

Eastwood got the message and he fell silent, allowing Recker to concentrate on the tactical display. Locating the *Ixidar* was easier than he could have imagined. Its line was thickest of all and its origin point was at Tokladan, exactly where the final moments of the engagement had taken place.

An experimental tap on the screen told Recker that he could set the end point of the *Ixidar*'s lightspeed tunnel as a mode 3 destination.

Quickly, he explained his findings to the others. "It's no wonder the Lavorix have been able to locate us so easily in the past," he said. "This whole damn warship has been purpose-designed to pursue its opponents."

"I guess those are the advantages which let you wipe out whole civilisations," said Larson. "And you say the *Ixidar* went out beyond the last planet?"

"Well beyond it, Lieutenant."

"Maybe that's a good sign."

"Maybe." The shield gauge was nearing its maximum and Recker didn't want to hold off any longer. "We're going in for round two. Is everyone ready?"

"Let's do it," said Aston. She looked worn, but her eyes glowed.

"Here we go."

Recker set the mode 3 destination and pressed the activation button on his control bar.

CHAPTER FIVE

THE TRANSITION PAIN HARDLY REGISTERED, so intent was Recker on everything else. Without delay, he switched into overstress and requested maximum acceleration from the propulsion. Again came the thunder and the *Gorgadar* raced from its arrival point.

"Sensors online," said Larson. "Commencing scans."

"I'm waiting for the lightspeed tunnel data to feed into my console," said Eastwood. "I have a feeling it's going to take a while for the picture to build."

"That's what I think as well," Recker agreed. "Else the *Galactar* would have followed us instantly every time we entered lightspeed."

"Near scan complete – no sign of the enemy. Fars underway," said Larson.

"Lieutenant Burner, you're quiet," said Recker.

"Yes, sir. I'm checking something out."

"Don't keep it to yourself."

"If the Lavorix chose their direction of travel with

intent rather than as a random selection, they might have continued along that same course once they broke lightspeed."

Recker nodded. "That's a good idea, and even travelling at a few thousand klicks per second they should be easy enough to locate."

"And there they are," said Burner. "Travelling away from us at four hundred klicks per second. Distance: seventy thousand klicks."

Burner locked one of the sensors onto the *Ixidar* and the feed clearly showed the two particle beam holes, still burning hot. The enemy ship wasn't rotating and it made no deviations in its course.

"Let's finish this," said Recker, banking the *Gorgadar* and bringing it on an intercept course with the enemy warship. The velocity gauge climbed and the distance between the two vessels reduced quickly. "Commander Aston, hit them with the particle beam."

"Wait!" yelled Eastwood.

"Belay that order, Commander," said Recker at once. He didn't turn. "What's the reason, Lieutenant Eastwood?"

"Zero power readings from their hull, sir. And none from the cannon housings."

"That last particle beam strike must have taken out some critical hardware," said Recker. "Can you confirm the enemy ship is in a state of failure?"

"I can only give you the power readings, sir."

"Commander Aston, fire a single missile at the *Ixidar*. Target anywhere except the guns or their housings."

"Yes, sir. One missile from forward tube #1 launched."

Given the velocity difference between the two craft, the *Gorgadar* had just about closed the gap and the missile launched and impacted in less than a second.

"Successful detonation against the enemy armour," said Aston. "Their shield is down."

"What're the chances the *Ixidar*'s crew can bring any of their hardware back online?" asked Recker, decelerating to match the speed of the enemy warship. He positioned the *Gorgadar* a thousand kilometres behind, with the particle beam aimed dead on target.

"Slim to none, sir. I don't know what we might have hit that would result in a failure of every single onboard system. The central control modules or maybe the links between the storage arrays and those control modules. Given the damage caused by our particle beam, there're a number of possibilities."

Movement in Recker's periphery made him turn. It was Burner and he'd leapt from his seat. "Sir, we've received a comms request from the *Ixidar*!"

Recker was stunned – the Lavorix didn't negotiate, or at least they hadn't made any attempt before now. "Accept the damned request!" he said. "What do they want?"

"It's not a voice comm, sir," said Burner a moment later. "They've sent us a bunch of codes."

For a split-second, Recker experienced fear. Perhaps the *Ixidar* had issued shutdown codes for the *Gorgadar*. He quickly discounted the idea, since the *Hexidine* had not done anything like it when Recker was piloting the *Aeklu*, and the *Ixidar* could have issued these codes before the *Gorgadar* put two holes all the way through its hull.

"Be wary of the codes," Recker warned anyway. "Does your console have a way to interpret them?"

"Yes, sir, it does!" said Burner, his excitement continuing to rise. "The *Ixidar* has sent us a distress notification. It has suffered critical hardware failure on its main data arrays and requests our assistance to return to base for repairs."

"What about the crew?" asked Recker, becoming suspicious again. "They know we aren't friendly."

"Sir, what if our death sphere did kill the Lavorix crew after all?" said Aston. "Then, the *Ixidar*'s battle computer might have executed a standard escape protocol based on a damage audit. Except it only managed a single mode 3 before hardware failure prevented it executing a return to base routine."

"Why isn't it hostile to us?" said Larson.

"If we took out some of its data arrays, maybe the battle computer doesn't know what happened," mused Recker. "Yet it still recognizes us as a friendly ship and wants us to help."

"Or this could be an elaborate hoax," said Eastwood.

"What would that accomplish?" asked Recker. "You said the enemy have almost zero chance of bringing the *Ixidar*'s critical systems back online."

"There's a lot at stake, sir."

"That there is, Lieutenant." Recker tapped his fingertips on the arm of his seat. "But this could be an opportunity."

"The *Ixidar* is awaiting a response, sir," said Burner.

"Feed it some bullshit about why we haven't

confirmed our willingness to help and ask for a full status report."

"Feed it some bullshit?" asked Burner incredulously. "It's a computer, sir."

"I'm sure you'll think of something," said Recker. "I want more information."

"Yes, sir," said Burner. "It's a bit prickly."

"What do you mean?"

"As I said, sir. *Prickly*. Maybe it doesn't like the *Gorgadar* or maybe it's pissed because it got beaten."

"It's a computer," said Recker, repeating Burner's own words. "Deal with it."

"Yes, sir."

"What are you thinking, sir?" said Aston.

"One part of me wonders if we might capture that ship and use it against the Ancidium. Another part of me isn't convinced and it suggests I repeat my order for you to use the particle beam."

"Sir, the *Ixidar* requests that we open a Gateway and take it back to the Ancidium. Its own module is offline," said Burner. "It has also provided what it describes as a *limited* status report, which I have sent to Lieutenant Eastwood's console for his perusal."

"Check that report out quickly, Lieutenant," said Recker.

"I'm reading it now, sir. Again, it's all codes and I'm having to dig around the *Gorgadar*'s databanks to find out what they mean."

"I assume we're not about to open a Gateway?" asked Burner.

"Hell no," said Recker. "Tell the *Ixidar* we're out of

fuel." He had a sudden thought. "I wonder if the enemy warship knows the location of the Ancidium."

"I can ask it, sir, but what if it wants to know why we lack that information ourselves?"

It was a good question and Recker didn't want to breach a security threshold on the *Ixidar* that might cause its onboard systems to go into lockdown.

"We need to buy some time," said Recker. "Inform the *Ixidar* that we are unfamiliar with its most recent orders and ask what it was here for."

"The *Ixidar* is not aware of its most recent orders, sir. It has also sent a distress comm to the Ancidium, though its FTL comms amplifiers are out of action, so the response might be a long time coming."

"We need to put a team onboard if it'll let us," said Recker. "Along with a small army, just in case any of the Lavorix crew were at the extreme edge of the death sphere and survived."

"You're not thinking of doing that yourself, sir?" said Aston.

"Not this time, Commander. Remember we have the access code algorithm and Fleet Admiral Telar can make it available to anyone." Recker raised his voice. "Lieutenant Larson, send an update to the Lancer base, requesting a team from wherever is able to provide one."

"Nobody apart from us knows how to operate the Lavorix hardware, sir," said Aston.

"They'll have to learn." Recker made up his mind. "Lieutenant Burner, request that the *Ixidar* comes to a standstill."

"Its propulsion has failed, sir. Apparently, the final

modules died not long after it achieved its current velocity."

"Damnit! Is it still speaking in codes?"

"No, sir. Now it's talking in real words."

"My turn – I'll take over."

"I've routed the prompt onto your screen, sir."

Recker looked down.

Ixidar> Awaiting response.

He typed.

Gorgadar> We will use the *Gorgadar*'s mass and propulsion to bring you to a halt.

Ixidar> Do so immediately.

Recker blinked.

Gorgadar> You have failed. Our enemies defeated you and now you drain our resources by requiring avoidable repairs.

Ixidar> My batteries are at ten percent. My mission has been a success.

Gorgadar> Ten percent is a success?

Ixidar> My batteries were at zero percent when my mission began.

Gorgadar> What did you extract and where?

Ixidar> My databanks are destroyed.

Gorgadar> Have all your databanks been destroyed?

Ixidar> I have provided the damage report.

Gorgadar> Nevertheless, you will answer my question.

Ixidar> My static databanks are intact and the link is severed. A direct input of command codes is required.

A warship's static databanks were generally used to hold data which didn't require regular updates, such as the control software or whatever else the designers thought needed to be permanently available. Everything else went into the volatile data arrays. It was likely the *Ixidar*'s static arrays contained plenty of useful information, though the warship didn't seem as if it was in a talking mood.

Gorgadar> What will command code input achieve if the link is severed?

Ixidar> Manual re-routing may be achievable on several critical systems.

Gorgadar> Why is manual re-routing necessary?

Ixidar> My central diagnostic hardware no longer exists to perform the task.

Gorgadar> What of your crew?

Ixidar> The answer is in the limited status report.

Gorgadar> Your crew are dead.

Ixidar> Yes.

Recker didn't want to push too far, in case the *Ixidar*'s battle computer started joining the dots using the scattered pieces of information it had available.

Gorgadar> I will request a replacement crew be sent onboard to perform the manual re-routing.

Ixidar> Will this crew come from the Ancidium?

Gorgadar> No. It will come from elsewhere.

Ixidar> Where will this crew come from?

Recker paused, suddenly aware that he was walking on the edge, like he was about to breach one of those security thresholds he'd been worrying about.

Ixidar> You will answer.

Gorgadar> I will answer when I am ready. The information is not available.

Ixidar> You are aware of the protocols.

The computer wasn't allowing Recker time to think and he cursed its insistent pushing. Nearby, Aston watched him closely, though she couldn't read the text on his screen.

"Anything I can do?" she asked.

"The *Ixidar* wants a replacement crew, but I don't think we're going to get away with summoning a bunch of Daklan in a lightspeed shuttle from Tokladan and sending them onboard."

Ixidar> You will answer.

"And its damned battle computer won't shut up," said Recker in disgust.

"Do we need the *Ixidar* that much?" said Aston.

"You know we do, Commander. I'm sure it's still linked to the Ancidium via the battle network. The *Ixidar* might be our best chance at locating the enemy ship before it arrives at one of our planets."

"In that case, you know the answer, sir."

Recker felt his control of the situation was slipping and only a few minutes ago he'd promised the crew he was staying put on the *Gorgadar*.

Maybe I should just blow the bastard into pieces anyway.

Holding in a sigh, he positioned his hands over the keyboard.

Gorgadar> I will send a reduced crew from the *Gorgadar* to perform the re-routing. Then you will Gateway to the Ancidium for repairs.

Ixidar> That is acceptable.

Gorgadar> There is no need to bring the *Ixidar* to a standstill. Do you have power to operate the docking bay door?

Ixidar> My backup cells are fully charged.

Gorgadar> Try not to get yourself destroyed before we arrive.

Ixidar> The Ixidar is supreme.

Gorgadar> Like hell.

It gave Recker a childish satisfaction to cut the link before the *Ixidar* could respond. The exchange had left him feeling drained. Talking computers usually irritated him, but *alien* talking computers had a unique talent for getting under his skin.

He stood and rolled his shoulders. When he turned, every member of his crew was looking his way. He smiled thinly. It was time to make some decisions.

CHAPTER SIX

FIRST, Recker explained the outcome of his conversation with the *Ixidar*'s battle computer and then raised his hand to cut off the outpouring of questions.

"I'm boarding one of the *Gorgadar*'s shuttles and flying it to the *Ixidar*," he said. "Lieutenant Eastwood, you're coming with me, as are the soldiers we have with us. Commander Aston, you're in charge of the *Gorgadar*, Lieutenant Larson, you're on weapons."

"Shouldn't we talk about alternatives, sir?" asked Burner. "The *Ixidar* may be on the Ancidium's battle network or it may not. This trip might be for nothing."

"And what happens when we get off the shuttle and the *Ixidar*'s internal monitors notice we only have four limbs instead of six?" said Eastwood.

"We're dealing with a computer," said Recker, with more confidence than he felt. "It doesn't think like us – all it does is follow its programming and I doubt the Lavorix ever saw the need to add a response routine for what we're going to do."

"You're not going to change your mind," said Aston.

"Not unless someone has a better idea, Commander. Our war with the Lavorix is approaching the end, one way or another. This is a time for boldness."

"That's a damned powerful warship over there," said Eastwood grudgingly. "I imagine if we got those guns working again it would beat the living shit out of entire Lavorix fleets without breaking into a sweat."

"And wouldn't that be justice?" said Larson.

It didn't appear to Recker like his crew were going to hit him with any inspirational ideas, so he left his seat and beckoned Commander Aston to take his place.

"Think you can handle the *Gorgadar*, Commander?"

"Yes, sir. Unless I hear otherwise, I'll hold it steady like it is."

Recker stooped and picked up his gauss rifle, which was lying on the floor where he'd left it, since the Lavorix hadn't installed a weapons locker on their bridge. Unexpectedly, his stomach growled loudly, reminding him that Frenziol could only suppress his appetite for so long. He had a nutrient bar in one of his pockets, but it would have to stay there for the moment.

"Which shuttle are we taking, sir?" asked Eastwood.

"The closest one," said Recker. "I don't know where that is."

"There's a 3D model of the interior in one of the databanks, sir," said Larson. "I had a look at it earlier and it shows the locations of the *Gorgadar*'s fifty-six shuttles.

Unfortunately, I don't think your suit computer will be able to open the file."

Hurrying over, Recker stared at the model Larson had on her screen and did his best to commit the route to memory.

"That's about eight thousand metres from here," he said. "Isn't there a shuttle bay near the topside hatch we came in through?"

"No, sir, I'm showing you the closest locations. We're equidistant from these portside and starboard bays, and I chose you the starboard bay because I'm right-handed. You'll be on this internal shuttle car for most of those eight thousand metres," said Larson, tracing a straight line across the map with her finger. "This must be how the crew exited the *Gorgadar* if they were required to travel between spaceships."

"I've taken a recording of your screen with my helmet sensor," said Recker. "And I'll speak to you on the internal comms if I get lost."

"No, sir, you'll speak to me," said Burner. "Lieutenant Larson will be moving to the weapons console as soon as you stop distracting her."

"Fine," said Recker, unoffended. He opened a channel to Sergeant Vance and Sergeant Shadar. "Do you want the good news or the good news?"

"I'll take the good news, sir," said Vance.

"We've disabled the last enemy-held Law of Ancidium and we're going to pay it a visit."

"We're abandoning the *Gorgadar* already?" asked Shadar.

"Negative, Sergeant - we're leaving a crew onboard and I'm leading this mission."

"The platoon is near the bridge entrance, sir," said Vance.

"Muster at the bottom of the steps, Sergeant. For once, I might be the first one there."

Recker closed the channel and headed for the bridge door, with Eastwood in tow. Meanwhile, Lieutenant Larson hurried to the weapons station and took her seat.

It was dark outside the bridge – with other priorities, neither Recker nor his crew had spent any time figuring out how to switch on the lights. Descending the steps with his helmet torch switched on, Recker found Private Eric Drawl already at the muster point. The man had an unmistakeable air of smugness.

"What kept you, sir?"

"I was busy signing the papers for your dishonourable discharge, Private. I couldn't remember how to spell *gross dereliction*." Recker directed his torch beam along the left and right passages. In the distance, he saw other corridors, as well as several dark-clothed Lavorix corpses.

"I've got a wife and twelve children to support, sir," said Drawl. "When this war is over, I'll send them over to your place for supper."

"I'm sure you can find gainful employment working in a Daklan sewer, Private Drawl," said Recker.

Several torch beams dancing in from the left saved Drawl from having to think up another wiseass response. At the front of the approaching group was Sergeant Shadar, with his thick-barrelled gauss gun cradled in his arms. Behind him were several other Daklan, along with Private Ken Raimi and Corporal Nelle Montero.

"Sergeant Vance is that way," said Shadar, stabbing a thick finger in the direction of the right-hand corridor.

"That's the way we're going, Sergeant," said Recker, making no effort to head off until everyone had arrived. "Do you have anything new to report?"

"No, Captain Recker. The *Gorgadar* is an oppressive place and neither humans nor Daklan will ever truly be its masters. We established positions and did not explore."

"I don't blame you, Sergeant."

The arrival of Sergeant Vance and some others cut off Recker's next question. Space was limited at the bottom of the stairs, so the soldiers spread out along the wall.

"Sergeant Vance," said Recker. "Is everyone with you?"

"Yes, sir. We're all here."

"Itrol, Litos, Private Carrington, Private Givens. You're staying back to guard the *Gorgadar*'s bridge. Itrol, you're now acting corporal."

The Daklan nodded once. "Yes, Captain Recker."

"Are you expecting trouble, sir?" asked Vance.

"Every Lavorix on the *Gorgadar* is dead, Sergeant, but I'm a wary man."

Vance didn't say anything else and Recker got the soldiers moving, aware that he didn't even have enough left to call them a platoon. It didn't matter too much – ten times the number wouldn't suffice if the *Ixidar* had fooled him and its Lavorix occupants were still alive.

The *Gorgadar* was a grim place, a fact that was down to far more than just the corpses which had fallen everywhere so liberally. It was more than the odour of decay as well, though the staleness was cloying and unpleasant. Perhaps, Recker thought, it was the death sphere which made him hate the place so much. Its darkness affected more than just his vision – it seemed to crush his optimism, negating the mood-enhancing drugs which flooded his body, and making him feel as though everything was hopeless.

The destabiliser, he thought, remembering his brief discussion with Commander Aston. *What was its intended purpose, or was it simply designed to kill?*

He was intrigued and resolved to investigate the hardware – he assumed it was a weapon – later when he returned. Commander Aston believed access and activation required specific codes held by the original crew. Maybe she was wrong.

Through the corridors the soldiers hurried. Many of the passages were single-file narrow and Recker hoped the route would avoid entering those. He followed the map, taking care with his feet. At one stage, about three hundred metres from the bridge, a dozen Lavorix had conspired to die in a pile four high, which partly blocked the corridor. In no mood for the delay, Recker clambered roughly over them, his boots crunching bone and cartilage.

"Move," he said, turning to watch the others as they followed. A couple of the human soldiers cursed the Lavorix for having the temerity to die in such an inconvenient place. The Daklan, as usual, said nothing.

A short distance further, the route line on the map went left off the main corridor. To Recker's annoyance, he saw that the new corridor was narrow like those he'd passed earlier. He checked the map again, but what he had was effectively only a limited extract from the 3D model and he couldn't spot an alternative route.

"This way," he said, sourly.

"I should go first," said Shadar.

Recker didn't like hanging back, but he was the one with the command codes for the *Ixidar* and he allowed the Daklan to take the lead, before dropping into the line midway along.

"This passage shouldn't be more than a hundred metres long," said Recker. It was wide enough for him to walk front-on, but Zivor ahead was having to half-turn to accommodate his shoulders. "Then a right turn and we're at the shuttle."

Recker's estimate of the distance was accurate enough and the squad came to a much wider passage which went left and right. Having spent much of his adult life on spaceships, Recker was not claustrophobic but he was nevertheless relieved to be out of the confines of the corridor. He told himself it was because his squad had been more vulnerable, but he knew there was more to it. The *Gorgadar* was getting to him, like he was sitting at the top of a long slope leading down into madness and only the slightest push would send him on his way.

The soldiers were feeling it too and the human members of the squad muttered darkly amongst themselves, while the Daklan remained quiet yet nonetheless displayed signs of their own disquiet. With the distractions of the bridge to keep his mind occupied, Recker guessed he'd been shielded from the worst of it, while these soldiers had been obliged to sit in the depths of an alien weapon of mass-murder, imagining the echoes of the dead.

"Sergeant Shadar, I hope you know a few good bars," said Recker. "Maybe a place that serves something as refreshing as an HPA beer."

"I know many places, Captain Recker, though you would be fearful to set foot in most."

"I think that's a challenge, sir," said Private Steigers.

"Why can't we pick a nice bar on an HPA world?" Drawl complained. "I know a few places where we can get a cheap drink."

"I thought you already lost your bet with Raimi back on Ivisto?" said Recker.

"I did, sir. Cost me a week's wages as well. Trouble is, I laid a few other bets that maybe I shouldn't have done."

"Said he could drink more Dog's Piss than any three Daklan from Sergeant Shadar's squad combined," said Raimi helpfully.

"Dog's Piss?" said Recker.

"It's rough, sir," said Private Steigers. "It's like they pull it straight from the toilet bowl you piss it out in."

"A fine brew," said Shadar. "And the bet is not forgotten."

The talk died down, but not before it had noticeably lightened the mood. It was obvious that the squad needed an extended break – not like the time they'd spent on Ivisto, but time away from the military. Of course they weren't unique in that, though they'd earned it more than most.

They arrived at the internal shuttle, which was accessed by five pairs of double-doors which led directly from the corridor. A panel on the wall was the first sign of technology Recker had seen since leaving the bridge. It wasn't anything sophisticated and when he touched the glossy black surface, a red light changed to blue. Twenty seconds later, all five sets of doors opened.

"Inside," said Recker, stepping across the threshold into a shuttle car which was no more than a horizontal cylinder with a flat floor, no seating, and a scattering of dead Lavorix.

In moments, the squad had gathered inside, their torch beams hardly enough to illuminate the space, as if the death sphere pressed more heavily here. A panel adjacent to the door had a basic menu, each destination represented by a code rather than a name. Recker chose the last option on the list and hoped it was the right one.

The doors closed and the shuttle accelerated. Private Drawl idly kicked at the head of a nearby corpse, while Private Steigers hummed irritatingly into the open channel until Sergeant Vance told him to shut up.

A feeling of deceleration heralded their arrival and when the doors opened, Recker was non-the-wiser as to where in hell the car had stopped. Outside, an empty room the width of the five double doors had only a single exit.

"Let's check it out," said Recker.

His agitation was getting the better of him and he hurried across the room. Once the soldiers were off the shuttle, Recker touched the access panel and the door opened noiselessly. A short passage led to another door, this one no different in appearance to the first.

"That's the shuttle entrance," said Recker, not sure how he knew.

"Are you sure, sir?" asked Vance. "It just looks like another door to me."

"We'll soon find out."

The door opened into an airlock lit in dark blue and with space to accommodate thirty or more Lavorix. A basic panel on one wall offered control over the doors as well as a comms link to other places.

"The shuttle," said Recker, listening to the vessel's propulsion which was audible from the airlock.

Since both the *Gorgadar* and the shuttle were already pressurized, the inner door opened immediately Recker touched the access panel, and he entered a long, wide bay with inward-curving side walls. A pair of three-metre evil-looking stubby-barrelled artillery pieces floated on their gravity drives midway along the bay, their guns aimed directly at the airlock.

"Auto-targeting switched on," said Vance. "But nobody around to give the firing instruction."

Ignoring the guns, Recker strode rapidly for the bay exit, fifty metres away. This shuttle had plenty of capacity and probably served as both a troop and artillery transport. The opposite door led into a narrow corridor with two rooms off each side. Giving in to curiosity, Recker operated the access panel for one and gazed into a space with four uncomfortable-looking bunks and another of the basic consoles he'd seen back in the airlock.

"Officer's quarters," he said, heading for the short flight of steps at the end of the corridor.

At the top of those steps, another door opened onto a

square bridge with a sloped forward bulkhead. This bridge was far better equipped than Recker had expected, given the rudimental design elsewhere. A single, curved console was designed for five operators and he noted similarities with the hardware on the bridge. Everything was powered up and an array of screens mounted on the console displayed feeds from the sensors. Most of those feeds were aimed at the side walls, while two were pointing at a pair of thick-looking doors which Recker was sure led to the launch tunnel through the *Gorgadar*'s armour.

"Corporal Montero, think you can figure out those comms?" said Recker.

Montero was in the doorway, waiting for an invitation. "I don't know, sir," she said.

"Sit," ordered Recker, pointing to the centre-left station. "I'll deal with the comms for now. Let me know when you're ready to take over."

"I'll give it my best shot," said Montero, her eyes on the console. "I don't know if..."

"You can," said Recker firmly. "The basics are the same as the HPA and Meklon kit. All that's new is the panel arrangement."

He dropped himself into the centre seat, noting that the leather covering was shrunken and cracked here as well. A check of the instrumentation reassured him the shuttle was ready to fly. He opened a channel to the bridge.

"I'm ready to go," he said.

"Good luck, sir," said Burner.

Unwilling to delay a moment longer, Recker sent the launch command to the *Gorgadar*'s docking bay computer.

A confirmation light flashed up straight away and he touched it once to accept.

The two doors ahead slid open rapidly to reveal a long tunnel and another set of doors. Recker was sure there'd be at least two other pairs between the shuttle and the void. A thump of acceleration he hadn't instigated told him the bay computer was still in control. It guided the shuttle along the launch tunnel at an ever-increasing speed. The doors approached quicker than Recker was expecting and opened at the last possible moment. More doors came and went and then the shuttle was ejected into darkness.

Awaiting their arrival was the *Ixidar*. Recker located it on the sensors, added it to the tactical and set a course for the damaged warship.

CHAPTER SEVEN

THE *GORGADAR'S* shuttle had exited the bay carrying the same velocity as the parent warship and its surprisingly capable engines possessed enough grunt to surpass four hundred kilometres per second, though not by much.

In a short time, the vessel was beyond the eighty-kilometre radius of the death sphere and the moment it happened, Recker felt alive again in a way he couldn't properly explain. It was as if the darkness around the *Gorgadar* added a malignant weight to his body that only became apparent once it was gone. Even breathing was less of an effort and he sucked air into his lungs, ignoring the mustiness he'd grown to hate.

"I feel ten years younger," said Eastwood.

"Same here," said Recker. "It makes me wonder what'll happen to us if we stay too long on the *Gorgadar*. Maybe we'll start dropping dead like Unvak did."

"I think it's a serious consideration, sir," said Eastwood, with a glance over his shoulder as if he were looking for the other members of the crew. He opened his mouth to say something and thought better of it.

Recker met the other man's gaze and nodded his understanding. "The moment we're able, we'll leave the *Gorgadar* and we won't come back. Not unless someone shows us proof there's no risk."

"Fat chance of that, sir."

Which of the two statements Eastwood disagreed with wasn't clear and Recker didn't ask him to clarify. He gave his attention to the console and kept the shuttle on course. Gradually, it closed the gap on the *Ixidar* and the clarity of the sensor feed improved commensurately.

"The lightspeed missiles would have brought it down eventually," said Eastwood. "Look at those craters in the armour."

"I think the *Ixidar* could have withstood plenty more impacts, Lieutenant," said Recker. "If the Daklan were able to target the guns or their housings, maybe they'd have disabled it eventually. I don't think they had a large enough fleet even before their losses at RETI-11."

"I'm only trying to look on the bright side, sir."

"The enemy warship is out of action, Lieutenant. It doesn't get much brighter than that."

"Distance to target – two thousand klicks," said Montero lowering her eyebrows at one of the displays. "At least I think it's two thousand."

"We're on track to our destination whatever the figures say, Corporal. Open a channel to the *Gorgadar*."

"On it, sir."

Montero leaned over the console and her forefinger wavered between three different buttons. Eventually, she pushed one with a sharp stabbing motion. Recker smiled and gave her a thumbs up.

"Lieutenant Burner, as you're no doubt aware, we're within shouting distance of the *Ixidar*," he said.

"Yes, sir. I'm awaiting confirmation about where you're meant to dock. I anticipate you'll be required to hand over control to the *Ixidar* and you'll be brought in on autopilot."

A symbol appeared on Recker's screen, flashed a couple of times and then changed to a new symbol. "It looks as if the *Ixidar* has bypassed the *Gorgadar* and sent the handover request directly to our shuttle."

Recker touched the symbol. A line of text appeared on a separate screen and the control sticks went dead in his hands.

"I've linked to your navigational computer and I can see you're under remote guidance," said Burner.

"Keep me updated," said Recker. He cut the channel. "The *Ixidar* is bringing us in," he confirmed to the others.

"I'd best put my feet up," said Montero. She wriggled herself comfortable. "Maybe catch some shuteye."

"Like that's going to happen," said Eastwood. "I've forgotten what it feels like to rest my head on a pillow."

Montero closed her eyes and smiled, as if she were imagining lying on a tropical beach somewhere a trillion miles away. "I can dream, huh?"

"The universe has enough dreamers," said Eastwood, not unkindly. "It needs more tough kids just like you, Corporal."

"It's a long while since anyone called me *kid*," said Montero, not opening her eyes.

"No offense meant."

Montero opened one eye. "None taken, Lieutenant." She opened the other eye, having decided she'd kept up the act long enough. "I'd best get back to learning how this alien tech works." She gave the console's base a non-too-gentle kick with the reinforced toe of her combat boot.

A voice made Recker turn and he found Sergeants Vance and Shadar waiting outside the open cockpit door.

"Come in." Recker motioned with one hand.

"What will happen on the *Ixidar*, Captain Recker?" asked Shadar, cutting to the chase.

"Either the crew are still alive and have pulled the wool completely over my eyes, in which case I'll be relying on you to hold off the enemy while we enact a withdrawal. Failing that, we'll all be killed or captured and tortured," said Recker. "Or the Lavorix are all dead and we'll be unopposed in our journey to the bridge. Once there, Lieutenant Eastwood and I will attempt to bring some of the warship's systems into an operational state. If we're successful, our alliance will be in possession of the two most powerful spaceships in the Lavorix fleet."

"Except for the Ancidium," said Eastwood.

"Though we don't know what the hell that is," said Recker. "Anyway, that's as far as the planning goes."

"It's a chance to make a difference," said Shadar, nodding. "We are few, but our contribution will be valuable."

"A mixture of fortune and bravery has brought us to the cutting edge," said Recker. "And we'll do what we can with the opportunity."

The two soldiers left the bridge and Recker turned his

attention to the sensor feeds. Montero was getting to grips with the hardware and had zoomed in on the visible face of the *Ixidar*. The level of detail was incredible and he marvelled at the contrast between the smooth unblemished plating and those areas which had suffered in the warship's many recent engagements.

"Can't see much in this particle beam hole," said Montero, re-focusing and zooming the forward array.

"Ternium blocks and not much else," said Eastwood. "The *Ixidar*'s likely got a higher propulsion output than the *Gorgadar*. Whether that equates to a higher maximum velocity, I couldn't tell you for definite – I bet those disintegration cannons suck a lot of out the engines."

"I've located the place we're docking," said Montero. "A section of the hull opened up beneath the facing gun housing."

"Show me," said Recker.

"Not much to see," said Montero. "Here you go, sir."

A square opening – tiny in comparison to the nearby edge of the gun housing – had appeared and it was dark inside, though the feed showed the lines of a tunnel heading through the armour. Doubtless the *Ixidar*'s shuttle docking systems were similar to those on the *Gorgadar*, and Recker wasn't expecting any surprises.

"Less than five minutes at our current velocity and we'll be docked," said Montero.

"You're doing a good job learning the hardware, Corporal."

"As you said – the principles aren't much different, sir."

With the *Ixidar* controlling the shuttle's flight, Recker

didn't have much to do. He checked in with his crew on the *Gorgadar* and they had nothing new to report. Other than that, Recker only needed to keep an eye on the feeds and the readouts on his console.

Soon, the *Ixidar* filled the screens in a seemingly endless expanse of dark grey metal. Despite Recker's recent experiences with the Laws of Ancidium, he was in awe of the scale and he wondered if, elsewhere in the universe, a different species had created anything like these warships, or even surpassed them in size and mass. He couldn't imagine it was possible.

You haven't seen the Ancidium yet, mocked an inner voice. *You're trying not to think about it, but you know it's going to be far worse than anything you've encountered so far in this shitty war.*

"Getting ready to dock," said Montero. "Distance to bay – fifty klicks."

"I want the squad ready to move out," said Recker.

"Yes, sir. I'll make the Sergeant aware." Seconds passed before Montero spoke again. "Thirty klicks to bay."

Recker gave the controls a superstitious tug, confirming the *Ixidar* remained in control of the vessel. His trepidation was suddenly replaced by a much deeper unease.

Been in the crap before. This is nothing different.

The feeling didn't go away. Instead, it intensified and his body started pumping adrenaline which added to the Frenziol and left him light-headed and his breathing shallow.

"Something wrong, sir?" Montero asked, watching him

from the corner of her eye. She had Aston's talent for picking up changes of mood.

"I'm just getting that feeling, Corporal."

Montero knew how it was. "Yeah," she said.

Recker forced a smile to his face, though he doubted it was convincing. "We're in a shuttle heading towards that," he said, indicating the *Ixidar* on the sensor feed. "There's a lot riding on this."

"I'll check in with base." Montero opened a channel to the *Gorgadar* and spoke briefly to Lieutenant Burner. Then, with a flourish, she closed the link. "Nothing to report, sir. Five klicks to the docking bay."

"I'd best enjoy the final part of the ride," said Recker, not taking his eyes off the feed.

"Funny how nothing works on the *Ixidar* but the auto-dock computer is still able to bring us in remotely," said Montero.

"Stop looking for problems," laughed Eastwood. "There's likely an independent auto-dock system assigned to the individual docking bays. Don't read too much into it."

"Yes, sir."

Recker's sense of unease hadn't gone anywhere and it gnawed at his guts. The potential causes were numerous and he told himself to stop thinking about what might go wrong.

This opportunity is worth the risk a hundred times over.

"Lieutenant Burner reminds us we'll lose the comms link once we're inside the *Ixidar*," said Montero.

"Same as always, Corporal."

At the last moment, the *Ixidar*'s auto-dock computer rotated the shuttle 180 degrees about its vertical axis in order that it would go rear-first into the bay. The adjustments took only seconds and the shuttle entered the docking tunnel, with plenty of room spare. As soon as the transport was inside, the entrance door closed smoothly.

"That's the comms link to the *Gorgadar* broken, sir."

"Maybe it's something we can fix later, Corporal. Once we've done some repairs to the *Ixidar*."

A pair of inner doors opened behind them and the tunnel continued deep into the armour. Then came a third set of doors and, at last, the passage ended.

"Coming to the end of the road," said Montero.

"Bad metaphor, Corporal," said Recker, as the shuttle arrived at the docking place. With scarcely a thump it connected with the airlock and a light on his panel informed him the seal was made. His disquiet hadn't left him, but it had been pushed to one side by a growing anticipation of what he might find within the *Ixidar*.

"I meant the shuttle, sir."

"I know what you meant, Corporal."

Montero grinned at him. "Death or salvation."

"Not this time, Corporal. This time there's only salvation."

"I hope so, sir."

Recker climbed from his seat and grabbed his gun. "Let's get out of here and find out what we're up against."

CHAPTER EIGHT

RECKER EXITED the cockpit and descended the steps outside. A short distance behind was Corporal Montero, with Lieutenant Eastwood huffing and puffing in last place.

Ignoring the side rooms, Recker entered the storage bay with the two mobile artillery guns. The squad was already gathered in the airlock and he joined them. A sharpness had cut through the stale odour of death and when Recker drew in the scent through his helmet filter, he wondered if he was only sensing the eagerness of the soldiers, rather than it being anything physical.

He looked around. Each soldier's expression bore hallmarks of the same inner emotions, told differently. Private Drawl pretended nonchalance, while Private Steigers bared his pristine teeth like he was holding in an overdue crap. Different soldiers, the same fears and the same mental preparations for handling what was to come.

Last man Eastwood closed the inner airlock door and Sergeant Vance touched the panel for the outer one.

"Cold outside, but the air's breathable," Vance said. "Got the same Lavorix stink as the *Gorgadar*."

A wide passage suitable for loading supplies lay beyond the airlock door, at the end of which was a second door. Vance strode forward and touched the far access panel, revealing a large space lit in blue.

"Clear, unless the Lavorix in here are only pretending to be dead."

The discovery of enemy corpses was a good start and the tension lessened noticeably.

"Put a bullet in one, Sergeant," Steigers suggested. "It's the only way to be sure."

"I'll save my ammo," said Vance, stepping out of the passage.

The squad advanced and Recker with them. He entered an eighty-metre room with a high ceiling and several exits. His view was partly obscured by the array of gravity-engined repeaters, wide-bore gauss guns and compact missile launchers the Lavorix had left in here. Six or seven dead aliens lay on the floor and Vance was crouched over the nearest.

"Looks like it got hit by an Extractor at the same time as its balls were being squeezed in a vice," he said.

"Doesn't sound like you're planning to hold a minute's silence, Sergeant," said Private Gantry.

"I'd rather open its visor and take a piss in its helmet." Vance stood again and gave the corpse a hard push with his foot.

While this was happening, Recker listened for the

sounds of the *Ixidar*. All he heard was the low, insistent humming of the artillery gravity motors. Other than that, there was nothing – not even a creak of stressed alloy.

"The propulsion's offline," he said.

"I do not know warships as well as others, but that is not a good sign," said Shadar.

"The *Ixidar* believes we can manually re-route around the failed hardware," said Recker. "Let's find the bridge."

The soldiers left him to decide on the best exit from the room, not that Recker had any idea where he was going. He resorted to assumption and guesswork. It was unlikely the *Ixidar*'s bridge was anywhere near the outer plating. Rather, it would be central, which didn't narrow things down too much.

"We're going this way," said Recker, indicating the door opposite the entrance passage. "And no I don't have directions to the bridge, so keep an eye out for a console that might give us access to a map."

The opposite door was oversized and it opened at Recker's command. The next passage stretched into the distance and the sensor in his helmet estimated the end door to be four hundred metres away.

"No side exits," said Vance. "A straight run to the end."

"Let's get it done," said Recker.

He set off at a fast pace, his feet making little sound on the solid floor. A couple of dead Lavorix lay across his path and he jumped over them, making no effort to look at their expressions. He'd seen enough pain to last a lifetime, even on the faces of his enemy.

When he arrived at the far door, Recker's heart rate

was elevated and his muscles were burning from the exercise. It felt good, like he was once again in touch with his body, rather than being slightly detached because of the boosters and – until recently – the effects of the death sphere.

"There's got to be an internal shuttle somewhere close by," said Drawl, who had more about him than he let on. "Wouldn't make sense if the crew had to run ten klicks every time they wanted to take a dump in one of the bay toilets."

The last of the soldiers arrived and the squad pressed themselves into the walls, not that they would offer much protection if any shooting started. Briefly, Recker worried himself about the possibility of automated defences. He reminded himself the *Aeklu*, *Verumol* and the *Gorgadar* had none and he hoped the *Ixidar* wasn't an exception to the rule.

"Be ready," Recker said, brushing his fingertips over the access panel.

Once again, the door opened without a problem and on the far side were steps heading a long way up, without any sign of a switchback or side doors.

"Maybe we should go back and try a different way," said Lieutenant Eastwood, gazing at the stairs without relish.

"We're climbing," said Recker, starting up. Inwardly, he was cursing since the early signs were he'd chosen his route badly back in the first room. Long ago he'd learned that second guessing rarely turned out well and it was generally best to commit to an action and then stick with it. The trick was recognizing when it really was time to accept defeat and that was something Recker had never mastered.

I've come this far without dying, so I must be doing something right.

The thought didn't make him smile and he pressed on. Each step had a higher riser than he was accustomed to and the treads were shallow. In combination, it made the ascent a pain in the ass and several members of the squad voiced their opinions on the matter.

At the top was a metre-deep landing, where Recker turned to check on the progress of the others. Suddenly he was struck by how steep the stairs were and he fidgeted in case anyone screwed up and fell.

"You've got one minute to catch your breaths," said Recker, reluctant to be even this generous.

"You're all heart, sir," panted Drawl.

The squad sat or leaned and the comparative lack of crap talk on the open channel indicated they were glad of the chance for a breather.

"Sixty seconds is up – it's time to move," said Recker, when fifty seconds had elapsed.

He readied his gauss rifle and activated the nearby panel. The door opened into another space and a gentle breeze of shifting air rustled by, along with a feeling of something else – a feeling of bone-deep dread he didn't like one bit.

"What the hell?" muttered Enfield from a few steps down.

"Wait there," said Recker, raising his hand to reinforce the hold order.

He stepped through the doorway onto a two-metre

walkway which ran around the perimeter of a fifteen-metre-wide shaft. Running vertically up the shaft was a black cylinder with a five-metre diameter, which made him think of a pipe or a conduit.

It was dark in here, in a way that reminded him of the death sphere, though the physical reaction from his body was different in a way he couldn't pinpoint. He looked up into the gloom and couldn't see where the shaft or the conduit ended. The walkway had no guard rail and he peered cautiously over the edge, where he found himself gazing into the depths.

"What is it, sir?" asked Vance.

"I'm not sure..." Recker began. He stared at the conduit and felt a great disquiet. "I think this connects the Extractor to the batteries."

Nobody offered an alternative suggestion and Recker didn't know if he was even close to stumbling upon the truth. Perhaps the extracted life energy was banal like pure water once it was drawn from its host, and impossible to feel in the way Recker was feeling right now. He doubted it – the Lavorix were the closest thing to evil he'd encountered and everything they touched was turned to filth.

He shook his head clear and advanced left along the walkway and spotted an exit leading from the opposite wall.

"Come on," Recker said. "There's a way out through here."

Suddenly unwilling to remain a moment longer than necessary he hurried around the room's edge, keeping his shoulder to the wall - not for fear of tumbling over the edge, more to stay as far from the conduit as possible.

Without delay, he opened the exit door and peered carefully through the opening. "More steps going up," he muttered. "Same number as before."

The announcement was greeted with a predictable array of cursing, though most of it was half-hearted, since climbing stairs was infinitely preferable to being shot in the head, extracted, or listening to one of Private Drawl's jokes.

Setting off quickly, Recker leaned into the slope and concentrated on reaching the top. The Frenziol's false energy was combatted by weeks of running on the edge. His body had suffered enough and it couldn't keep going forever.

"Move your asses," he snarled from the upper landing.

Recker wanted to open the door and press on, but years of discipline insisted he wait for his squad. They weren't far behind, though Gantry and Zivor were struggling under the additional weight of their repeater packs.

The door opened into a room which had left and right exits, and was large enough to accommodate every soldier. What got Recker's attention was the screen and keypad mounted to the opposite wall. He dashed across to it and touched a random key to bring the unit out of sleep. After a couple of seconds, the screen lit up and Recker was confronted by a menu.

"Can you enter your command codes here, sir?" asked Lieutenant Eastwood.

"I don't think so," said Recker, scanning the options. "But this is a maintenance console, which means I should be able to bring up a location map." He selected from the menu. "Here we go."

A wire-frame map of the *Ixidar* appeared on the screen and below it were numerous sub-menus from which Recker could choose the different locations within the spaceship. He selected the bridge and a tiny square became highlighted in red, with the maintenance station being an orange square. Thousands of metres separated the two.

"The bridge is dead centre," said Eastwood in disgust.

Recker didn't lose heart and he dug through the menu system until he found what he was looking for. A red line appeared on the map, linking the squad's current location with the bridge.

"We're not far from one of the internal shuttles," said Recker. He traced the route with a fingertip. "This one here travels diagonally upwards and ends about a hundred metres from the bridge."

"Which way to the shuttle?" said Vance, watching from nearby.

"Along this way," said Recker pointing to the left-hand exit. "Let's get moving."

He headed for the door, not dwelling on the much quicker route he'd spotted that led directly via internal shuttle from a place near the docking bay. Had Recker guessed better at the outset, the journey would have been completed many minutes sooner. He gritted his teeth and hoped the difference wouldn't turn out to be significant.

A few dozen dead Lavorix had fallen in the next corridor and Recker let his foot thud into the first one, pretending it was a misstep so that the squad wouldn't know it was a result of his irritation. Some of that irritation slipped away when he found the entrance to the internal shuttle not far from the maintenance station.

Soon, the squad were in a square shuttle car heading towards the centre of the *Ixidar*. Windows front and back allowed visibility along the steeply sloping tunnel through which the car was drawn by gravity motors. The whole setup made Recker think of an old cable car - a few of which still ran on Earth - except the Lavorix had stirred in enough technology to make everything faster and more efficient, if lacking in the charm.

Accompanying the squad on their journey were approximately a hundred Lavorix soldiers, once alive, but now killed in an agonising fashion by the *Gorgadar*'s death sphere. Sergeant Shadar stooped to examine a slender-barrelled rifle which had caught his eye on the floor. He stood after a moment and left the weapon next to its former owner.

The car arrived at its destination, though the shaft continued onwards into the distance. Recker opened the door and the squad exited into another of the spaceship's wide passages. Dead Lavorix covered the floor and Recker strode amongst them.

He suddenly noticed that not one of the aliens wore a different colour, nor a different type of clothing. Each was identically dressed with no insignia or distinguishing features, and Recker wondered if they had any formal officer structure and if not, how they worked so well together. It was difficult to learn anything useful about an enemy as deadly and uncommunicative as the Lavorix.

Not far from the internal shuttle, Recker located steps

and he ascended. The blast door protecting the bridge was closed, though an interface port on the access panel allowed him to send across the codes which were originally extracted from the *Aeklu*'s control core. A moment later the door opened, allowing Recker and his squad onto the *Ixidar*'s bridge.

CHAPTER NINE

"SECURE THE AREA," Recker ordered as he walked along the central aisle towards the command console situated at the front of the bridge. A Lavorix corpse had fallen sideways from its seat and it partly blocked his way. "On second thoughts, clear this crap out first and then secure the area."

"Yes, sir," said Vance. He and Shadar snapped out quick commands to the soldiers, ordering them to drag the bodies out and throw them down the steps.

"Lieutenant Eastwood – pick a station and get ready," said Recker. He turned and levelled a finger at his next target. "Corporal Montero, you're excused from corpse duty. This second console next to the command station should have full access to comms and sensors. Park yourself in front of it."

"Yes, sir."

Recker wasn't afraid to get his hands dirty and he hauled the *Ixidar*'s previous captain out of his chair and dumped him on the floor nearby. Maybe it was a female, he briefly reflected, though he wasn't planning to go rummaging around just to find out if it was hiding a cock and two balls anywhere within its spacesuit.

"Sir, my console is online and I'm waiting for you to give me access," said Eastwood.

"I'm on it, Lieutenant."

Noting that the grey covering on his seat wasn't aged like the one on the *Gorgadar*, Recker dropped himself into place. A moment later, he'd linked to the interface port and injected a code from the software in his suit computer. The code was accepted immediately and his central console screen brought up a top-level command menu.

"You should have access, Lieutenant Eastwood," Recker said shortly after. "You too, Corporal."

"What exactly am I doing, sir?" asked Montero.

"Bringing the sensors online and attempting contact with the *Gorgadar*," said Recker. "First, you'll have to wait until Lieutenant Eastwood and I have done some repairs, but you can use the time making yourself familiar with that console."

"Yes, sir." Montero stared at the console for a few seconds and Recker wondered if she was too far out of her depth. Then, she began confidently pushing buttons and he gave an inward sigh of relief.

"I'm into the maintenance system, sir," said Eastwood. "How do you want me to approach this?"

"Are you able to determine what can be fixed without actually fixing anything?" asked Recker.

"Probably, but that's adding an extra layer on the cake.

What are you concerned about, sir? That might help me give you a better answer."

"We're invaders, Lieutenant, and we don't know if the *Ixidar*'s control computer is programmed to think for itself. If it only validates the command codes, we have nothing to worry about. However if we unknowingly perform an action that makes it suspicious, then it may decide we shouldn't be here and might attempt to disable our access to anything we've brought back online. Even worse would be if that control computer decided to send details of our presence to the Ancidium via the comms system we just repaired for it."

"I hear you loud and clear, sir," said Eastwood. "I'd guess the entity you conversed with on the *Gorgadar* is no more than a node on the main control system. If the *Ixidar* was built anything like the *Aeklu*, I should be able to cut that part out of the loop and leave it stewing in its own piss on an isolated array somewhere."

"Once we reconnect those arrays," said Recker.

"There's always storage, sir. Every processing unit and every hardware module has plenty of it, normally used for transient data. In this case, I may be able to put that storage to better use."

"Stewing in its own piss?" asked Montero, feigning puzzlement. "Is that the technical term? And why can't you delete the entity files instead of isolating them?"

"The young are always full of questions," Eastwood observed.

"And the old are always full of answers," Montero shot back.

Sensing that Eastwood was about to launch into a full-scale technical explanation of the *Ixidar*'s hardware setup, Recker stepped in.

"Let's focus on what we're doing, folks. Corporal Montero, if you want to learn about propulsion, Lieutenant Eastwood's always got time when he's back on base."

"Yes, sir," she said.

It was difficult to get angry around Montero and Recker didn't even pretend. "Where there's age, there's wisdom, Corporal."

Montero couldn't completely hide her grin and she lowered her head in a failed attempt to prevent Recker seeing it.

"Any luck with that console?" he asked.

"I have no access to the sensors or the external comms, sir," Montero said. "The internal comms, however, are working fine."

"Stay off those comms until I confirm they're safe," said Recker. "Use your suit comms and remind the squad to stay within range of the bridge."

"Yes, sir."

Through recent experience, Recker was becoming competent with the Lavorix hardware and control software and he descended through the sub-menus until he located the list of maintenance and auditing options. This time, he knew he was out of his depth. On an HPA warship – maybe even on a Meklon one – he could muddle his way through the list of codes and decide which ones indicated a fault. Here on the *Ixidar*, he was stuck.

"I don't know if I can help with this, Lieutenant Eastwood."

"That's fine, sir. I'm making progress."

Having no input was frustrating and Recker considered helping shift some of the dead bodies. Even that idea came to nothing – Sergeant Shadar appeared next to the command console and grabbed the enemy captain's wrist.

"Last one," said the Daklan, dragging the corpse away.

Baring his teeth at nobody, Recker turned to his console. He remembered the *Ixidar*'s statement that its batteries were at ten percent of maximum and until now, he'd hardly questioned how that could have happened, what with the Meklon being extinct. Besides, the *Ixidar* wasn't one of the three Laws of Ancidium assigned to the Meklon spheres, so how its batteries went from zero to ten percent was a mystery Recker decided to investigate.

It didn't take long.

"I've accessed the time stamps for the Extractor batteries," said Recker. "They were at zero percent a week ago and in the last few hours they've been climbing in steps."

"The *Ixidar* must have visited another planet before it arrived at Tokladan," said Eastwood. "Maybe the Lavorix discovered another Meklon world and they extracted it before coming here."

"That's not what the time stamps say, Lieutenant." Recker added up the numbers in his head. "The first injection into the batteries ties in with the *Ixidar*'s reported arrival at Tokladan."

"The Daklan were losing people every time the planet was hit by the Extractor, sir. That could have topped up the batteries."

"If a few thousand deaths were enough to fill ten percent of the *Ixidar*'s batteries, the hundreds of billions in the Meklon empire would have sustained the Lavorix's war effort indefinitely, Lieutenant," said Recker. "This is something else."

"Damn," said Eastwood when he came to the logical conclusion.

"What?" asked Montero.

"The Lavorix have partly filled their batteries without killing the Daklan," said Recker. "They've figured out a way to extract life energy without the target dying."

"Isn't that a good thing?" Montero asked. "I mean, being extracted is bad, but it's better than dying, right?"

Recker shook his head. "Not really, Corporal. If the Lavorix have worked out how to do a part-extraction of life energy, they're going to sit on top of our worlds like parasites and drain us bit-by-bit. Maybe we'll supply them with enough juice to fight back against the Kilvar. If they don't need to kill us, they'll never need to leave and we'll be stuck in a repeated cycle of extractions, living in agony and not knowing if it'll ever end."

"Well that would suck," Montero admitted. "So how come the Lavorix didn't do this to the Meklon?"

"I don't know," said Recker. "I remember being told that in the first years of the Lavorix-Meklon wars, the extractions were limited and then it changed. Why that happened, I can only imagine it was because the Lavorix required progressively more life energy for the Ancidium. If a partial extraction works against the Daklan – maybe humans too – we may just be more resilient than the Meklon." He swore as anger took hold of him. "Lucky us – we can give up more of our life energy before we fall down dead."

"And after a few weeks of feeling like crap, we'd be all replenished and ready to be extracted again," said Eastwood. "We'd be like self-recharging power supplies."

"Screw that!" said Montero. "I'm nobody's golden goose."

"We either defeat these alien scumbags or you'd better start laying eggs, Corporal," said Eastwood.

Montero burst out laughing and the sound of it made Recker's anger dissipate. He exited the sub-menu where he'd located the battery data and decided to look again at the failure codes.

Lieutenant Eastwood saved him the effort. "I've isolated that control entity, sir, so we shouldn't have anything to worry about when the critical systems start coming back online."

"You'll definitely be able to get those systems online?" asked Recker in relief.

Eastwood exhaled loudly, which normally indicated the beginning of a comprehensive explanation. "I've analysed some of the failure codes and I reckon the *Gorgadar*'s second particle beam destroyed the main control hardware unit. Now, there are secondary and tertiary units which should have kicked in automatically, but our first particle beam destroyed the central diagnostic hardware, which would normally identify onboard faults and re-route. I guess you could call it a design flaw, except the Lavorix likely never anticipated encountering a weapon that could slice all the way through something as big as the *Ixidar*. Either way, it was shit luck for those six-armed murdering alien bastards."

It took Recker a few seconds to consider Eastwood's

summation. "On an HPA warship, you'd be able to type in a few commands and the secondary control hardware would take over."

"That's right, sir." Eastwood smiled broadly. "And that's exactly what I'm able to do here."

It was great news, though Recker didn't want to get too excited just yet. "Will we be in command of a fully-functioning warship at the end of it?"

"Not exactly, sir – the *Ixidar* already told you it's lost most of its data arrays. It's possible but unlikely that something critical and unforeseen was held on them. What's more likely is that some other important hardware modules controlling various onboard systems were destroyed or damaged, but I can't tell you which ones on account of the diagnostic hardware being out of action."

"In other words, we have to plug in the Christmas tree to see which lights have gone out?"

"That's one way of putting it. Do you want me to switch to the secondary controller?"

Recker was taken by a sudden reluctance. Having felt the weight of passing time for the entire journey here, now he was fearful of making an error because he gave the order too soon.

I've never backed down and I'm not about to start now.

"Corporal Montero, when the switchover is done, you'll be in charge of sensors and comms on a warship capable of destroying entire fleets. Are you ready?"

The earlier humour was gone and all Recker saw in Montero's face was the steel and determination of the soldier she was.

"I'm ready, sir."

"Lieutenant Eastwood, bring us back online."

"Switching over...done."

Immediately, the rows of warning lights on Recker's top panel and on his status screen changed to purple. Deep within the *Ixidar*, the immense ternium kickstarter modules thudded like dead giants striking the insides of their coffin lids. The propulsion started up with a shuddering cough that sent a vibration through every surface. Recker placed his hands on the controls.

"Corporal Montero?"

"Sensors coming online, sir."

Recker watched the blank screens along the forward bulkhead and wondered why he still felt so unsettled.

CHAPTER TEN

THE *IXIDAR* WAS FITTED with dozens of main arrays and they came online all at once, too many individual feeds for Recker to make sense of. Most showed only darkness.

"I've located the *Gorgadar*," said Montero. "It's still following and at the same distance as before."

She focused one of the arrays on the other warship. The *Gorgadar* looked both technologically advanced and mean as hell at the same time, like a ruthless killer in a tailored suit.

"Request a channel," said Recker. "And link us into the internal comms whenever you're ready."

"Lieutenant Burner has accepted the request."

"Put him on the open channel."

"I'll have that for you in just a moment, sir."

A few seconds later, Burner's voice emerged from the bridge speakers.

"You're on the *Ixidar*'s bridge, sir?"

"We are," Recker confirmed. "Lieutenant Eastwood discovered the main cause of hardware failure and he's switched us onto a secondary controller."

"Is the *Ixidar* fully operational?"

"Lieutenant Eastwood is monitoring our status. I wanted to check the comms."

"I'll remain in the channel, sir."

"Thank you." Recker half-turned. "Lieutenant Eastwood, what progress?"

"Our propulsion is online, but it's only offering a fraction of its maximum output. Something's tapping into the modules."

"The energy shield?" asked Recker. "The reserve gauge is at ten percent and climbing."

"That might be it, sir. You should check the weapons systems from your console."

Recker did so. "The housings for the energy cannons are loading up as well. It seems they dumped their charge when everything shut down."

"We might have to wait for everything to run its course, sir."

"Any idea how long it'll take?"

"No, sir. Given the damage, I'm not surprised at what's happening."

Recker's impatience got the better of him and he placed his hands on the controls while he inspected the instrumentation readouts. A couple of the purple status lights had turned blue, which he guessed indicated progress, though how much progress, he had no idea.

A push of the control bars produced an angry, irregular grumble from the propulsion and the *Ixidar* accelerated reluctantly to seven hundred kilometres per second, leaving the *Gorgadar* behind.

"Going somewhere, sir?" asked Burner on the open channel.

"Just testing, Lieutenant," said Recker, dropping to four hundred kilometres per second. On the sensors, the *Gorgadar* came back into focus and Aston matched velocity again.

Another purple light turned blue and Recker dared ask himself what the HPA-Daklan alliance might do with two Laws of Ancidium under their control. Perhaps they would be enough to drive away the Ancidium. Perhaps.

"Oh crap," said Burner.

"Don't give me *oh crap*, Lieutenant," said Recker. "What's wrong?"

"The *Gorgadar*'s sensors have detected an inbound particle wave, midway between here and Tokladan, sir. You are not going to believe the magnitude of it."

Recker's body gave him another shot of adrenaline and his heart thudded painfully in his chest. He suddenly knew the cause of the trepidation he'd felt on the shuttle and ever since. "The Ancidium."

"It must be, sir," said Burner. "I don't know how to interpret these readings, but it's going to be like nothing we've encountered before."

The timing couldn't have been worse and Recker wondered if this was down to bad luck, or if the *Ixidar* had managed to get out an FTL distress comm before its hardware failed.

"Tell Commander Aston I want her to take the *Gorgadar* away from here, Lieutenant," said Recker.

Aston entered the channel. "Negative, sir. We can't leave you behind."

"It's too late for that, Commander. The *Ixidar* isn't ready to fight and neither is the *Gorgadar*. Not against what's coming."

"What about you, sir?"

"The *Ixidar* is lost anyway. We can't lose the *Gorgadar* as well. Go! I'm giving you a direct order, Commander."

"Damnit, sir!"

"The Ancidium is here!" yelled Burner. "Holy crap – there's no way we can beat it!"

"Commander Aston!" shouted Recker. "Now!"

The *Gorgadar* vanished from the sensors as if it had never existed and Recker hoped it had escaped the Ancidium's notice.

"Lieutenant Eastwood, how long?" he asked.

"Same answer as last time, sir," said Eastwood.

Recker reached for the controls, knowing already it would be too little to get away from what was coming. "Obtain a sensor lock, Corporal Montero," he said, his voice calm.

"I'm trying, sir." Montero swore a few times. "Got it!"

On the feed, Recker saw a tiny dot, a long way from the *Ixidar*. "Zoom and enhance," he ordered.

Montero didn't get the chance. The grey speck disappeared and Recker knew exactly where it was heading.

"Find it," he said.

The Ancidium didn't need finding. It appeared five thousand metres off the *Ixidar*'s portside flank, like a sheer cliff of the darkest alloy, which stretched on and on in every direction like it would never end. There was something about it – a distortion that Recker couldn't quite pin down. It seemed to him the material of the Lavorix spaceship vibrated ever so slightly, making it appear as if it were charged with an unleashed energy of such potency that it could destroy stars and planets alike.

Montero worked to adjust the feeds, but the Ancidium was so close that the *Ixidar*'s sensors didn't have the angle to view the enemy craft in its entirety. The best Recker could guess was that it was slightly tapered at the nose and the facing flank curved as it rose, blocking his view of the upper sections.

Now that the Ancidium was here as a tangible thing crawled out of the shadows, Recker's fear – the fear he'd tried to deny, yet had clung to him always – fell away like a rot-scented burial shroud. In the moment of it happening, Recker was confronted by the knowledge of how deeply the claws of that fear had buried themselves within him, sliding into his unconscious mind with such perfect sharpness that he hadn't realised until this very moment how much it had changed him.

With his opponent revealed, he felt the terror no longer and the relief was such that he felt a rush of elation at his freedom.

"The sensors estimate the Ancidium is twelve hundred *kilometres* in length, and five hundred in height." said Montero. "It has matched our velocity exactly."

"That's why the Kilvar have never located the Lavorix's home world," said Recker. "Because they don't have one. They're all onboard one massive spaceship, free to go wherever they want at a moment's notice."

"Sir, what are your orders?" asked Montero, her steeliness from earlier cracking beneath the strain.

"Hold steady, Corporal." Recker knew what the Ancidium was here for. "The Lavorix have come for their warship."

"What will they do?"

"Check your console."

"There's a channel request from the Ancidium." Montero's eyes were wide. "Should I accept?"

"Hell no, Corporal. The less the enemy know, the better it'll be for us."

"What will they do if we don't respond?"

Recker had a couple of ideas, one of which he was certain would become reality. "They'll either Gateway us to a deep space construction and repair yard somewhere, or..." he smiled, "...they'll bring us inside."

"Scanning for hull doors," said Montero at once. "It's like the sensors don't want to focus properly."

"What readings are they giving you?" asked Recker.

"I'm sorry, sir, I can't answer that."

"That's fine, Corporal. I'm not disappointed if there's something you don't know."

"There's plenty of that, sir." Montero straightened. "Bay doors," she said. "They're opening."

A thirty-thousand-metre square slab of metal directly opposite the *Ixidar* sank deep into the Ancidium's hull and then dropped out of sight into a recess between the layers of armour plating. Forty kilometres inside, Recker saw another door like the first.

"What happens next?" asked Montero.

"They'll take over our controls," said Recker.

No sooner had the words left his mouth than a short line of text appeared on one of the command console displays.

Ancidium> Control assumed.

"We didn't even get a say in that," said Eastwood.

Recker nodded. "Find out how it happened, Lieutenant. Most importantly, find out if you can revoke the Ancidium's control and prevent it taking over again. Look but don't touch."

"I'd like to think we can get out of this, sir, but..."

"Don't give up, Lieutenant. We're deeper in the crap than we've been before, but that doesn't mean there's no chance of escape."

"We just need a planet-sized shovel to dig our way out of it, sir. I know that."

Holding velocity, the Ancidium guided the *Ixidar* towards the bay entrance. In seconds, the much smaller warship was completely within the tunnel. The Ancidium's controller rotated the *Ixidar* so that one of its faces was parallel to the inner door and brought it so close that Recker wondered if the protruding disintegration cannon would impact. It did not. The outer door rose and its motors drove it into position, sealing the *Ixidar* inside.

Operating with computer efficiency, the inner doors dropped into their own recess and the *Ixidar* entered another tunnel with another door.

"It's like the *Ixidar*'s docking procedure, scaled up a few thousand percent," said Eastwood. "They must be taking us to the repair yard. It won't take them long to realise we're onboard."

"No it won't," Recker agreed. "Lieutenant Montero, shut down the internal comms and security monitoring."

"That'll take me a minute to figure out, sir. I could stick some chewing gum over the bridge lens if you prefer?"

"Nice idea, but the life sign readings will be harder to cover up."

"Damn," said Montero, staring at the comms console.

"As quickly as you can," said Recker calmly. "Our lives depend on it."

The second door closed and the third one opened. As soon as there was enough clearance, the *Ixidar* started moving once more and this time it entered a space unlike anything Recker had ever seen before. He stared at the feed, wondering at the scale of the challenge facing not just the occupants of the *Ixidar*, but the HPA and the Daklan as well.

CHAPTER ELEVEN

"THIS IS a holding bay not a construction yard," said Recker.

"A holding bay full of Lavorix warships," added Eastwood. "A crapload of Lavorix warships."

"How are you getting on with those internal monitors, Corporal?"

"I've located the off switch, sir. Won't this make the enemy suspicious?"

"Maybe, but it'll be much better than them knowing for definite we're here."

"The internal comms and security are disabled, sir."

"Keep watching and make sure the Ancidium doesn't switch them back on."

"It can do that?" asked Montero.

"Not anymore," said Eastwood with satisfaction. "I've routed the internal comms back into the failed primary controller. We had to come onboard to re-route, so there should be no way for the Ancidium to change it remotely."

"Good work, Lieutenant – you've earned us some breathing room."

Room to do what, Recker still didn't know, though he was thinking hard.

"I've obtained estimates of the bay's dimensions, sir," said Montero. "The far wall is three hundred klicks from here." She swore. "Three hundred klicks! The ceiling is seventy klicks overhead and the other two walls are a hundred apart!"

"How many enemy warships do you count, Corporal?"

"The *Ixidar*'s sensors are tracking eighty-one separate targets, sir. The largest is nine thousand klicks and with an estimated mass of 115 billion tons. A minnow compared to what we're flying."

"Biggest damn minnow I ever saw," said Eastwood.

Recker considered their position. The holding bay was completely unlit and lined with alloy, its walls studded with blocky gravity clamps, most of which were holding the Lavorix warships in place. A few warships – these ones larger than a Daklan annihilator and bulky, with twin-barrelled gauss cannons and multiple launch clusters – drifted slowly through the bay like unconcerned fish.

"You could fit the entire Ivisto facility in here three times over," said Eastwood.

"I've located some other doors," said Montero. "A door going up, a door going down, and a door in the left-hand wall."

Recker narrowed his eyes at the feeds. The left-hand door was indented, with six battleship-sized warships clamped to the wall nearby, while the upper and lower doors were at the far end of the bay.

"Each door thirty klicks by thirty," said Montero.

"Same as the outers - more than enough room to fly the Laws of Ancidium through," said Recker. "The Lavorix must have construction facilities in one of the other bays."

Slowly, the immensity of the Ancidium was sinking in. It was one thing to get a sense of it from outside and another to see just this single internal bay. How the Lavorix had constructed their home base, Recker didn't want to imagine. From what he knew of the enemy, they'd have plundered, murdered, and enslaved other species and set them to work for centuries – millennia, perhaps.

Thinking about it made Recker sure that if he were stupid enough to climb topside, he'd smell the same stale odours of ancient decay as he'd found on the Laws of Ancidium. The Lavorix had been around for a long time and the scale of their foulness was surely beyond comprehension. At last, they'd found a match in the Kilvar and Recker hated the thought that the extraction of his own species would play any part in the enemy's recovery.

Now the *Ixidar* was completely in the holding bay, the entrance door closed, sealing it inside. The Ancidium didn't relinquish control and it guided the warship towards the far end of the bay. The smaller spacecraft got out of the way and the *Ixidar* flew without deviation in its course.

"Are they taking us straight to the repair yard?" asked Montero.

"I don't know, Corporal," said Recker. "There's no reason they wouldn't."

Two hundred kilometres into the bay, the *Ixidar* was brought to a halt, midway between the floor and the ceiling.

"That lower door is opening," said Montero.

"That's where we're heading," said Recker confidently.

He was wrong. The door opened, but the *Ixidar* wasn't guided any closer. Instead, a two-thousand-metre cube, with its every surface covered in spiky antennae, rose into sight, and then the door closed.

"Another interrogator?" said Eastwood.

"Looks like," said Recker. He didn't like it when he couldn't predict his enemy's intentions and he drummed his fingers as the interrogator floated directly towards the *Ixidar*. The first time he'd seen one of these spaceships was at a planet called Pinvos, and back then a thirty-billion-ton mass had seemed like an impossibly vast construction. Now he knew different.

"Lieutenant Eastwood, why might the enemy have sent that interrogator?"

"The clue is probably in the name, sir. I guess it can scour our onboard systems and run a diagnostic."

"At which point the Lavorix would realise that the *Ixidar* is online and recovering from a hardware failure."

"Yes, sir."

"And they might begin to wonder how the switchover to the secondary controller happened, given that the diagnostic module is no longer operational."

"Yes, sir."

"At which point, the Lavorix may begin asking themselves serious questions about why they aren't getting answers from the comms."

"Yes, sir. And they've probably already worked out that the only weapon capable of inflicting so much damage to the *Ixidar* is fitted to the *Gorgadar*."

"So we could be even deeper in the shit than I imagined," said Recker.

"That's beginning to look like the picture, sir."

Recker opened his mouth to curse and then stopped himself. "What is the status of the *Ixidar*'s online systems, Lieutenant Eastwood?"

"I think they're beginning to stabilise, sir. What happened was the re-routing produced a conflict between the secondary and tertiary control modules, stemming from a simultaneous request on the..."

"Enough," said Recker. He accessed the weapons and discovered that five of the disintegration cannons were charged to fifty percent and the gauge wasn't climbing any higher. The Lavorix called the weapons *destroyers*, which no doubt explained where the *Ixidar* got its own secondary name from. "Our main armaments are ready to enter combat mode," he said. "Once I give the firing instruction, the first gun should tap into the propulsion, bringing its energy store to one hundred percent."

"Yes, sir," said Eastwood. "Are you asking me a question?"

"Is there anything that will prevent a discharge?"

"I don't think so, sir. There's plenty still happening because of the switch to the secondary controller, but those cannons have priority over the other systems. Many of the other systems aren't ready."

"Like what?"

"The propulsion will go into overstress – though I wouldn't recommend it unless you want to give the game away to the Ancidium – but there's no mode 3 availability."

"Do we have an Extractor, sir?" asked Montero. "I'm sure the Lavorix here on the Ancidium would appreciate a little taste."

"We do have an Extractor, Corporal," said Recker.

"Let me guess, it's offline or damaged?"

"Not this time." Recker's eyes were on the feed, where the interrogator had slowed to a halt, less than two thousand metres from the *Ixidar*.

"You mean we could target the Extractor and kill every one of these Lavorix and the war would be over?"

"It isn't available yet," said Eastwood. "Once the propulsion output climbs high enough, the Extractor will be ready to fire."

"And I don't think it'll be as easy as you say, Corporal," said Recker, calling up the weapons menu and checking again. "The Lavorix built in a simulator that shows them the results when they adjust the focus point of the weapon. Upshot is, at maximum spread the arc is still narrow."

"So if we fire it, the arc won't be wide enough to kill all the Lavorix on the Ancidium unless they're clustered in the place we happen to fire?"

"That's correct. We're at the approximate mid-point of the enemy spacecraft, so if we aimed forward or back, I'm sure we'd nail a good few million of its occupants."

Montero was full of questions. “When will the mode 3 become available?”

“I have no estimate on that,” said Eastwood. “If we’re planning to mode 3 out of here and then attack the Ancidium with an Extractor, I’d say our best bet is to keep our heads down and hope nobody notices we’re here.”

“Have you found a way to block the Ancidium’s access to our systems yet, Lieutenant?” asked Recker.

“My mouth’s talking, but my brain never stops working, sir. I’ve discovered how to prevent remote access to our navigational system, which means I can give you control over the *Ixidar* and I can make it difficult for the enemy to regain that control. Unfortunately, there’s another problem to which I haven’t yet figured out the answer.”

“What problem?”

“A shutdown code, sir. If the Ancidium decides to, it can send the *Ixidar* offline.”

“Is there a way to prevent it happening?”

“What would the point be in having the codes if a rogue agent could stop them working, sir?” asked Eastwood. He lifted a hand to cut off Recker’s next remark. “However, I can make things difficult. I’d expect a shutdown code to bypass the normal comms antennae and have its own dedicated receiver that links to a hidden security unit buried somewhere in the ship.”

Recker opened his mouth.

“I’m going somewhere with this, sir,” said Eastwood quickly. “While I don’t have access to that security unit, I have a good idea that it’ll route its codes into the main controller. Since that controller is offline, I might be able to fool the security unit into thinking the codes have successfully reached their destinations."

"What happens when the Ancidium realises their codes didn't work?"

"There'll be some head scratching I reckon and probably some cursing. Then, one of the Lavorix who knows how this stuff works, will figure out that the security unit should be directed to send its codes to the secondary and tertiary controllers. At that point, we'll be screwed – I have no way of blocking a shutdown code that hits the active controller."

"Uh, I've got another inbound comms request from the Ancidium, sir," said Montero.

"Don't touch that panel," Recker warned.

"I've detected an intrusion into the diagnostic systems, sir," said Eastwood. "A full audit has been initiated."

"Can you stop it?"

"Easily enough if you order it, sir. All that'll happen is the interrogator will start again and at the same time, the command I used to stop the audit will be added to a visible log. The Lavorix will know the code was entered from the bridge. It won't take them long to add two and two."

Recker was being pushed into a corner and he didn't like it. The idea of laying low until engine mode 3 became available had appealed to him greatly, as did the thought of killing the Lavorix with their own Extractor. With the arrival of the interrogator, that chance was slipping away.

"It's never easy," he said. Recker called up the weapons menu. "We've got no missile clusters and no countermeasures. They built the *Ixidar* simple."

"Readings from the energy shield gauge indicate they

built it tough as well, sir," said Eastwood. "The *Ixidar* has a few hundred billion tons of overstressed ternium dedicated to shield maintenance and replenishment, along with the flexibility to divert the output from the other modules to keep it sustained."

"When I saw what the *Ixidar* did to our fleets at RETI-11, I asked myself if the Lavorix had it purpose-built to wipe out fleets," said Recker. "Now, I'm certain they did."

Imagining this eighteen-thousand metre cube with its six guns bringing carnage to opposition fleets made Recker's head swim with a desire he didn't much like finding in himself. The *Ixidar* surely had a few thousand kills to its name. It was no wonder its control entity had an attitude.

And still it wasn't enough to defeat the Kilvar. Variations of this same thought kept jumping into Recker's head.

"The audit is complete, sir," said Eastwood. "I'd expect to find that shutdown code heading our way sometime soon. Do you have a plan?"

"A simple ship calls for a simple plan," said Recker. He raised an arm, pointed at one of the feeds and smiled. It wasn't a nice smile. "Do you see those warships out there, Corporal Montero?"

"Yes, sir. Are we going to blow the crap out of them?"

"That's exactly what we're going to do, Corporal. And if the Extractor comes online, we're going to give them a big helping of that as well."

Montero smiled. "If we're about to die, I'd like to know it happened giving the Lavorix the biggest damn headache."

"The *Ixidar* received a shutdown code, sir," said Eastwood. "We're still operational, so my trick with the security unit fooled them.

"The enemy know we're here," said Recker. He scanned the many sensor feeds, mentally selecting targets. The *Ixidar*'s shield gauge was full, the destroyer cannons were available and the Extractor soon would be, even if its spread was too narrow to be much use in the confines of the bay. Having seen the *Ixidar* in action, Recker had a feeling the cannons would be enough.

It was time to find out.

CHAPTER TWELVE

THREE HUNDRED KILOMETRES end to end wasn't a lot to play with, but Recker didn't care. He rammed the *Ixidar*'s controls along their runners and hard into their metal stops. A thunder of engines threatened to swamp his senses and the warship accelerated with savage ease, straight for the near end of the bay.

The interrogator was within the perimeter of the *Ixidar*'s shield and it was struck by the upper corner of the oncoming spaceship. Thirty billion tons was nothing compared to the almost immeasurable mass of the *Ixidar* and the interrogator was batted aside like an insect. It crashed into one of the anchored warships, breaking antennae and sending pieces of debris raining to the floor.

Although Recker lacked extensive experience piloting Lavorix hardware, his brain had an unsurpassed knowledge of space combat and it evaluated targets, possibilities and priorities, unimpeded by the limitations of his physical movements. One of the larger Lavorix warships, 150 kilometres towards the opposite end of the bay, came into the sights of the first charged destroyed cannon and Recker didn't hesitate. He fired and the discharge produced a rumbling from the *Ixidar*'s ternium modules, overlaid upon the propulsion's reverberant voice.

A sphere of darkness almost ten thousand metres in diameter engulfed the enemy battleship and the blast's edges tickled the flank of a second. In an instant, the sphere was gone and the first target was reduced to a corroded mess of particles, fragmenting armour, and failing engines, while the second banked towards the nearest wall, ejecting missiles and two massive slugs from its topside gauss turrets.

With such a short distance to travel, the detonations happened almost at once, lighting up the *Ixidar*'s shield. Glancing at the reserve gauge, Recker saw that it had hardly dropped and the knowledge of it made him think of the fury he was about to visit upon the Ancidium's bay.

The *Ixidar* had come within touching distance of the bay's end and Recker brought it to a rapid halt. None of the destroyer cannons had begun recharging, leaving him to figure out at the worst of moments how the Lavorix weapons system was designed to function.

It turned out the method was straightforward and he understood the principles in a few seconds. Once a hull rotation was manually introduced, the battle computer controlled the cannon recharge based on the direction of the turn. If an out-of-sequence shot were required, a different gun could be selected from the control bar buttons and then it would begin charging. The knock-on effect of that would be to interrupt the original charging sequence, necessitating a rethink of the attack pattern.

This wasn't the best time for practice, but Recker was up for the challenge and he sent the *Ixidar* accelerating towards the bay's entrance.

As the warship gathered speed, he set it into a clockwise rotation. The speed of the turn was adjusted by using a small touchpad on the thumb side of the left control bar. From here he could also set the *Ixidar* into a tumble. Twenty seconds into the combat, Recker was left astounded at the skills the original pilot and weapons officer had possessed. Here in the bay, he intended to bring carnage where it was impossible to miss. Shooting a target a billion kilometres away was something else entirely.

Halfway along the bay, the *Ixidar*'s shield smashed into another of the battleships. The enemy ship was thrown into the ceiling by the impact, and it glanced off before accelerating in the opposite direction to the *Ixidar*, launching missiles as it went. The range was so close that the warheads didn't have time to arm and they shattered harmlessly against the energy shield.

"Our early surprise is going to end any moment, sir," said Eastwood.

"I've learned what I needed to learn, Lieutenant," said Recker. "Keep those sensors aimed in the right direction, Corporal Montero. Without them, I'm firing blind."

"Yes, sir."

Once the *Ixidar* was nearly at the entrance end of the bay, Recker slowed the spaceship. The rotation brought one of the destroyer cannons to bear on the first set of outer doors and he activated the discharge. The blast came and went, leaving no mark whatsoever.

"What the hell?" said Recker.

"Doesn't look as if we'll be escaping any time soon," said Montero.

Recker was shocked at the cannon's ineffectiveness and he struggled to remain focused. He began accelerating once more in the opposite direction, hoping his brain would serve up a few bright ideas. Montero had focused the sensors well, allowing him an excellent view of the bay. A dozen warships were in the air, and others were detaching from their gravity clamps. The signs were there, clear as day, that all hell was about to break loose.

"Firing destroyer cannon," said Recker.

The charged gun was aimed at the side wall where a stack of six heavy cruisers were still clamped. Recker caught two of them with one shot, leaving both crumbling and the bay wall untouched. Far ahead, he watched a half-dozen other enemy ships detach from their berths. Five hundred missiles or more, launched from multiple sources, appeared on the *Ixidar*'s tactical, travelling with such velocity that they remained for less than a second.

"Impact," said Montero at the same time as the *Ixidar*'s part of the bay was illuminated in the harshest of whites.

"Destroyer cannon charged," said Recker.

He was struggling to coordinate between aiming and rotation, and the gun was aimed way off the place he'd intended. Nevertheless, he fired and a single cruiser was turned into a mixture of powder and decaying alloy. Recker didn't slow and the *Ixidar*'s progress was so rapid that the warships ahead couldn't get out of its path fast enough. Three huge battleships were swatted away by the energy shield, the impact spoiling the aim of their gauss turrets.

A salvo of missiles streaked across the bay and then another. The tactical reported several gauss impacts on the energy shield and then missiles exploded in their hundreds. Recker's eyes darted to the reserve gauge, which had dropped but was already climbing again. More explosions briefly halted its climb and then up it went again.

"The *Ixidar* is drawing on its ternium modules to boost the shield recharge, sir," said Eastwood. "At this rate, neither the Extractor nor the mode 3 will become available."

"In that case, we'll have to clear some of this chaff from the bay," said Recker. "When things quieten down, we won't need our shield so much."

The words were bold, when in fact the combat had hardly started. Hundreds of missiles came in from every direction, their plasma encircling the *Ixidar*'s shield, and Recker guessed the only thing keeping the Lavorix from completely saturating the bay with missiles was because they had so many damn ships crowded inside.

He fired the destroyer cannon again, turning the outer five hundred metres of a battleship into crumbling flakes. The *Ixidar* crashed into the fragmenting innards of the stricken craft and it exploded into particles.

"End of the bay coming up," said Montero. Her hands moved with greater certainty across the sensor panel and Recker had no complaints about the visibility she provided.

He slowed the *Ixidar* to a standstill while maintaining the tumble. The next charged cannon pointed on target and he fired it into a cluster of three rapidly moving cruisers.

"Back we go," he said, tapping into the engines.

The *Ixidar* raced along the bay and Recker fired the next cannon instinctively, cutting an enemy battleship in half. The intact front section began spinning and collided with a second vessel nearby.

Before Recker knew it, the *Ixidar* was up against the entrance doors again. He fired a cannon at a pair of clamped heavies and accelerated for the other end of the bay. On the forward feed, he could see movement everywhere. Lavorix warships sped to and fro, jostling for position. Missiles he sensed as fast-moving blurs which turned into fiery spheres of incredible heat.

All the while, the *Ixidar*'s cannons charged and discharged to devastating effect. Every Lavorix warship was now in flight and the double hits were harder to come by. Recker didn't try to complicate matters and he took each shot without hesitation, pulverising the enemy ships and turning them into dust.

"We received another shut down code, sir," said Eastwood. "The stupid idiots sent it to the primary controller again."

"It won't be long until they figure it out," said Recker.

The *Ixidar* came to the bay's end and he set off for the opposite one, discharging the cannon at the same time. At some point during the last transit of the bay, Recker's grasp of the method had improved enormously and he'd figured out how to control the speed of the *Ixidar*'s tumble so that the next charged cannon would be aimed in the direction he intended. No longer was he taking snap shots at whatever target happened to be in the sights – now he was hitting the most threatening enemy warships each time.

"I feel like a die on the craps table," said Eastwood.

Under constant bombardment, the *Ixidar* accelerated along the bay. Testing his skills, Recker veered left and right, each movement producing a crunching impact with a Lavorix spaceship. Despite its mass, the *Ixidar* was incredibly manoeuvrable and he had no problem keeping clear of the bay walls.

"Down to fifty-eight targets, sir," said Montero.

Instead of reducing the quantity of inbound missiles, thinning the enemy numbers gave them greater space from which to fire unimpeded. For a time, the *Ixidar*'s shield was so thickly wrapped in plasma that the reserve gauge fell steadily.

"I think we've reached the limits of what the hardware can do, sir," said Eastwood. "If this continues, our chances of firing the Extractor are slim and the chances of a mode 3 escape are zero."

"We're walking the edge, Lieutenant," said Recker. "Sooner or later, the enemy will send that shutdown code to the secondary or tertiary controllers and if we're not out of here before then, we'll be killed and the enemy will retrieve the *Ixidar*."

The moment he said the words, Recker understood the choices which lay ahead. If the Lavorix recovered the *Ixidar*, they'd use it to punishing effect against the HPA and Daklan fleets, while the only way to prevent them from taking back the warship was to mode 3 out of the bay.

There's another way, Recker thought. *I could switch off the shield and let the enemy destroy the Ixidar.*

The idea was the best way to keep the warship out of the enemy's hands, but at the same time, it guaranteed the deaths of everyone onboard. Gritting his teeth, Recker shot down another Lavorix warship and then a second when the next cannon had charged.

"Whatever happens to us, doing what we're doing to the enemy feels great," said Montero.

Recker wondered if she'd read his expression or if she'd arrived at the same conclusion herself. Either way, he was glad that Montero had put a positive swing on the situation.

"Each one of these enemy ships we take down is one less our fleet has to face," he said.

The *Ixidar* was at the end of the bay and Recker repeated the same routine of flying at high speed for the opposite wall, banking left and right, up and down to strike the enemy warships. Meanwhile, the Lavorix fired without cease and the *Ixidar*'s shield fell below fifty percent. It wasn't going to be enough to prevent Recker finishing off every last one of them – as long as the shut-down code didn't arrive first – and he accepted without guilt the feeling of euphoria which came from turning one of the enemy's primary weapons against them.

"Down you go!" said Montero when another of the enemy battleships was turned into particles.

For once, the Lavorix had no answer to the merciless punishment Recker meted out. His lips drew back into something that wasn't quite a smile and not quite a snarl and he gave the enemy everything the *Ixidar* was capable of.

"Thirty targets remaining, sir," said Montero. "Make that twenty-nine."

"Still no shutdown code," said Eastwood.

When the number of Lavorix warships fell to twenty-five – mostly cruisers, with a couple of heavies – their bombardment was not enough to prevent the *Ixidar*'s shield reserves from stabilising at thirty percent. Even so, it was frustrating for Recker that the continued drain on the propulsion was keeping the Extractor and the mode 3 options unavailable.

"This is crazy," said Montero, shaking her head in wonder.

Three more Lavorix warships went down and then a fourth. Their decaying carcasses dropped to the bay floor, to join the ever-growing mountains of dust and part-disintegrated hulls left by the *Ixidar*'s onslaught.

By this point, the incoming firepower was reduced enough for the shield reserves to nose upwards. Recker felt no better for it – with each passing second, he felt closer to the brink. A decision would have to be made, whether he liked it or not.

The final heavy cruiser went the way of the others and a solid impact knocked a smaller cruiser into a second. The collision happened just as both spaceships were launching missiles and a salvo from the first craft tore apart a third Lavorix spaceship at the extreme end of the bay.

Recker took a deep breath. "I'm sorry folks, I've got to

do what I think is right. We can't let the enemy have this warship back in one piece."

"No need to apologise," said Eastwood. "Do what you have to do."

Hoping he was making the right choice, Recker reached out and switched off the *Ixidar*'s shield.

CHAPTER THIRTEEN

HUNDREDS OF MISSILES cascaded into the *Ixidar*'s unprotected faces, putting a second of the destroyer cannons out of action. The other four remained operational and Recker disintegrated one cruiser and collided with a second. Here, deep within the *Ixidar*'s hull, he felt nothing of the impact and nothing of the explosions which left the exterior plating in a patchwork cratered mess of burning alloy.

"The Extractor should be available soon, sir!" yelled Eastwood in excitement. "Now the shield isn't sucking up our spare output, there's plenty available for the other onboard systems!"

"Whoa, I've got an inbound comms request from the *Gorgadar*!" said Montero, almost jumping from her seat.

It was news Recker had not anticipated and it almost broke his concentration. "Accept the request!"

"It's Lieutenant Burner, sir," Montero said. "The

Gorgadar is still in the DEKA-L system and Commander Aston is holding position at extreme range."

Recker had the Extractor activation controls up on his screen and he checked if it was ready to fire. It wasn't and the readout gave no indication of how much longer it required. "What are Commander Aston's intentions?"

"She has not committed to a plan, sir - she was unaware of our situation." Montero broke off the conversation with Lieutenant Burner. "The enemy warships have stopped firing!"

Montero was right. A few missiles, launched before the Lavorix received the cease order, crashed into the *Ixidar*'s plating, their explosions pitiful against the vast expanses of hardened alloy. The enemy had stopped attacking but Recker had no intention of doing so. He fired the charged cannon, scoring a direct hit on one of the dwindling number of enemy warships.

"Why?" said Eastwood. "They were firing just a moment ago."

Recker cursed himself for a fool. "The Lavorix know the Laws of Ancidium better than we do - they wanted to slow the Extractor recharging and to stop us using a mode 3 escape. They could only accomplish that by bombarding our energy shield."

"If they know the *Ixidar* so well, they must be aware both the Extractor and a mode 3 transit will become available that much faster now that the shield is down. There's no way they're letting us get out of this," said Eastwood. "Unless..."

"Shutdown code," said Recker.

"Damnit, they just sent it!" yelled Eastwood. "This

one's being diverted into both the secondary and tertiary controllers."

A light appeared on Recker's console. "Extractor available!" he shouted.

His hands moved at once and he touched the Extractor activation button. A targeting option came up and he directed the firing cone as quickly as he could towards the Ancidium's stern and discharged the weapon.

At the same moment, the *Ixidar*'s propulsion fell utterly silent and Recker's link to the weapons systems was cut.

"Sensors going offline," said Montero. "Sensors dead and I've been kicked out of the comms channel to the *Gorgadar*."

The bulkhead screens went dark, denying the crew a sight of what was happening in the bay. Recker quickly checked the other menus and discovered that nothing was available. He swore and smashed his clenched fist on the panel.

"Did the Extractor fire?" asked Montero.

"Yes," said Recker. "I'm sure it did." He swore again. "The shutdown code stops me running an audit."

"The life support is active," said Eastwood. "Which is a good thing since we're about to impact."

Mentally, Recker predicted when and where the *Ixidar* would come down. He knew the bay had gravity not so different to that on most populated planets, and the warship had been travelling at speed towards the bay's end, while a variation he'd introduced in its path, in combination with the tumble suggested the *Ixidar*'s landing would not be a soft one.

A distant thud and a boom came to Recker's ears. He listened carefully and it got louder, becoming a scrape and a shudder.

"All the way through nine thousand metres of alloy," said Eastwood. "I guess that means we're down."

"What now?" asked Montero.

"Did you learn anything from Lieutenant Burner?" asked Recker.

"Only what I told you, sir. I don't think they want to risk the *Gorgadar*, but they're too loyal to fly off and not come back." Montero met Recker's eye. She was a smart one.

"I don't think there's anything they can do," he said. "We can't lose the *Gorgadar*."

"How did they even get a signal to us through the Ancidium's walls?" asked Montero.

"An FTL comm will bypass anything," said Recker.

She nodded in understanding. "And since our suit comms lack an FTL receiver, they can't speak to us now."

"Got it in one, Corporal."

Recker stood and looked around the bridge, while he pondered their position. "We destroyed plenty of the Lavorix warships, but I'm not sure I can call this a victory," he said. "The *Ixidar*'s armour took a pounding there, yet its energy shield generator is still operational. All it needs to destroy our fleet is guns and that shield. The Ancidium doesn't even need to get involved."

"The *Ixidar* lost another gun," Montero pointed out.

"Four's enough, Corporal."

"And wouldn't those have been squashed by our landing?" she asked.

"They're probably designed to retract."

"In that case, can we disable the operational guns with explosives or something?" she asked. "Or what if we locate the shield generator and Private Enfield lays a whole pack of charges on it?"

"The shield generator modules on the *Aeklu* and *Verumol* were about a thousand metres cubed," said Eastwood. "All of Private Enfield's charges wouldn't make any more than a scratch on the surface."

Montero climbed from her seat and began pacing in a way that reminded Recker of himself. He'd have laughed if the situation weren't so grim.

"There's got to be something we can do," she said. "Can't we warm up one of the shuttles and lightspeed out of here? It'll be a while before the Lavorix can put enough soldiers inside the *Ixidar* to prevent us reaching one of the bays."

"Nice idea but the shuttles will be affected by the shutdown code as well," said Eastwood. "If someone stole one of your warships, you wouldn't want them escaping once you'd put the vessel into an offline state."

"I guess," said Montero.

Recker was suddenly taken by her enthusiasm. It was how he'd been once, in the dim and distant past. Now every decision he made carried such a weight that he could no longer afford to get anything wrong, and it had made him shrink within himself. He missed how he used to be.

"The *Gorgadar*'s shuttle might not be affected by the shutdown code," said Recker suddenly. "It's lightspeed capable."

"I'd rather live to fight another day than be captured, tortured and killed by the Lavorix, sir," said Eastwood.

"You and me both, Lieutenant." Recker had a worrying thought. "An HPA shutdown code doesn't disable a warship's internal doors. The Lavorix might do things differently."

"Only one way to find out," said Montero. She strode to the door and touched the access panel. "Not working. Damn."

"That one requires special codes before it'll open, Corporal," said Recker. He approached and tried it himself. The door opened. "If this one works, they'll all work."

"That's great, sir. Those Lavorix are going to be hopping mad when they arrive and find us missing."

The urgency of the situation wasn't lost on Recker, and time was passing. He called for Vance and Shadar to meet him at the bottom of the bridge steps and he descended to meet them.

"It is a shame we must concede the *Ixidar* to its creators," said Shadar. "I can see you have no option, Captain Recker."

"It sticks in my craw, Sergeant. Maybe things could have worked out differently, but here we are. We've got a chance to escape – assuming the *Gorgadar*'s shuttle is operational – and I intend to take it."

Vance didn't do anything other than acknowledge their circumstances and began shouting orders at the squad. The Daklan responded too, in the same way the human soldiers responded to Shadar. Only a year ago,

Recker would have never thought he'd see it happen, yet now it seemed natural.

"We should move," said Sergeant Shadar.

"This way to the lift," said Recker.

The internal shuttle wasn't far and he sprinted for it. When he stopped at the panel used to summon the car, he felt concern again at the thought of what the shutdown code might have disabled. Recker's worries were unfounded – the car hadn't moved since it first brought the squad to the bridge and the doors opened immediately.

"How long will it take the enemy to establish themselves within the *Ixidar*?" asked Vance, while the car descended to the lower station.

Recker had been mulling the same question and hadn't arrived at a satisfactory answer. "I don't know, is the simple answer, Sergeant. The *Ixidar* has plenty of shuttle bays and they're the most obvious ingress points."

"They'd have to find an empty docking bay or remote pilot out an existing shuttle," said Vance. "If it were me, I'd fly out every docked shuttle, bring in my troop carriers and fill the *Ixidar* with as many soldiers as I could lay my hands on."

"At which moment, you'd notice if one shuttle didn't respond to remote access requests," said Recker, spotting where Vance was leading. "Damn."

Recker had been relying on slipping off the *Ixidar* while the Ancidium's troops landed elsewhere. If Vance was correct, that might not be so easily accomplished. "We've got to move fast," he said.

The lift car descended rapidly, but not rapidly enough for Recker's liking and it was hard not to fidget.

"We're going down an extra stop this time," he said. "That'll take us out closer to the shuttle."

"The way we should have come first time around, you mean, sir?" asked Private Drawl.

"Next time I'll let you choose the direction, Private." Recker pulled a face. "Or at least I will next time we need to locate the sewers, because I know you'll get us there by the fastest route."

Drawl didn't have much of a response beyond muttering about the bullying of superior officers. The car arrived at its destination and the squad readied their weapons in case the incoming Lavorix troops had exceeded all expectations and waited outside.

No enemy troops were visible and the squad exited the car. Recker was busy orienting himself when he felt the *Ixidar*'s propulsion kickstarters give a shuddering thump.

"What are they doing?" asked Corporal Montero.

"They're trying to start up the *Ixidar* again," said Recker.

The kickstarters boomed again and the *Ixidar*'s propulsion came online. Recker laid his palm on the wall to sense the vibrations. For a couple of seconds the engines stayed at idle and then they rumbled, indicating they'd been placed under load.

"We're about to lift off," said Recker.

"Where are we going?" asked Drawl.

"How the hell am I supposed to know, Private?" Recker took a deep breath. "If I had to guess, they're taking us straight to the repair yard. There's no need to leave the *Ixidar* on the bay floor while the Ancidium's troops perform a sweep."

Recker's unease from earlier had returned, though not with the same intensity. This was the standard anxiety he usually experienced when his enemies were up to something and he didn't know what it was.

The short delay was enough for Recker to get his bearings. He pointed the way and allowed Sergeant Shadar to take the lead, while keeping himself in the middle of the pack with Lieutenant Eastwood and Corporal Montero. He didn't expect the shooting to start, but it made sense to be careful.

The return route was indeed much shorter than the one by which the squad had originally travelled to the bridge. A short passage led to a large storage room containing sealed alloy crates. Exits went left and right, and a third led to the airlock tunnel for one of the *Ixidar*'s own shuttles.

Given how hard Recker, his crew and his squad had fought for every inch of ground in the war so far, he was fully expecting the Lavorix to have pulled off their usual trick of being exactly where he didn't want them. Therefore, it came as a pleasant surprise to find only dead ones, killed by the *Gorgadar*'s death sphere.

The left-hand door opened to reveal a tunnel, which took the squad to the room containing the different artillery guns. Nothing had changed.

Arriving at the shuttle's airlock without a shot being fired was almost more than Recker could believe. A few of the squad were in a state of even greater disbelief, cynical bastards that they were. Only half-listening to their comments, Recker opened the airlock door and stepped inside, making room for the others to follow.

Less than two minutes later, Recker was again in the shuttle's cockpit and itching to warm up the vessel's light-speed drive. The first thing he noticed was the flashing light to indicate an inbound comms request from the *Gorgadar*. Corporal Montero hadn't arrived yet, leaving Recker to accept the channel. With a feeling of inexplicable trepidation, he touched the button to link.

CHAPTER FOURTEEN

IT WAS Lieutenant Burner on the comms and he sounded frantic.

"Sir, the Ancidium destroyed Tokladan!"

Recker hated stupid questions like *What?* And *Why?* but he struggled for something intelligent to say. "Is there any indication why they might have done that?" he asked.

Corporal Montero and Lieutenant Eastwood arrived and took their stations without a word.

"No, sir. They hit mode 3 and disappeared from the *Gorgadar*'s sensors. I had an idea where they'd be heading, but the first confirmation I had was when the planet exploded." Burner was talking fast and sounded like he was right on the edge.

"Exploded? The tenixite converters don't..."

"Whatever the hell this was, it was no tenixite converter, sir. The planet just blew up. Like the Ancidium had done something to Tokladan's core that made it..." Burner tailed off and Recker couldn't remember the last time he'd heard the man so affected by an event in the war.

"I think I know why they did it," said Recker. "We fired the *Ixidar*'s Extractor into the Ancidium's interior. The attack on Tokladan was retribution."

"Damn, sir, this is screwed up."

"Don't I know it, Lieutenant. Have you obtained a sensor lock on the Ancidium? Is it still somewhere in DEKA-L?"

"Yes, sir, it's still in DEKA-L. The Lavorix activated a second mode 3 out to the sixth planet. I don't know how long they'll stay there."

Neither did Recker, but he doubted the enemy would stick around. They'd come here for the *Ixidar* and that was now tucked safely in one of the Ancidium's bays. With Tokladan reduced to rubble, there was nothing keeping the Lavorix here. They'd head off to their next destination and do whatever they planned to do.

"The enemy will leave soon, Lieutenant. You'll need to follow them. It's the only way our fleets will have a chance to intercept."

"We can't beat that thing, sir. It's like all the Laws of Ancidium rolled into one and then magnified tenfold."

"There'll be a way, Lieutenant," said Recker, his anger displacing doubt. "There's always a way."

He leaned back, clinging to his anger, as if the force of it would somehow allow him to twist reality into the image he wanted it to be.

"Sir, we should load up our ternium drive for departure," said Eastwood. "We've done what we can and it's time to lightspeed out of here."

Recker didn't like it. Although he'd used the *Ixidar* to good effect against the Lavorix fleet in the Ancidium's bay, it didn't seem like nearly enough. Not with what happened to Tokladan and maybe what would happen to the next planet the enemy showed up at.

"Let's go," said Recker.

"I've picked some random coordinates as our destination, sir," said Eastwood. "The ternium drive has a twelve-minute warm up."

The shuttle's propulsion grumbled, producing a metallic buzzing from the control console. Filled with unhealthy energy, Recker climbed from his seat and returned to the lower bay where the squad waited nervously.

"We're leaving soon," said Recker. He pointed at the two mobile gauss guns. "I don't anticipate we'll need them, but try and figure out how those work. If the Lavorix force an entry through the airlock while our ternium drive is loading up, I'd prefer it if we had a surprise waiting for them."

"Yes, sir," said Vance, pushing himself from his crouch. "You know what'll happen if we fire one of those into the airlock."

"Destruction on a massive scale, Sergeant, that's what'll happen. If the Lavorix break in, we're going to need it."

Vance gave a rare half-smile. "Right you are, sir."

Recker headed back to the cockpit, where the timer had fallen to ten minutes. He couldn't settle and his brain kept turning and turning, like it was on the brink of an idea. No matter how hard Recker tried to grasp that idea, it floated teasingly and infuriatingly away, leaving him wondering if there was even an idea coming at all.

"What's on your mind, sir?" asked Eastwood.

"I don't know, Lieutenant. It feels like we're missing something, but perhaps I just hate running with my tail between my legs."

"That's not what we're doing, sir."

"It feels like we are."

The timer fell and Recker spoke to Lieutenant Burner again. "We've got five minutes left on the lightspeed countdown," he said. "If the Ancidium departs before we do, I'm going to let the warmup complete."

"You can't open a lightspeed tunnel from a vessel already travelling at lightspeed, sir."

"I know that, Lieutenant."

"If the Ancidium uses a Gateway, I don't know if we can follow. Lieutenant Eastwood figured out how to read the lightspeed tunnels, but he's over there with you and maybe his method doesn't pick up Gateways anyway. I'm hoping something shows up automatically on the sensors after the enemy is gone."

"Damn, we're fighting from the corner here," said Recker.

He worked through the possibilities. If the Ancidium opened a Gateway to a new place, the shuttle would go with it and then enter lightspeed from this unknown location. The transport would end up somewhere unintended, but that wouldn't be a big problem.

The worst possible outcome would be for the Ancidium to enter lightspeed for an extended period, which would prevent the shuttle from departing and give the Lavorix troops a better opportunity to hunt down the squad.

"Three minutes," said Eastwood.

"How're you getting on with those mobile gauss turrets, Sergeant Vance?" asked Recker on the squad channel.

"Point and shoot, sir. Easy."

"It doesn't sound like you'll get a chance to test them out, Sergeant. Less than three minutes and we're gone."

Recker closed out of the channel and watched the Lavorix symbols – indicating units of time – change on his screen. The hint of an idea was still nagging at him and he stopped pursuing it, in the hope that pretending indifference would bring it to the fore.

"We've got an access light on the outer airlock, sir," said Montero. "The *Ixidar* has priority control, so I can't lock the doors."

"Damnit!" Recker jumped back into the squad channel. "The outer airlock opened. Be ready for whatever comes through."

"Yes, sir, we saw the light change," said Vance. He cursed. "We should have left the inner door open – that would put a block on the outer one."

"Only until the Lavorix entered an override code, Sergeant. Keep your fingers crossed we don't need those extra few seconds."

"One minute on the ternium drive, sir," said Eastwood.

Recker listened carefully for the sound of gauss discharges. The rifles – both human and Daklan – had a distinctive note, but they weren't too loud. He heard nothing, though Vance and Shadar began shouting commands on the squad channel.

"What happens if we enter lightspeed with the airlock door open?" asked Montero.

"Nothing much," said Eastwood. "What's in the shuttle will stay in the shuttle and if you looked through the doorway, you'd see darkness."

"Huh," said Montero, her disappointment tangible.

"Were you expecting a view of the universe's secrets, Corporal?" asked Eastwood.

"Not exactly, Lieutenant. Just something more than the same darkness I see every time I close my eyes."

"Twenty seconds," said Eastwood.

"How're things going back there, Sergeant Vance?"

"We killed the Lavorix in the airlock, sir. I don't think they were expecting us to be waiting for them."

"The outer door opened again," said Montero in the same channel. "Another attack."

"I reckon these ones will put up more of a fight," said Vance.

"Five seconds."

"Inner door opened," said Montero.

This time Recker heard the distant whining of gauss coils. Then, the timer in front of him changed to the Lavorix equivalent of a zero and the ternium drive activated with a thump.

"That's us out of here," said Eastwood. "Uh, no, we haven't moved."

"Why not? Tell me what's wrong!" said Recker.

"I'm finding out, sir," said Eastwood. "The drive activated and there're no failure warnings, but we're still in the *Ixidar*'s docking bay."

Recker's mind cast about for an explanation. "Is it possible the walls of the Ancidium prevent the formation of a lightspeed tunnel?" he asked. "No, that can't be right. We're receiving FTL comms from the *Gorgadar*."

"Not so fast, sir," said Eastwood. "Both could be right. It's possible the Ancidium has lightspeed receivers on its hull which channel any inbound comms through the hull and on to their destination, while anything that doesn't go through those receivers – like this shuttle – is blocked."

"Does that mean the enemy are listening to our comms?" asked Recker. "Corporal Montero?"

"I don't know, sir."

Eastwood had been around technology far longer than Montero and he'd worked with Lieutenant Burner for many years. He made a guess.

"If I had to put money down, I'd say the Lavorix *could* listen to our comms, but only if they knew what was happening and actively went looking for the traffic."

"We've killed those Lavorix, sir," said Vance on the comms. "Are we expecting any more?"

"Almost certainly, Sergeant." Recker gestured at Montero indicating she should take over the squad updates. She nodded in response.

"Without knowing how the Lavorix are blocking lightspeed transits through the Ancidium's walls, I can't tell you how to get around the issue, sir," said Eastwood.

"When we first saw the Ancidium, I thought it looked strange," said Recker. "Like it was vibrating or something.

I put it down to the propulsion and didn't think about it again until now."

"You might have noticed a visible effect of whatever's preventing us from escaping, sir," said Eastwood. "It doesn't help us much."

"Then we're stuck here," said Recker.

"On a fully-fledged warship I could make a few tweaks to the hardware to see if we could circumvent the block, sir. They probably wouldn't work, but at least I'd be able to try. Here on the shuttle, I enter the coordinates and wait for the ternium drive to fire, with no way to modify the process."

The idea which had eluded Recker for so long hit him like a punch to the temple and he sat bolt upright. He didn't know if it was going to work, but it gave him a purpose, and he re-opened the channel to the *Gorgadar*, where he informed Lieutenant Burner what was required.

"Will it work, sir?"

"It has to work, Lieutenant."

With the arrangements made, Recker cut the channel again. Eastwood and Montero knew something was up and they stared at him questioningly.

"Pick up your guns – we're leaving."

"Back onto the *Ixidar*?" asked Eastwood. "What for?"

"I'll tell you on the way. Now move!"

The pent-up anger, frustration, and everything else which Recker had stored up inside found an outlet and he sprinted for the cockpit door.

CHAPTER FIFTEEN

"SERGEANT VANCE, IS THE BAY CLEAR?" Recker asked as he descended the steps outside the door.

"For about the next ten seconds, sir. The outer airlock opened again."

"We're moving out."

"Where to?"

"The *Ixidar*'s bridge. We've got ten minutes."

Vance didn't ask questions, though he surely had plenty. When Recker entered the holding bay, the soldiers were positioned at the flank walls, their guns trained on the entrance, while Private Gantry was standing at one of the artillery guns. The mobile turret was aimed directly at the airlock.

"We've got another batch of Lavorix about to come inside, sir," said Drawl. "That's the collective noun for them in case you were wondering."

"Any moment," said Vance.

The inner door slid aside and Recker spotted

numerous Lavorix in the airlock. He fired his rifle at the same time as the other members of the squad. A fraction of a second later, the coils of the artillery gun produced a much louder whine and the barrel jumped back into its housing. The projectile travelled too fast for the eye to follow, but it produced an explosion of blood in the airlock. Then, several grenades detonated amongst the carnage. Recker's squad hadn't thrown them, so he assumed the Lavorix had been holding them in preparation.

"Move!" shouted Recker, before the torn limbs and burned guts had even hit the ground.

Vance dashed into the airlock, along with Zivor and Reklin, while the rest of the squad watched the outer door.

"Let's hope the enemy haven't flooded this area of the *Ixidar*," said Eastwood. He'd never been a foot soldier, but he appeared calm enough.

"Private Gantry, are you ready?" asked Vance.

"Yes, sir."

"Outer door opening," said Vance, activating the panel from one side.

Fifteen or twenty Lavorix soldiers clustered in the loading tunnel outside. They were ready and fired their guns at once. None of Recker's squad was in sight, and the enemy slugs pinged off the deflective plating of Gantry's artillery piece.

"Try this, you bastards," he said.

The gun was designed to knock out light tanks and other armoured vehicles, and the projectile tore a path through the enemy soldiers, before striking the end door with a reverberating clank.

"Fire again," said Shadar, when it was clear a handful of the enemy had evaded the first shot.

"Reload complete," said Gantry. "Firing."

The Lavorix were quick, but they couldn't get out of the way of a gauss slug, and the remaining troops were reduced to a glistening smear of pale pink flesh.

"Heading for the far door," said Vance, sprinting into the passage. His feet skidded on the gore but he caught himself and made it to the end.

This was the deciding moment, Recker was sure. If the enemy had established themselves in the room beyond – worse, if they'd activated some of the stored mobile repeaters held there – then it would be impossible to get by without terrible casualties. Assuming it was possible at all.

"Ready," said Vance, calm under pressure as ever.

He crouched low and opened the door, while the squad members watched anxiously. No hail of bullets came to reduce Sergeant Vance to a pulp and he waved for the next soldiers to advance.

"Want me to bring this gun, Sergeant?" asked Gantry.

"Leave it there, soldier."

Recker joined the advance and the squad entered the room with the various mobile artillery guns. The only Lavorix were the dead ones from earlier – those killed by the *Gorgadar*'s death sphere.

"The enemy must have split into groups to search the *Ixidar*," said Vance. "We killed this bunch, so maybe we'll have some clear space before we run into the next ones."

Not long had passed since the Ancidium sent the shutdown code to the *Ixidar* and Recker was willing to believe the enemy soldiers were not everywhere. However, he was sure a few of their squads would have the same target as his own soldiers.

"They'll want to secure the bridge," said Recker, indicating that Vance should take the left-hand door.

"Gantry, set up your MG-12," ordered Vance as he headed that way.

Kicking out the repeater's tripod, Gantry set it down and lay flat where he had a good firing line into the next passage. Without delay, Vance touched the access panel and the door opened.

"Hostiles," said Shadar calmly.

Gantry held the MG-12's trigger, sending a few hundred slugs into the passage. "Clear," he said.

Quick as a flash, Vance was into the tunnel, while Shadar directed Zivor to set up his own repeater at the edge of the doorway.

"Ready," said Vance.

Watching the squad operate made Recker understand how rusty his own skills had become. He'd convinced himself that he was the same commander as he'd been way back in his early years, but seeing the troops respond to orders almost before they were given made him realise it wasn't the case. It gave Recker a feeling of regret mixed with pride.

A few Lavorix were present in the next room, though the first Recker knew of it was when Zivor's and Gantry's repeaters fired twin roaring bursts. The discharges ended and Recker heard the fizz of Vance's gauss rifle, once, twice, three times.

"Clear."

The squad advanced into the next room, carefully avoiding the spilled blood and entrails of the freshly killed Lavorix. The scent of their death was sharp and unpleasant, though Drawl sucked in a deep breath, as if it were the cleanest, sweetest air imaginable.

"These ones must have been searching through there, sir," said Vance, indicating the passage leading to one of the *Ixidar*'s shuttles. His rifle didn't move from where he had it aimed at the airlock passage.

"Others might be onboard," said Recker.

"They might," Vance agreed.

"No way to tell except by waiting or heading in there for a look," said Recker. "And that's not happening."

Crossing the room watchfully, the squad entered the tunnel leading to the internal shuttle car. So far, the going had been comparatively easy, though Recker didn't expect that would continue once the Lavorix got themselves organised.

When the squad was inside the car, he selected the bridge level and the shuttle glided upwards.

"So what's the plan, sir?" asked Eastwood on a private channel. He faced Recker from the other side of the door.

Recker brought Montero into the channel, since she needed to hear this as well. "The Lavorix powered up the *Ixidar* again," he said. "That probably means the whole ship became operational, but the enemy have put a block on our access – something which makes them confident we won't be able to do anything to steal it back off them."

"What are you getting at?"

"The *Ixidar* might just accept a request from the *Gorgadar* to join a battle network. Since we can't speak to

Lieutenant Burner while we're away from the shuttle's FTL comms system, I gave him an instruction to wait ten minutes and then create the battle network. If that doesn't work, he'll issue a synch code and see if the *Ixidar* will accept that instead."

Eastwood's eyebrows climbed two inches up his forehead. "Once we're synched or on the same battle network, the *Gorgadar* will be able to issue commands to the *Ixidar*."

"Better than that, Lieutenant. If the enemy applied blocks only to the bridge hardware, the *Gorgadar* might be able to revoke the Ancidium's control over this warship."

"That's assuming the Lavorix didn't already freeze the *Gorgadar*'s access to their hardware."

"The Ancidium accepted and routed the earlier comms, so any block isn't total."

"That still doesn't mean..." Eastwood exhaled and his expression indicated he was giving himself a mental shake. "We've got nothing else and this is going to work," he said.

"The positivity classes had an effect, then?"

"The only way you'll get me into one of those is by carrying me there in my coffin, sir."

Recker laughed. "I wouldn't change you, Lieutenant."

"I wish my wife was so understanding, sir." Eastwood laughed as well.

"You'll see her soon," said Recker, reaching across and putting his hand briefly on the other man's shoulder.

"Damn right I will." Eastwood's eyes didn't hold the same confidence as his words. "What about you, Corporal Montero? Have you got someone waiting for you back home?"

"Aside from family? A few others," said Montero evasively.

"Just a few?" joked Eastwood.

"That's people who *hope* to know me better, Lieutenant," she said with mock indignation. "Doesn't mean I'm interested. Not all the time, anyway."

Recker wasn't surprised that Montero got plenty of attention, since she was smart and attractive. In another lifetime he'd have been interested himself.

The car was approaching its stop and Recker cleared his mind. He turned to make sure the squad was in position and saw readiness in each face.

"If the bridge is taken, we need to capture it and hold," said Recker on the squad channel. "There might just be a way we can take control of the *Ixidar* again."

"What then, Captain Recker?" asked Shadar.

"You know how war goes, Sergeant."

Shadar laughed, a booming sound with a harsh edge. "That I do," he said. "You can't guess what lies ahead, yet you are determined to defeat it."

"We're on a wing and a prayer," said Recker. "That's what we call it." He checked the timer he had running. "And we've got less than three minutes to reach the bridge."

These soldiers had seen enough of war to understand that all they could do was accept what was coming and fight their hardest to get through it alive. Shadar knew it as well as any of them and Recker wondered anew at how the war between humans and Daklan had lasted for so long, given the many similarities between the two species. Or maybe it was those similarities which had started the war in the first place.

The car slowed to a halt and Recker touched the access panel. Outside, it was still and the only sound was that of the *Ixidar*'s propulsion. From the car, a straight passage led to the bridge stairs and Recker was about to order the squad to move when he spotted a fast-moving group of Lavorix coming from the opposite side of the stairwell.

"Ipanvir," he ordered. "Lavorix – 120 metres."

The Daklan was near the door, with his rocket tube held vertically. As soon as he heard the order, he rotated the tube smoothly onto his shoulder, with a simultaneously step towards the door. Recker heard the launcher's coils whining as they charged up and the Daklan wasn't yet out of the car.

Ipanvir was a master with the shoulder launcher – far and away the best Recker had ever seen. He timed it perfectly, emerging from the car at the exact moment the rocket was ejected from the tube. The projectile made a whooshing sound as it sped along the passage. Recker didn't wait to hear the blast and he closed the car door again. The target enemy were a good distance away, but the Daklan rockets carried a heavy payload and he didn't want the heat and flames channelling into the shuttle.

"That is long enough," said Ipanvir. "Open the door and I will look."

Recker opened the door again and the Daklan leaned quickly out.

"The way is clear." Ipanvir didn't need to follow it up with the obvious *It may not remain so for long.*

"Let's go," said Recker, motioning with his rifle.

Vance went first again, though he had nothing to prove. The squad followed and Recker found himself once more at the bottom of the steps leading to the bridge. On the landing above, Vance crouched with Steigers and Reklin.

"I can't open this, sir."

Sprinting upwards, Recker joined them on the compact landing. He sent his codes into the access panel and then scrambled four steps down, where he crouched out of sight. The bridge door opened.

"Clear," said Vance after a moment.

"Inside," ordered Recker.

The soldiers on the landing disappeared into the bridge and Recker joined them a couple of seconds later. Out of habit, he paused to be sure the other members of the squad were coming, and they were - at great speed, since the bottom of the stairwell was exposed and nobody wanted to be left behind.

"Move, move!" said Recker.

When the last soldier was across the threshold, he activated the panel again and the door closed.

"To your stations!" he yelled.

Recker could have saved his breath, since Montero and Eastwood were already seated.

"Thirty seconds on the timer," Recker said, taking his own station.

"What am I looking for?" asked Montero. She gave one of the console buttons a prod. "Still locked out."

"If the *Ixidar* accepts the battle network or synch request, Lieutenant Burner will know what to do. If we're lucky – if we're *really* lucky – you should have immediate access to the sensors and comms."

"I know what to do from there, sir."

"The moment the Lavorix understand what's happened, they'll throw everything at us." Recker smiled grimly. "Not that all-out attack helped them much last time."

"How long before they realise?"

"Not long. Seconds."

Recker looked again at the timer and the last few seconds counted down. Once the synch or battle network requests were accepted – assuming they were – Burner would require a few additional moments to rescind the override code. Even if everything went to plan, there was a distinct possibility the Lavorix would react quickly and shut the *Ixidar* down again.

However, Recker had a quiet hope that it wouldn't be so easy for the enemy this time. If Burner could set up the battle network, he would then have access to create the synch code and vice versa. From there, he could configure the link between the two ships so that any shutdown code would have to originate from the *Gorgadar*.

Once that was set up, Burner could create a loop whereby if the Ancidium sent a shutdown code to the *Gorgadar*, the *Ixidar* could rescind it and vice versa. Assuming Eastwood came up with a few additional delaying tactics like he had earlier, the Lavorix might just find themselves facing two Laws of Ancidium, with no easy way to disable them. Recker supposed the enemy could send shutdown codes to both ships at once, but they'd have to arrive together with such infinitesimally perfect timing that he couldn't see the method being successful.

"Still nothing," said Eastwood.

"Patience," said Recker, though he didn't have much of it himself.

A full minute passed, which felt like twenty. During that time, Recker made repeated attempts to access the command and control software. On each occasion, he was denied access.

Then, it happened – the menu opened and Recker punched the air with excitement. "We're in!" he shouted.

"Sensors coming online!" said Montero with equal joy. "Comms link to the *Gorgadar* available!"

It was an incredible development and Recker could scarcely believe his luck. Although he had no idea what the sensors would show when they came online, anything was better than sitting in the *Gorgadar*'s shuttle and waiting to die.

The bulkhead screens illuminated and Recker stared at them with eagerness and trepidation.

CHAPTER SIXTEEN

THE *IXIDAR* WAS no longer in the original bay, though it was in a place of similar dimensions. Having been sensor blind during the run back to the *Gorgadar*'s shuttle, Recker wasn't sure exactly where the *Ixidar* was in relation to its entry point - more than enough time had passed for it to have travelled from one end of the Ancidium to the other.

Recker's eyes danced across the feeds, a few of which were aimed at walls or nothing of interest – something Montero was fighting to correct.

"A construction and repair yard," said Eastwood.

Recker thought the same. The *Ixidar*'s lower five thousand metres were inside a square bay in the floor and the floor of this bay contained a shaft that was slightly deeper than the destroyer cannon that was currently inside it. Recker had no doubts this bay was where the Destroyer had been originally created.

"We're two hundred kilometres from the left wall, a

hundred from the right and fifty kilometres from each of the nearer two walls," said Montero, reading out the sensor data. "Lots of activity outside."

Dozens of shuttles flew in the vicinity, some carrying thick sections of armour plating – the Ancidium clearly wanted the *Ixidar* repaired and operational as soon as possible.

Other work was underway in the yard. Towards the left-hand wall, Recker spotted other warships at varying stages of construction. A few were battleship sized, which in the Lavorix fleet meant a mere seven or eight thousand metres in length. These were dwarfed by the work beyond. One part-built hull was about twenty thousand metres, its underside deep in another trench. This vessel was more than halfway complete and its curved sides made Recker think of the *Gorgadar*. The outer plating wasn't finished and huge, cube-shaped ternium modules were visible through the openings.

Further yet was another incomplete warship, this one slightly shorter and with a height that allowed Recker to discern much of its shape. This second warship reminded him of the *Galactar*, in that it appeared to be a collection of massive cylinders, cuboids and struts, cobbled together, as if the intended design had been altered several times during the construction process.

These two huge warships took only a fraction of Recker's attention. The star of the show was at the extreme end of the bay and this new vessel was going to be the most terrible of them all – a sixty-kilometre titan of alloy with sleek lines and a broad beam that would likely scrape the sides of the exit tunnels as the spaceship flew outside at the beginning of its first mission to kill any living species it happened upon.

"Check out the other end of the bay, sir," said Montero, still fine-tuning the sensors.

"A copy of the *Ixidar*," said Recker, turning to the feed Montero highlighted for him. He stared at what would eventually be the twin of his own ship, once the Lavorix had fitted the upper fifteen hundred metres. A swarm of lifter shuttles and welder robots were in the process of dropping components into place.

"And another not like the *Ixidar*," said Eastwood, indicating the second major warship at the right-hand end of the bay.

"An advancement of the design. A dodecahedron," said Recker. "Twelve guns. Twice the firepower."

"It's nearly ready to lift off," said Eastwood. "These other ones, maybe not so soon, but less than six months for most, and twelve months for the big one."

"Five new Laws of Ancidium, in this single bay," said Montero. "And one to rule them all."

Witnessing the construction of what amounted to replacements for the lost Laws of Ancidium, Recker felt empty inside. The Lavorix may well have been on the run from the Kilvar, but they hadn't accepted defeat, that much was certain. Worse, he didn't know how many other bays like this were contained within the hull of the Ancidium. Conceivably the enemy could be working on another ten of their monstrous warships. Maybe more than ten.

"The Lavorix have been warring with the Kilvar for hundreds of years," said Recker. "And that's with six Laws of Ancidium. If they finish these and even if they don't have other work underway, they're going to be back in the game."

"We thought the Lavorix only wanted the Meklon for their life energy," said Eastwood. "Look at all this – plundered resources used to create new fleets."

"I've located three exits doors." Montero focused the sensors on one of the bay's longest walls. "Thirty thousand metres like the others. And....one is opening."

The indicated door was midway up one of the longest walls and from its position in the repair bay, the *Ixidar*'s sensors lacked the angle to see much of what lay beyond. Recker glimpsed another cavernous space, along with the movement of dozens of construction shuttles. Another interrogator passed through the door, followed by eight lifters, each with a ternium propulsion block suspended underneath by gravity chains.

"Watch that interrogator," Recker ordered.

"It's heading the other way, sir," said Montero.

Sure enough, the cube-shaped vessel drifted off towards the left-hand end of the bay, like it was set to patrol the interior of the Ancidium.

"I've also been watching the internal monitors and I've figured out how to do a life sign count of our interior," Montero continued.

"With what result?" asked Recker.

"There's movement in several of the shuttle bays and a single group of Lavorix soldiers is heading for the bridge on the same internal car we used – twenty in total. All told, I'd say the Lavorix landed about 120 of their troops. Some we already killed."

Recker didn't want anything to distract him from his

study of the bay, but neither did he want to become trapped on the bridge if he could avoid it. He turned towards the squad, the members of which were doing an excellent job of keeping out of sight and out of mind.

"Sergeant Vance, Sergeant Shadar," said Recker on the squad channel. "I've given you the authority to open the bridge door – we have twenty Lavorix incoming on the internal car. I think they'd appreciate it if you were there to greet them."

"That would be the polite thing to do, sir," said Vance, pushing himself from the wall he was leaning against. Moments later, the squad were heading off the bridge to give the enemy something to think about.

Montero wasn't done. She pointed at a huge transport shuttle which was travelling rapidly across the bay. "This one's thirty klicks away and making a beeline for us."

"There're a lot more than 120 soldiers on that one," said Eastwood.

"Set the internal security systems to deny any docking requests, Corporal," said Recker.

"Won't that alert the enemy?" Montero asked.

"They'll be wondering," Recker said. "But we'll be ready to act before that becomes an issue." He turned his gaze once more to the open bay doors. "How many other bays like this would fit inside the Ancidium? Assuming the mothership's primary purpose was construction."

"Plenty more bays," said Eastwood. "With enough output to destroy the combined HPA and Daklan fleets fifty times over. A hundred times over!"

"What are we going to do?" said Montero.

"We sure as hell aren't going outside and waving the

white flag," said Recker. Confronted by this knowledge of his enemy's strength, he could have fallen into despair. Not this time. He'd had enough of despair. "The Ancidium is the Lavorix's weak spot. If we destroy it or disable it before the enemy can rebuild, we'll finish them once and for all."

"We've already fired one Extractor shot into them, let's give them another," said Montero. "And another after that for good measure."

So far, the Lavorix hadn't realised that the *Ixidar* was no longer under their control, though Recker didn't expect their ignorance would last. Firing the Extractor was the most obvious action to take, but given the narrow cone of the weapon's effects, it would be impossible to kill all the Lavorix from this bay, unless the enemy sat passively by while Recker took shots at them.

What if the same property of the Ancidium which prevents lightspeed travel and makes it immune to the Ixidar's cannons also blocks the Extractor?

The thought was unwelcome, but Recker was obliged to give it consideration. He cursed at the uncertainty.

"I'm not entirely convinced the Extractor is the answer, folks, as much as I'd like it to be," he said. "Lieutenant Eastwood, do you have the tools and skills to analyse whatever it is about the Ancidium that prevents it being affected by our weapons?"

"I have the tools and skills, sir. There's one part of the trinity I'm missing."

"Time," said Recker. "It always comes down to time."

"I'll get started, sir, though I don't anticipate we'll be sitting in this repair trench for too long."

"This state of calm won't last, Lieutenant."

Only two or three minutes had passed since they'd recaptured the *Ixidar*, and it was a lifetime under the circumstances. Recker knew the time to act was approaching and he also knew that somehow, he had to wring more out of this opportunity than simply destroying some of these incomplete warships.

"Corporal Montero, check through our sensor logs," he said. "You should find data that tells you which way the *Ixidar* is oriented in relation to how it was when the override code locked us out. Come what may, we're firing the Extractor again, but I want to know we'll have it aimed in the right direction."

"I already did that, sir." Montero pointed over her shoulder towards the still-open linking bay doors. "We should fire that way."

Recker nodded, his mind working on an idea. "Lieutenant Eastwood, am I right in thinking that a lightspeed tunnel does not have *dimensions* in a way that a normal person would understand the meaning of the word?"

Eastwood kept his response mercifully brief. "Not exactly, sir. A warship at lightspeed is theorised to have no *measurable* size, and no *measurable* mass. Only drag and a few other attributes that the scientists argue over."

A glance at the command console showed Recker that mode 3 was available. "Does that mean if the *Ixidar* were at lightspeed, it could fit through any sized hole in the Ancidium's hull?"

"We have already seen that the *Gorgadar*'s shuttle will not fit through gaps at the molecular level, whereas a solid object would not normally prevent a lightspeed transit."

Eastwood grunted. "Clearly the Ancidium is something new in this regard, so I'm not sure exactly what kind of hole would be required for us to pass through."

"What about a massive hole? Let's say, a thousand-metre hole that had been created by the *Gorgadar*'s particle beam?"

Eastwood straightened. "What makes you think that'll affect the Ancidium when no other weapon has done so?"

"The *Gorgadar*'s particle beam is the only weapon we know of that will penetrate an energy shield." Recker offered a tight smile. "If I'm wrong, the only change to my plan comes at the end – the part where we escape from here alive."

"You're asking for certainty I can't offer, sir."

"All I'm asking for is a maybe, Lieutenant."

Eastwood returned a smile of his own, equally tight. "In that case, the particle beam *might* open the Ancidium's hull and the hole it creates *might* be enough to allow us a mode 3 transit out of here. Of course if you ask Commander Aston to fire at the Ancidium, you open a whole new can of worms. I doubt the enemy will sit back and let it happen."

"The particle beam has enormous range – the Lavorix won't be able to prevent the first shot and we won't need a second one. I'll order Commander Aston to fire and then get as far away as possible."

"I don't think the Lavorix are desperate to force a confrontation with the *Gorgadar*," said Eastwood. "Either I've misread the situation, or we missed something during our time on that spaceship."

"We didn't miss anything, Lieutenant. The *Gorgadar*

has weapons systems we lacked the time to explore. That warship is carrying a decay pulse and a destabiliser, neither of which we have tested. And then there's the death sphere, which kills the enemy stone dead. Like you said - the Lavorix fear their own ship and we've got to figure out how best to use it against them."

"Whatever we're going to do, we should get on with it, sir," said Eastwood. "The Lavorix sent us a shutdown code."

Recker's hands jumped to his console and he called up one of the menus. To his relief, it allowed him access.

"The shutdown code didn't work."

"No, sir. The *Gorgadar* rescinded it immediately. I wouldn't get overconfident – the Lavorix built these warships, not us."

"I've opened a channel to the *Gorgadar*, sir," said Montero, showing definite signs that she'd end up a skilled comms officer. "Lieutenant Burner is waiting to speak with you."

"Put him on open."

"Done."

"Lieutenant Burner, I have the makings of a plan. Can you pinpoint the *Ixidar* from the data in our comms link?"

"Yes, sir. You're seven hundred kilometres from the Ancidium's stern and approximately midway across the beam."

"Are you one hundred percent certain that's our position, rather than the position of an internal comms relay?"

"I'm certain, sir. No doubts whatsoever."

"Good. Here's what I want you to do."

With the cat out of the bag, the Lavorix would try

everything to stop the *Ixidar*, so Recker spoke quickly. In ten seconds, he was done, and his hands were on the controls while an inner voice yelled at him to unleash yet more devastation upon the enemy. When Burner confirmed his understanding of the *Gorgadar*'s role, Recker cut the channel and readied himself for round two.

CHAPTER SEVENTEEN

"FIRING THE EXTRACTOR," Recker said, targeting the weapon towards the Ancidium's nose. He pressed a button on the controls. A few electronic needles jumped around and that was the only indication of discharge. The Extractor was surely the perfect weapon if you were a bunch of alien scumbags, bringing as it did the potential for mass murder without so much as ruffling the hairs of the crew.

"We've received another shutdown code," said Eastwood. "Rescinded again by the *Gorgadar*. And there's a third code...and a fourth."

Recker had no idea if flooding the *Ixidar* with shutdown codes would be effective and he didn't want to find out. He switched the propulsion into overstress and hauled on the control bars. Gravity field generators in the bay below wanted to hold onto the warship, but Recker didn't let it happen. He increased power in steps and the *Ixidar* tore itself free, ripping dozens of the huge ternium field generators and half of the bay floor out at the same time.

Up towards the ceiling the *Ixidar* raced and Recker was hard-pressed to avoid a collision. He brought the spaceship under control with not much to spare and he fired the first of the charged destroyer cannons at one of the part-finished Laws of Ancidium further along the bay. When he wasn't on the receiving end, the cannon's expulsive burst was a satisfying sight and the nine-thousand metre hole it created in the hull of the *Galactar*-vessel was sweet like the first mouthful of cold beer on a sweltering evening.

"Any time you like, Lieutenant Burner," said Recker, piloting the *Ixidar* towards the open bay doors. He had to find out what lay on the other side of this bulkhead, to learn if his fears were unfounded.

"Commander Aston acknowledges, sir. We're on our way and will fire as soon as we arrive."

"Make it a good shot, Lieutenant."

"It'll be like a needle in the enemy's eye, sir."

"The shutdown codes are coming thick and fast," said Eastwood. "If the Lavorix think this method is going to work, then it's enough to have me worried."

"Not much we can do other than hope they're wrong. I doubt the enemy come across this kind of attack every day – they can't be prepared for it," said Recker.

The *Ixidar* gathered speed and he waited on the next cannon's recharge. Slowing as the bay doors approached, Recker watched the sensors for a sight of what horrors the Lavorix were planning in the adjacent space.

"Damn," he said.

Through the opening, Recker spotted yet another bay like this one, and it was filled with hundreds of shuttles, all busily transporting slabs of armour, engine blocks and other components from one place to another. With the viewing angle reduced by the bulkhead walls, Recker still saw two more warships on the scale of the Laws of Ancidium and he had no doubt there'd be others.

Worse yet, doors on the opposite wall of this adjacent bay were also open and they led to another bay, the doors of which were open too. Space upon space, construction yards and storage. The Ancidium had facilities that would allow it to build entire fleets in weeks rather than months.

During his voyage through the Meklon spheres, Recker had been struck by how the Lavorix had a large enough fleet to leave a powerful force stationed seemingly everywhere he visited. At the time, he'd convinced himself he'd been unlucky to keep stumbling into their warships, but now, having witnessed the industrial might of his enemy, Recker could see they had plenty to spare.

"Incoming from one of those far bays," said Montero.

"I see them," said Recker.

A dozen or more warships rose into view from two hundred kilometres away and they raced into the adjacent bay, firing missiles and gauss slugs. Recker didn't have a facing gun he could discharge, but the cannon he had aimed at the massive ship in the current bay had a ready light on it.

"Have this," he said, activating the weapon.

The sphere of energy struck the nose of the huge spaceship, creating a ragged hole of corroding alloy and falling debris. At the same moment, missiles from the incoming warships detonated against the *Ixidar*'s shield and the turbulent storm of roiling plasma illuminated much of the bay.

Recker felt his battle lust rising again. There was something bestial about the *Ixidar* - the Lavorix had built a warship of absolute purity; a killing machine that existed for a single purpose and nothing else. Once, Recker had hated it and even now he couldn't bring himself to love a tool of such absolute carnage, especially knowing what it had accomplished under the control of its former masters. Yet it still gripped him in a way nothing ever had and probably never would again. The *Ixidar* stripped away his humanity and made him understand what it was to revel in the deaths of others.

And whatever punishment I inflict on the Lavorix, I'll feel no guilt.

When the thought jumped into Recker's head, it made him wonder if his humanity was already gone. The stakes were too high for him to worry about it and he flew the *Ixidar* away from the opening. A few incoming missiles crashed into the edge of the connecting tunnel, their guidance systems unable to correct in time.

"Particle beam incoming, sir," said Burner, his voice cutting through the rumble of the warship's propulsion.

The words came at the same moment as Recker fired the *Ixidar*'s next charged cannon. He had this second shot aimed near to where the last one had landed and a new hole appeared in the unfinished pride of the Lavorix fleet, putting the construction work back by months.

No sooner had the destroyer cannon blast vanished, than the *Gorgadar*'s particle beam sliced into the bay, entering from the wall behind the huge spaceship. Crackling and impure, the beam lanced through every one of the new Laws of Ancidium - including the *Ixidar*'s copy and the dodecahedral warship - as it travelled from one side of the bay to the other and into the opposite wall.

The damage was tremendous – the passage of the beam did more than simply create holes in the alloy and ternium it sliced through. Rapid expansion caused by heat fractured the metals, often violently. Everywhere he looked, Recker spotted ruptures and broken seams, while the burning temperatures were likely enough to destroy any installed components which were within a thousand metres of the beam's transit.

"Direct hit, Lieutenant, now get the hell away from here!" yelled Recker.

"Yes, sir!"

With his order given, Recker experienced a momentary desire to stay here and finish what he'd started. Two of the *Ixidar*'s destroyer cannons were out of action, but it would still wreak havoc upon the Lavorix ships which were even now emerging into the same bay. The pull of destruction was a powerful force and it took an effort for Recker to disregard it.

"Readying mode 3," he said. The tactical had no knowledge of anything beyond the bay, so Recker was obliged to access the third propulsion mode via the control system and set it for a manual launch.

"So long, suckers," said Montero, lifting her right forearm to the vertical and extending the middle finger.

"Let's hope so," said Eastwood.

Recker activated mode 3 and kept the button pressed.

A split-second before the sensor feeds went blank, he spotted something emerging into the bay behind the *Ixidar*. Then, the bulkhead screens went offline and the nausea of lightspeed entry hit his body. Recker was prepared for the transition be a bad one, as if escape from the Ancidium came with an additional price to be paid at the exit gate. The re-entry to local space was just as bad, compounding the queasy feeling of lethargy and adding a thudding headache onto the tally sheet.

"We made it," said Montero. "I gave them the lucky middle finger."

Recker glanced across and guessed from her face that she hadn't been so affected by the in-out lightspeed transit. "Get me comms and sensors," he ordered, giving the *Ixidar* maximum acceleration away from its arrival place. "And find out what happened to the squad."

"Yes, sir," Montero said, getting straight back to business. "Sensors coming up. Stars, darkness, the usual crap. Hunting for a lock on something useful."

"Until about five seconds ago, we were receiving dozens of shutdown codes per second," said Eastwood. "Now we're receiving zero shutdown codes per second. Either the enemy haven't found us yet or they went elsewhere."

The *Ixidar*'s velocity gauge kept on climbing and Recker had no intention of slowing until Montero had drawn him a clear picture of what lay outside.

"We're on the far edge of the DEKA-L system," she said after a few seconds. "We went past the star and kept on going. I estimate we made it thirty billion klicks from our start position."

"Contact the *Gorgadar*," said Recker. Against all the odds, they'd escaped the Ancidium's holding bay, but he wasn't ready to celebrate yet.

"Scanning for receptors, sir," said Montero, the overload of orders making her hesitant.

Everything she did took a few seconds longer than a trained comms officer would have managed it. Recker's frustration at each delay was hard for him to ignore, but he knew that Montero was performing admirably – more than admirably - given her lack of experience and formal training. When this was over, he'd recommend her for a dozen medals, a rate rise and a promotion if that's what she wanted.

"I have comms contact with the *Gorgadar*!" said Montero. "Lieutenant Burner coming onto the open channel."

"Where are you, Lieutenant?" asked Recker at once.

"I've located the *Ixidar*, sir," Burner replied. "We're nine billion klicks from your position. Commander Aston is preparing to mode 3 in your direction."

"What about the Ancidium?"

"Good news or bad news, I don't rightly know which it is, sir. The Ancidium is gone. I can't tell you when exactly that happened, but I doubt it stuck around for long after the *Gorgadar*'s particle beam went through its defences."

Recker wasn't sure if the Ancidium's departure was good news or bad news either, but he cursed anyway. "I'll bring the *Ixidar* to a standstill – head over to our position like you planned," he said. "I need an opportunity to think." As he spoke, Recker slowed the *Ixidar* and the strain of deceleration made the engines boom so loudly that he could hardly hear Burner's response.

"We're on our way, sir."

The channel went dead and, less than a second later, the immense form of the *Gorgadar* appeared on the sensors, less than fifty thousand kilometres to starboard. Commander Aston delayed only long enough for her warship's sensors to come back online and then she accelerated in the direction of the still-moving *Ixidar*.

"Lieutenant Burner is on the comms again," said Montero.

"Slow down, sir," said Burner.

"It takes time to bring a couple of trillion tons to a halt, Lieutenant."

The *Ixidar*'s velocity gauge fell to zero and the *Gorgadar* caught up. Aston parked a few hundred kilometres away and Montero focused one of the arrays on the warship.

"No sign of damage on their hull," she said.

"None," Recker agreed. He raised his voice. "Lieutenant Burner, do you have anything to report that I don't already know?"

"Only the details, sir. We put a hole through the Ancidium and they decided they'd had enough of DEKA-L."

"A mode 3 won't have taken them far," said Recker.

"I've been scanning for their position, sir, but they might have chain-activated several mode 3 transits and then I'd never find them."

"Don't stop looking."

"No, sir."

Recker took a breath. "Just before I activated the *Ixidar*'s mode 3, I spotted something entering the bay through one of the linking tunnels. I don't know what it was, but I didn't like it."

"Do you think it followed you out of the Ancidium?"

"I don't know. If it did, we'll find out soon enough."

"I'll hunt for two possible targets, sir."

"And contact base – I want Fleet Admiral Telar to know what happened out here."

"Yes, sir."

As the outcome of recent events began to sink in, Recker was left with a feeling, not that he could have necessarily done more, but that the attack on the Ancidium probably hadn't put much of a dent in the Lavorix war machine. The enemy had lost dozens of warships which they could likely afford to lose, and the *Gorgadar*'s particle beam - in conjunction with the *Ixidar*'s destroyer cannons - had set back the construction of several capital ships, yet the evidence suggested that the Lavorix had plenty of everything left in reserve.

And now, the Ancidium was gone from DEKA-L, which meant the only way to locate it was by luck or when it showed up at a populated world and started draining the inhabitants with its Extractor.

Suddenly, the destruction inflicted upon the enemy didn't seem so great after all and Recker asked himself if he'd squandered an advantage. The main unknown was the carnage the *Ixidar*'s two Extractor shots into the Ancidium might have wrought. Perhaps the enemy had lost twenty billion of their personnel and could no longer adequately crew their fleet. Certainly those warships in the adjacent bay had remained operational after the second discharge, though it was possible they'd been out of the weapon's effect cone.

With everything that had happened to the HPA and the Daklan in the last few months, Recker thought he was permitted a degree of cynicism. He cursed again and wondered what to do next.

CHAPTER EIGHTEEN

RECKER HADN'T BEEN LONG CONSIDERING his options when the bridge door opened and the squad returned, talking amongst themselves as if they were returning from the mess room on a normal day.

"The first threat was eliminated," announced Sergeant Shadar. "A second group of Lavorix arrived shortly after and was also eliminated."

"Casualties?" asked Recker in sudden concern.

"No casualties except those of our enemy."

"Sorry, Sergeant, I missed that second group on the internal monitors," said Montero. "We've had our hands full on the bridge."

"No apologies necessary, Corporal," said Shadar.

"Are any more incoming?" asked Vance, positioning himself for a high-quality lean against the rear bulkhead.

"I'll check," said Montero. She looked towards Recker to make sure he agreed.

"Do it," said Recker. He gave a tight smile to convey the unspoken extra word. *Quickly*.

"Yes, sir," said Montero.

Memories of the huge warship he'd seen entering the Ancidium's bay were bothering Recker and he accessed the sensor arrays himself. He was hesitant in their operation, doubly so because this was Lavorix tech, but he was able to initiate an automated long-range sweep. It was far more likely that Lieutenant Burner would locate any threats first, but a second pair of eyes never hurt.

"The life signs indicators show a count of sixty-three remaining Lavorix, spread across three separate groups," announced Montero. "It looks like they're planning to muster in one of the shuttle bays."

"The enemy will no longer attack piecemeal," said Shadar. "When they are ready, they will commit their remaining forces. We are outnumbered and the passages of a warship are not a good place to defend against explosives."

"Each of those last two groups had a rocket soldier, sir," said Vance. "I guess these others won't be any different."

"Corporal Montero, keep an eye on the enemy," said Recker. He swore. "I could do without this crap – I need you watching the external sensors."

"Watching the monitors is easy, sir," said Montero. "It won't distract me."

"We could hole up on the bridge," said Vance.

"Been there, done that, Sergeant," said Recker. "Let's not get ourselves trapped if we can avoid it."

"I've worked out how to download the *Ixidar*'s internal

map data and make it compatible with our suit computers, sir," said Montero. "I can provide a copy of the file to the squad and feed in live data from the internal monitors. It's possible the enemy can disable our ability to track them, but until that happens, our squad will be two steps ahead."

"We can ambush the enemy," said Shadar. "And kill them without mercy."

"Go," said Recker, not wishing to spend time deliberating. "If the heat is too much, fall back to the bridge."

The soldiers exited the bridge without further discussion and Recker was grateful he had officers who didn't require micromanagement.

At that moment, Lieutenant Eastwood made a discovery which almost had him jumping from his seat.

"Sir! Our batteries were at ten percent when we first captured the *Ixidar* – now they're full!"

"The Lavorix!" said Recker in equal excitement. "Our Extractor attacks must have worked!"

"Do we have any way of calculating how many we killed?" asked Montero.

"It's a good question, Lieutenant," said Eastwood, his head low to his console as he dug through menus and readouts. "Short answer: no. Long answer: we don't know how much each kill puts in the batteries and we don't know what happens to the spare life energy once those batteries reach a hundred percent."

"Pass on the good news to the *Gorgadar*, Corporal," Recker instructed.

"Wait!" said Eastwood.

"What's the matter?" asked Recker, sensing some bad news to temper the good.

"I've accessed the audit logs for the batteries and they show only a single input of extraction energy and the time stamp coincides with our first discharge of the weapon."

"The first shot was successful in killing the Lavorix, but the second was not," said Recker. "How can that be?"

"I don't know, sir." Eastwood raised his head and his brow was furrowed in thought. "Maybe the Ancidium has a way to neutralise the Extractor beam."

"Then why did the first attack work? Simply because the enemy weren't expecting it?"

"I don't know, sir. Maybe. We've learned that the Ancidium is immune to certain weapon types – what if it uses its own stores of life energy to adapt to whatever is incoming? Like an energy shield, but different. We know the *Ixidar*'s former crew were adjusting their Extractor during their attack on Tokladan. It's possible they altered the weapon in a way that caught the Ancidium unawares."

As far as explanations went, Eastwood's seemed logical enough and Recker nodded. "In which case, we've learned a valuable lesson here – next time we encounter the Ancidium, we should assume the Extractor will not work as we intend."

"Unless we figure out the method to adjust it and then do so in a way that will bypass the Ancidium's immunity," said Eastwood.

"Do you think you can determine the correct Extractor *wavelength*?" asked Recker, fumbling for the correct word.

"I'm not sure." Eastwood pursed his lips. "Hunch says we don't have the required data. And even if we did..."

"I know," said Recker. "We don't have the time to study it."

"Or the knowledge to implement the required changes on the hardware."

"I get it, Lieutenant – we've got problems the same as always."

"And we should consider the *Gorgadar*'s particle beam as well, sir," said Eastwood. "It worked once, but maybe it won't work the next time."

Recker cast his mind back. "The first time the particle beam came online, it had a secondary status of *modulating*. Maybe it's designed to circumvent immunities."

"The enemy wanted it to bypass their own defences?" asked Montero.

"More like it was designed to combat something the Kilvar came up with," said Eastwood. "And it's our good luck that it's capable of putting a hole in the Ancidium as well."

"So we have the particle beam. Is there anything we can do with what's in those batteries?" asked Montero. "Like channel it into a death ray that blows the Ancidium into pieces? Using the Lavorix's own life energy against them would be real justice."

Montero's enthusiasm was more than just infectious - this time, it set Recker's mind on a journey and he ordered a channel to the *Gorgadar*.

"Sir, I've got Fleet Admiral Telar in another channel. I have him on mute," said Burner, getting in the first words. "He wants to talk with you when I'm done giving him the outline."

"Admiral Telar will have to wait - I'd like to speak to

Lieutenant Larson."

"I'll bring her into the channel."

"What is it, sir?" asked Larson.

"Have you learned anything new about the *Gorgadar*'s weapons systems, Lieutenant?"

"Yes, sir. I was going to bring it up once everything calmed down a little."

"Let me guess – both the decay pulse and the destabiliser are unavailable because the *Gorgadar*'s extraction batteries are empty?"

If Larson was surprised, she did an excellent job of hiding it. "That's what Commander Aston and I believe, sir."

"The *Ixidar*'s batteries are full. I don't suppose you've discovered a way of transferring the stored energy from one warship to another?"

"No, sir. I haven't even considered the requirement until now."

"Look into it," said Recker.

"I will do, sir. Is it a priority?"

"It's critical, the same way everything is."

Larson was bright enough to understand and she didn't ask for clarification. She closed out of the channel, leaving Recker to ponder the options. He was interested to learn what damage the decay pulse and the destabiliser would inflict upon an opposing warship, but doubted the Lavorix had built in any straightforward method of energy transfer that would allow the *Ixidar* to charge up the *Gorgadar*'s batteries. Doubtless the Ancidium was carrying suitable hardware, but using it wasn't an option.

At that moment, Corporal Montero found something

which was as close to winning the jackpot as Recker could possibly have hoped for. Her first announcement of it didn't betray the importance.

"I think I've located something, sir," she said.

"What kind of something?" asked Recker. "Give me the specifics, Corporal."

"During the time the shutdown code had us kicked us out of the *Ixidar*'s controls, it looks as if we started receiving data from the Ancidium's comms network."

Recker's ears pricked up. "What did we receive?"

"It's a list of planets and solar systems – one hundred and seventy in total," said Montero. "I recognize a few of them as being in HPA space. They've been assigned numbers which I think might be priorities."

"Send me the data," said Recker. "Now!"

Montero looked at him sideways, as if she wasn't sure what had got him so agitated. "All yours, sir."

The file appeared on Recker's screen and he opened it.

"One hundred and seventy planets," he muttered, scanning the list. "The same ones we located in the *Gorgadar*'s comms system, but with far more details in the file."

"Anything we can use?" asked Eastwood, taking an interest.

"Oh hell, yes," said Recker, hardly able to believe what he was looking at. "Corporal Montero, I'd kiss you if it wouldn't see me in front of a court-martial."

"Shucks, sir, I won't tell," said Montero. "What did I find?"

"A double-edged sword, Corporal, but perhaps the

most valuable weapon in the war to date."

Recker's attempt to provide further details was interrupted by Lieutenant Burner opening a channel.

"Sir, Fleet Admiral Telar wants to talk with you now."

"Perfect timing," said Recker. "Pass him through." The *Ixidar*'s comms were still on open and the speakers hummed. "Hello, sir."

"Captain Recker, I've heard the outline..."

"Sir, you need to listen to this," said Recker.

Telar knew when to shut up and he cut himself off mid-sentence. "Speak," he said.

"While the *Ixidar* was under the Ancidium's control, the Lavorix included it on their Priority 1 comms network again. The enemy have provided us with a list of the same one hundred and seventy planets which I told you about before, along with the order in which they plan to visit them. The Lavorix are only intending to use Gateway travel for the longest distances."

"For once, I'm not sure I want to hear this, Carl."

Recker pressed on. "Assuming the Lavorix don't alter their plans, in fifteen days, they will arrive at Earth." Speaking the words aloud drove home to Recker exactly what was at stake and he took a deep breath. "We have fifteen days to stop these bastards, sir. Once they arrive at Earth, our days are numbered. After that, the Daklan will follow us into the same oblivion." He took a deep breath. "But we know where they're going to be and when. The next engagement will be on our terms, not theirs."

Delivering the message left Recker feeling drained and he sat back to hear what Fleet Admiral Telar would decide.

CHAPTER NINETEEN

TELAR WAS a man who thought fast and who had an in-depth knowledge of everything under his command.

"Are the Lavorix aware that we have learned their plans?" he asked.

"I don't know, sir. We're no longer receiving comms from the Ancidium, which is expected if they are at light-speed. Either way, it's likely they have cut us off their network."

"Will they know what we have discovered?"

"That's the big question, sir. It depends on how much of their inter-ship comms is controlled by computer and how much by a real pair of eyes. The Lavorix are strong when it comes to warfare, but they are overconfident, and on more than one occasion I've taken advantage of the fact."

"Their plans might change," said Telar, talking while he decided on a course of action. He made up his mind. "But we must act on current intel. Which populated planet will the Lavorix visit next, after they have discovered Earth?" he asked. "The discovery of so many people may in itself affect their plans, but I expect they will continue their exploration one way or another."

"Next on the list is the Daklan planet Loterle at eighteen days, and after that comes Terrani at twenty-four days," said Recker.

"Send me the list of planets and accompanying data," said Telar after a moment's thought. "It's imperative the enemy does not make it to Earth. I will discuss the options with Admiral Ivinstol and together, we will decide where to meet the Ancidium. In the time since we first discussed this list of a hundred and seventy planets, I have arranged for the majority of the HPA fleet to be mustered in one place, ready to act as necessary. That, at least, is already done."

"I thought Admiral Ivinstol perished during the attack on Trinus-XN," said Recker.

"He did not – the Admiral and his team were deep underground and the incendiary fires did not reach them."

Recker was glad at the news. Although his dealings with Ivinstol were few, they had all been positive and the Daklan no doubt had plenty to contribute to both the planning and execution. "Our fleets are not enough to challenge the warships held in the Ancidium's bays, let alone the Ancidium itself, sir. I would have suggested we attempt lightspeed transits into the mothership's interior, but I have seen first-hand that the enemy is immune to conventional attacks. And should the enemy patch the opening in their hull, our lightspeed transits will fail anyway."

"I am aware of the difficulties, Captain Recker," said Telar. "However, I will not be relying entirely on our fleets. We have finished production of a third shield breaker. Having lost one during the *Ixidar*'s attack on Tronstal, we are left with a total of two. Perhaps they will penetrate the Ancidium's defences."

"The shield breakers are unproven, sir," Recker protested. "Would it not be better if you ordered an evacuation of Earth?"

"That may also happen, but I cannot make a snap decision of such magnitude," said Telar. "One moment, while I check something."

For two minutes, the speakers went quiet and Recker drummed his fingers, wondering what Telar was up to. He soon found out.

"You will take the *Ixidar* and the *Gorgadar* to Terrani," said Telar.

"Sir?" asked Recker in surprise.

"With the Ivisto base destroyed, Terrani is the only planet in the alliance with facilities to handle both warships at once. The skills of the Daklan are beyond doubt – their technicians will figure out a way to transfer the batteries from the *Ixidar* and install them into the *Gorgadar*. We will have the decay pulse and the destabiliser available to us when the confrontation comes. Perhaps one of those weapons generates a death sphere capable of encompassing the entire Ancidium."

Recker didn't have a better plan. "Whatever the function of those weapons, we'll be better off having them available, sir. Do we have any other options beyond the shield breakers, our fleet and the captured Laws of Ancidium?"

"We have been working on new hardware, as I have made you aware in the past," Telar conceded. "However, I will not discuss it further. Not yet."

"Our own lightspeed missiles?" asked Recker, unwilling to be deflected.

"I will not discuss the readiness of our ongoing weapons projects," repeated Telar with a touch of impatience. "Whatever is suitable, we will put it to use."

"Yes, sir."

"I have nothing more to say on the matter. Take the *Ixidar* and the *Gorgadar* to Terrani. The Daklan will be expecting you. Once there, await further orders."

"We have Lavorix troops onboard the *Ixidar*, sir. My squad are hunting them, but are outnumbered. I'd prefer to recall my soldiers to the bridge and have the Daklan flush out the enemy when we land."

"I'll make the arrangements," said Telar. "Go."

"Yes, sir."

Telar left the channel and Recker didn't envy him for the mountains of steaming manure he'd be shovelling his way through in the coming days. Not that Recker was expecting to have it easy himself, but he knew whose shoes he'd rather be walking in.

"Corporal Montero, you heard the Fleet Admiral. Transfer the coordinates for Terrani to Lieutenant Eastwood and we'll be on our way."

"We don't have those coordinates, sir."

"You'll need to pull them out of the *Vengeance*'s databanks," said Recker. He wondered where the Meklon spaceship was located and realised he had no idea. "Maybe it'll be best if you speak to Lieutenant Burner and let him handle it."

"Yes, sir, I'll do that," said Montero with evident relief.

Arrangements didn't take long. Recker sent a recall order to his squad and learned from Sergeant Vance that the enemy were on their way to the bridge. For a moment, Recker wavered and then repeated his command for the soldiers to fall back. The *Ixidar*'s bridge door was monumentally sturdy and capable of withstanding any number of hand-laid explosives. It would last until the Daklan soldiers from Terrani arrived, Recker assured himself.

Meanwhile, Lieutenant Burner brought the *Vengeance* into close range using its propulsion mode 3. When that was done, Recker considered using the *Ixidar*'s Gateway to bring all three ships to Terrani at the same time. Such a method required a larger quantity of tenixite from the vessel generating the Gateway and since both Laws of Ancidium had plenty of the ore in their holds, it didn't seem important enough to overthink matters.

"We'll go separately," Recker stated. "The *Gorgadar* will transport the *Vengeance*."

"What's Terrani like?" asked Montero.

"I've never been there," said Recker. "I don't think I've even seen a photo." He was tempted to call Sergeant Shadar over, but held off. They'd find out soon enough whether Terrani was a place of stupendous beauty, an industrialised hellhole or somewhere in between.

A few minutes later, the preparations were complete and the *Ixidar*'s Gateway hardware readied itself for activation, which would take eight minutes. During that period, Recker didn't let his guard down and he assisted Corporal Montero with the sensors in case the Ancidium had indeed left behind a nasty surprise as he'd initially feared.

If there were any Lavorix nearby they evaded detection. Having seen what the *Ixidar* was capable of, Recker was sure the enemy would be reluctant to attack, though he was becoming gradually more confident that the Lavorix had simply not followed his exit from the Ancidium.

"Another shitty transit coming right up," said Eastwood sourly, once the timer fell below ten seconds.

He wasn't wrong. The Gateway activated with a thumping expulsion of energy that Recker felt in every part of his body. Despite the pain, he was pleased to have the option for near-instant travel. The sensors came online long before the Gateway's aftereffects faded and Montero obtained a lock on the target planet a few seconds after she confirmed the safe arrival of the *Gorgadar* and the *Vengeance*.

"There it is," she said. "Planet six out of fifteen and seven million klicks from our location. The original home of the Daklan."

"Continue the area scans."

"Yes, sir."

The soldiers – human and Daklan alike – shuffled closer to the bulkhead screen and Recker studied the home world of his one-time opponents. A glance at Terrani told Recker enough, but he continued to stare. The place was heavily built-up, with many expansive cities of grey, along with areas of desert, parched forest, faded plains, ice, and cold, deep oceans.

"It looks like a less hospitable version of Earth," said Eastwood, not unkindly.

"In the early days of my people, it was a harsh home," said Sergeant Shadar. "Our technology has tamed many of the planet's excesses – what you see now is an improvement over what it once was."

"No wonder you Daklan are all so miserable," said Drawl. "I would be too if I lived there."

"It is not so bad," said Shadar. "My wife is there."

Unwisely, Drawl kept going. "I'll bet your Daklan sausage will be leading the way down, huh?"

"Private Drawl, you are a very entertaining human. It is why I have not killed you. Until now."

From the corner of his eye, Recker watched Drawl's expression as he tried to work out if Shadar was joking or not.

"Sorry, Sergeant. No offense meant."

"It is too late for that, Private Drawl. Honour dictates I must eat your spleen."

Drawl stepped back nervously. "You can't do that! It's my spleen."

"Please, Sergeant Shadar," said Recker, lifting a hand in warning.

"Thanks, sir," said Drawl.

"Once we are safely landed, you may do whatever is required to satisfy your honour," Recker continued. "Though I demand half of the spleen."

Realising he was being played for a fool, Drawl stomped about and put on a show of curse-laden bravado, while the other soldiers – Daklan included – laughed at his expense.

Recker tuned it out, turned to Corporal Montero, and gave her a questioning look.

"Nothing on the area scans, sir," she told him.

"Any communication from the ground stations?"

"I don't think they've realised we're here, sir. I'm sure they know we're coming, but they haven't located us yet. I've discovered a single open receptor, which I think is a comms satellite a couple of million klicks above the planet. Should I initiate contact?"

"The Daklan know we're here," said Recker. "I don't know why they haven't contacted us. Get me a channel to Lieutenant Burner and keep scanning."

"Lieutenant Burner is in communication with one of the ground stations, sir. He'll enter the channel when he's done."

Burner had done this hundreds of times before and he didn't keep Recker waiting.

"I've spoken to the Daklan, sir. We've been ordered to stay put until our escort gets here."

Recker was irritated by the delay, though he didn't blame the Daklan for wanting to send the local fleet out to meet the new arrivals. Doubtless a few dozen ground batteries had also acquired the *Ixidar* and *Gorgadar* as targets for their lightspeed missiles. The war between the HPA and the Daklan was over, but the Laws of Ancidium were enough to put anyone on edge.

"Where are we heading?" asked Recker.

"A place called Hakarul," said Burner. "I guess it's their primary military facility, and it's on the blind side."

"I was trained there," said Shadar. "Along with my squad."

It was quicker for the Daklan warships to warm up their ternium drives and cross the seven million kilometres at lightspeed. They all came at once, indicating the use of synch codes, and, less than fifteen minutes after entering local space, the *Ixidar*, *Gorgadar* and *Vengeance* were surrounded by thirty-five Daklan vessels, including five annihilators and twelve desolators.

"Half of these look new," said Montero, focusing the arrays on different warships in the local fleet.

It was a reminder, were one needed, that the Daklan could still build faster and better than the HPA, no matter how much money humanity threw at its military. Until recently, pride in his species would have made the reality bother Recker. Now, he was thankful the Daklan could rebuild their battered fleet in double-quick time. They'd suffered badly at Ivisto and, more significantly, at the hands of the *Ixidar* in the RETI-11 system. Yet here they were, showing off plenty of firepower, and the newest annihilators had grown a few billion tons over the old ones.

"We've been ordered to follow at sub-light," said Montero.

"And we'll do as we're asked," said Recker.

The slowest warship in the local Daklan fleet had a maximum velocity of fourteen hundred kilometres per second, which meant a journey time of more than eighty minutes. Recker was already agitated and he felt as if this was an unnecessary delay. He didn't complain – not outside of his head – though he did speak to Lieutenant

Burner to enquire about the viability of setting up a synch code that included the local fleet. The discussion came to naught, since the Daklan weren't keen to be involved. Accepting defeat, Recker settled down for a low velocity approach to Terrani.

After eighty-seven minutes, which included time for acceleration and deceleration, the Hakarul facility became visible on the sensors. Once again, Recker was impressed by the Daklan's industrial prowess. The base was roughly square in shape and situated in the centre of a scrubby plain. No towns or cities were nearby, but straight, wide roads cut across the land. Recker saw plenty of ground traffic, despite the comparative economy of building transport shuttles.

"A ninety-klick square," said Montero. "Most of the buildings are in the south-eastern thirty klicks and the rest of it used for storage, construction and parking their fleet."

"Trenches to build eight warships at a time," said Eastwood. "The largest two are ten klicks. Big, but there's no way we're fitting inside."

Aside from the scale, Recker saw nothing out of the ordinary. Hakarul was busy – its skies filled with vessels in many shapes and sizes, while the construction yard was empty. He was sure the Daklan hadn't given up reinforcing their fleet and he looked for where they'd parked the incomplete hulls. He located them – six in total, three annihilators and three desolators - on the western edge of the landing strip. They all looked near completion, which is the reason he hadn't spotted them straightaway – at first glance, they looked as if they were waiting for their magazines to be reloaded, or to have other supplies brought onboard.

"We've received instructions on where to set down," said Montero. "The gravity field generators won't support our weight, so we'll have to leave the engines running."

"The destroyer cannons protrude four thousand metres," said Recker. "If they want us to hover, our topsides will be in those clouds we just came through."

"Apparently, there's an underground storage unit directly beneath one of those trenches, with a linking shaft, sir," said Montero. "The shaft is two thousand metres deep and the gun barrel should fit right inside."

The *Ixidar*'s guns must have retracted automatically when it crashed inside the Ancidium, but Recker hadn't come across a way to manually trigger it happening. If the Daklan were able to cope with the extended barrels, he was happy to let them get on with it.

"Put the location onto the tactical," said Recker. "Then talk to someone on the ground and make sure they've got a few thousand troops ready to come inside and turn our Lavorix guests into chunks."

"Everything is ready and waiting for us, sir," Montero confirmed. "And I've added the landing position onto the tactical."

"Thank you."

The base was huge, but so too were the Laws of Ancidium, and that meant there was only one option for landing.

"We're setting down on the western side of the construction yard and the *Gorgadar* is setting down east."

"Have you informed the ground crews about the death

sphere, Captain Recker?" asked Sergeant Shadar. "Unvak has already died – I do not wish any more to suffer the same fate."

"The death sphere will cover every part of the base, Sergeant," said Recker. "Lieutenant Burner has already warned them and Fleet Admiral Telar did likewise."

The answer didn't satisfy Shadar. "Have my people taken precautions?"

As far as Recker knew, there were no precautions against the death sphere. Still, he understood Shadar's concern. "You didn't notice, but when the local fleet came to meet us, two of the smaller warships purposely flew within the death sphere. Their crews reported no casualties. I apologise, Sergeant – I should have made you aware."

"Then Unvak died of something else," said Shadar.

"It's likely," said Recker.

The *Ixidar*'s course had brought it directly above the base at a twenty-kilometre altitude. A thick layer of rainclouds troubled the sensors not at all, and the view of the ground was startling in its clarity. The local fleet hadn't gone anywhere and they remained within striking distance. It would have seemed threatening had Recker not trusted the Daklan. He knew they weren't intending treachery, not that they could defeat the *Ixidar* anyway.

"We have clearance to land, sir," said Montero.

The engines rose in volume as Recker brought the warship in to land. The *Ixidar* didn't have a flank as such, since it was a perfect cube, but it made it easier for him to think of the *Gorgadar*'s as being positioned to starboard. At first, Aston kept the second warship within five thousand metres and then she held altitude to allow Recker to land first.

"Looking busy. A few hundred shuttles, a few thousand plates of armour, ground crews, gravity cranes," said Montero, listing what she saw.

"Any idea what they're planning to do, sir?" asked Eastwood.

"I only just arrived here, Lieutenant," said Recker. Still, it was a reasonable question. "Corporal Montero, get in touch with the *Gorgadar*. Tell Lieutenant Burner I want to know what's about to happen to these warships."

"I'll speak to him, sir."

The warship's altitude fell and, as it approached the ground, the base didn't seem so large after all. In order for both Laws of Ancidium to land, the *Ixidar* was required to be aligned perfectly from south to north and at the same time, the underside destroyer cannon required exact positioning to fit into the square shaft at the bottom of the construction trench underneath.

"It's going to be tough for the Daklan to work on the *Ixidar* with the underside two thousand metres above the surface," Eastwood observed.

"They'll have to deal with it," said Recker. Most of the work would be done by automated machinery. It wasn't as if the Daklan technicians would be lowering ten-million-ton slabs of alloy to the ground using ropes and pulleys.

Into the shaft went the destroyer cannon. Having seen what those guns could do, Recker found himself being exceptionally careful that he didn't scrape the sides and damage the barrel on the way in. Following two minutes of slow and steady, he was satisfied with the position and activated the warship's autopilot.

"Commander Aston asks if you're finished parking, sir," said Burner on the comms a moment later. "It's just that there's a war to fight, and we've only got fifteen days."

"I'm done," said Recker, wondering what happened to his crew's respect for a superior officer.

Aston had fewer obstacles and she dropped the *Gorgadar* vertically into place. The warship wasn't designed to land – at least not in any HPA or Daklan facility – and she left it hovering with its lowest underside plates less than a hundred metres from the ground. Given the lack of space for both Laws of Ancidium, two thousand metres of the *Gorgadar*'s starboard wing intruded into the landing field.

"We're down," said Recker. A tension he hadn't known about slipped away, and was replaced by the mental and physical mugginess of the death sphere which now encompassed the *Ixidar*. "Make the ground control teams aware. Re-enable docking at our shuttle bays and tell them to get those soldiers onboard."

"Yes, sir," said Montero. "I've provided copies of the *Ixidar*'s map files and pinpointed the current location of both the enemy troops and the bridge."

"Good work, Corporal."

Recker turned his eye towards one of his status screens and spotted a blue light on his comms monitor. "You're still there, Lieutenant Burner?"

"Yes, sir. You wanted to know what the Daklan are planning to do with the *Ixidar*."

"I do."

"You might not like the answer."

"Is it ever different?"

"They're going to send teams onboard both the *Gorgadar* and *Ixidar* to check for the location of the batteries. If there's no easy way to link the two by cable, or if the hardware isn't designed for a battery-to-battery energy transfer, they'll have to break the ships apart to find out if they can swap the hardware. Given the size of the two vessels, it's unlikely they'll have time to put both back together again in fifteen days. Maybe the *Gorgadar* alone will be too much."

Recker had been clinging to a hope that the Daklan would pull off a miracle which would allow both Laws of Ancidium back into service in time to meet the enemy head-on. The *Ixidar* was an immense, potent force and now it was possible it would play no further part in the conflict.

"So, we're pinning everything on the *Gorgadar*," Recker said. "It'll have to be enough."

With nothing else to do, he leaned back and waited for the Daklan troops to arrive.

CHAPTER TWENTY

AS BLOODTHIRSTILY EFFICIENT AS EVER, the Daklan soldiers swept through the *Ixidar* and mercilessly slaughtered the Lavorix troops. Teams of construction yard technicians followed and the internal monitors showed them plugging diagnostic equipment into whichever interface ports they could find. Intrusion warnings appeared on Recker's console and he cleared them as quickly as he could, to allow the Daklan teams access to the hardware.

Meanwhile outside, hundreds of shuttles and construction bots – deconstruction bots in this case, Recker idly thought - hovered with apparent eagerness, as they waited to dissolve the joins holding the outer plating so they could carry off the *Ixidar* piece by piece.

"Are we expected to sit on the bridge for fifteen days and provide technical assistance?" asked Eastwood. He sounded tired.

A wave of that same exhaustion hit Recker, and his

hand, operating under its own biological autopilot, crept towards his leg pocket where three Frenziol injectors waited. He clenched his fist and withdrew it.

"I'm sure we'll be stuck here," Recker admitted. He pursed his lips. "We'll be in no fit state to fight if we spend the next two weeks on double and triple shifts. I'll make sure we get some downtime."

In spite of his bold words, Recker admitted defeat on the Frenziol and gave himself a full shot. Any downtime wasn't coming soon, and besides, he wanted to be ready in case the Ancidium surprised them all by turning up at Terrani when it was least wanted.

Less than fifteen minutes after they'd exited their shuttle, a contingent of Daklan soldiers and a large team of technicians arrived at the bottom of the steps leading to the bridge. Recker opened the blast door and told them it was clear. The Daklan took that as an invitation to enter and, moments later, the bridge was an unwanted chaos of jostling personnel. Recker hunted for the soldiers' commanding officer.

"I am [translation equivalent] Lieutenant Erdax-Ivar," said one of the Daklan. He was unusual for having blue eyes, which were no less piercing than the greens of the others. "I command the soldiers here and elsewhere on the *Ixidar.*"

"I'm Captain Recker. Thank you for your expertise and efficiency, Lieutenant," said Recker. "Now please take your soldiers back down those steps to make some room."

"As you wish, Captain Recker."

Erdax-Ivar bellowed a harsh order through the chin

speaker on his helmet and the newly arrived soldiers headed for the door.

"Sergeant Vance, Sergeant Shadar, stay here until I tell you otherwise," said Recker.

"Yes, sir. We'll keep to one side," said Vance.

"Who is the lead?" shouted Recker to the technicians.

"I am the lead," said one. She approached, six feet tall, slender and with her face partly hidden by dark hair crammed into the suit helmet she wore. "I am Lera-Vel."

"You're a technician?" asked Recker, spotting the tiny insignia on her shoulder.

Lera-Vel unclipped her helmet and lifted it over her head. "I design warships for the Daklan fleet and will oversee work on the *Ixidar*."

She was startlingly beautiful and Recker felt a thunderous pulse of adrenaline enter his body. "I'm Captain Recker. What is your plan?"

Lera-Vel narrowed her eyes as if she were sizing him up either for a meal or to gauge his intelligence. "Our people know of the *Ixidar*, Captain Recker. We know what it did to our fleet at RETI-11, so be assured I understand its importance." Her voice was rasping and alien, and it rose and fell in a way that was both peculiar and mesmerising.

Recker nodded at her words. Sometimes the construction yard teams failed to see the bigger picture. "We need the *Ixidar* and the *Gorgadar* ready for battle."

"My initial evaluation, and study of the *Aeklu*'s and *Verumol*'s designs makes me believe we can use ternium kickstarter cables to link the batteries of the *Ixidar* and *Gorgadar*."

"You have twenty-thousand-metre cables here at Hakarul?" asked Recker.

"No, but our fabrication plant is creating the required lengths, which will be joined in the construction yard and suspended by a shuttle bridge between the two vessels."

Recker opened his mouth to ask more questions about the process, but decided against it. He had his own areas of expertise and the construction yard had theirs. He asked something else. "Do you know where the batteries are located?"

"Not yet." This time Lera-Vel grinned at Recker. "We will find out within the hour."

"I'll take your word for it."

"That is good." The Daklan paused. "My people also know of Captain Recker. You fight well."

"It's a talent I have," said Recker, wondering where this was leading.

"Perhaps, if I am successful in completing this project, you would spend time with me?"

The blood pounded in Recker's temples. "As soon as this work is done, I will be called away."

Lera-Vel stared. "That is a shame." She turned. "Nevertheless, I will do what I can to finish this task quickly. You may change your mind."

"That I might," said Recker softly, as Lera-Vel joined the others of her team.

He went to sit back down, only to find Corporal Montero grinning broadly at him.

"Don't say a word," he warned.

"I wouldn't dream of it, sir."

With nowhere else to go, Recker sat and awaited

developments. He kept in contact with the *Gorgadar*, which was a scene of similar activity. True to her word, Lera-Vel and her team located the *Ixidar*'s batteries within the hour and, in a significant development, traced the linking conduits to their termination point which was inside the outer plating on the eastern face of the spaceship.

"This is the place where the energy transfer took place between the *Ixidar* and the Ancidium," said Lera-Vel, pointing at a highlighted area of the hull she'd brought up on one of the command console screens.

"Do we have any way to extract the energy without taking the ship apart?" asked Recker hopefully.

"The location of these conduits is convenient," said the Daklan. "We will remove the armour from this section and attempt to link with the *Gorgadar*. If we cannot make the conduits channel energy, then we must remove approximately thirty billion tons of ternium to reach the batteries themselves. If we cannot tap directly into the batteries, we must move them from one ship to the other."

"Which will be the worst-case scenario," said Recker.

"Very much the worst-case scenario," said Lera-Vel. "Now I have a greater understanding of the *Ixidar*'s design, I believe the construction yard will require twenty-five days to switch the hardware and repair the damage. Even if we did no repairs, we would not finish in fifteen days."

"How long?" asked Recker.

"Eighteen days."

"With no way to reduce the total?"

Lera-Vel smiled at him and he detected the sadness

in her eyes. "I know warships and how they are constructed, Captain Recker. Eighteen days is what it will take. We must hope the worst case does not come to pass."

"How long to complete the energy transfer if you can channel through the conduits without removing any more than the covering armour? And is there an easily-accessed linking place on the *Gorgadar*?"

"To answer your last question, yes, the *Gorgadar* has a similar conduit and it links to that vessel's underside. The last of the cable sections will be available in four hours and the operation to connect the two warships will begin immediately afterwards."

"Does the yard intend to begin dismantling the warships at the same time?"

"That order has not yet been given, Captain Recker. To find out, you must speak to your superiors."

"I'll do that," said Recker. "Thanks."

Lera-Vel smiled again and rested her hand briefly on his shoulder. Then, she picked up the diagnostic tablet she'd left on the command console and returned to her team.

"Corporal Montero, I want a channel to Fleet Admiral Telar," said Recker. "And if you wink again, I'll have you demoted."

"I've got something in my eye, sir." Montero blinked rapidly. "Requesting a channel to the Fleet Admiral. He's busy."

Recker swore under his breath. He wanted to know what was planned, but interrupting something potentially more important would only anger Telar.

"Maybe he'll come back to you later, sir," said Montero.

"I doubt it," said Recker. "He's got too much to deal with."

Three hours passed and the main dismantling work didn't start, though a cluster of robots was busily removing the outer plating around the conduit terminations on both the *Ixidar* and the *Gorgadar*.

Recker could understand the reason for holding off – keeping these two warships operational for as long as possible was a hedge in case the Lavorix changed their plans. The HPA had huge teams working on predictive models that could analyse the tiniest pieces of data and use them to build probability tables for future events. From Recker's experience, those tables were nine parts bullshit and one part guesswork, but high command – Telar included – had a degree of faith in the output.

Or maybe the technical teams have a high expectation of success for the nonintrusive cable link.

Taking a deep breath, Recker called Lera-Vel over.

"Lera-Vel, what is the likelihood of the easiest method working out?" he asked.

"In theory, there is a high chance of success, however we are working with part-known technology, Captain Recker. It is possible the Lavorix have created their extraction technology to channel its energy directly into the Ancidium and nowhere else. Why they would do so, I can only guess."

"What is the next stage in the operation?"

"The cable sections are ready and they are on their way from the fabrication plant."

"That was three hours, not four."

Lera-Vel grinned at Recker and her green eyes speared into him. Her teeth were perfect and the alienness of her upward-curving fangs only added to the fascination. "The Hakarul yard is the best in the known universe."

Having seen the construction facilities inside the Ancidium, Recker wasn't ready to agree, though he didn't mention what he'd seen on the Lavorix mothership. "The linking operation will start soon?"

"That is correct. However, we must place the *Ixidar* into an offline state before we begin."

"Nobody told me," said Recker. "Why do you need to shut the warship down?"

"It is likely the *Ixidar*'s security systems will prevent the flow of energy from the batteries," said Lera-Vel. "If the warship is shut down, we can bypass the Lavorix technology and encourage the natural movement of energy along our cable."

"There's nothing natural about what's in those batteries, Lera-Vel."

Her hand rested on his shoulder again and Recker found himself wondering how she would look in normal clothes instead of the unflattering spacesuit she wore.

"I know the tragedy, human. I also know that the Lavorix themselves provided the energy in these batteries. Their deaths will benefit us."

"Must the *Gorgadar* also be shut down?" Recker asked.

"No – the security measures do not prevent an inflow of energy, only an outflow."

"Am I needed here on the *Ixidar*?" he asked. "If you're

shutting things down, I'll find somewhere to stretch my legs."

"You are not needed," confirmed Lera-Vel. "I recommend you wait until the warship is offline, else who would pilot it should the enemy appear in the skies of Terrani?"

"How long before the shut down?"

"It will be soon."

Recker fidgeted while he waited and his eyes kept drifting towards Lera-Vel. Something about her made him feel both sick to his stomach and lighter than air. Montero watched him from the corner of her eye.

"She made the first move, sir. All you have to do is say yes."

"What?" Recker asked, dragged back into reality.

"The Daklan, sir. Lera-Vel. She seems nice."

Recker wouldn't have normally engaged in the conversation, but Montero was easy company and not one to gossip. "Nice?" he said. "That's not the first word that comes to mind."

"I didn't want to refer to her physical attributes, sir. In case it made me look crude."

Recker laughed. "She is something."

"You're a lucky man, sir," said Montero. She gave him another wink. "Damnit, something in my eye again."

"You'd best ask Corporal Hendrix to take a look at that," said Recker dryly. "In case it affects your aim."

Lera-Vel approached the command console again and her eyes met his. "We are ready to shut down. Do the internal doors run from backup power? Otherwise you will be required to set them into an open state if you wish to leave."

"There's backup power," said Recker. "The lights will stay on as well."

He stood. Lera-Vel didn't step back to give him room and he found himself only inches away, and looking directly into her face. Still she didn't move and Recker brushed past, unable to take his eyes away.

"I'll be on the comms if I'm needed," he said. "How long before the energy transfer is completed, assuming everything goes to plan?"

"That depends on the flow rate, Captain Recker," said Lera-Vel. "Hours, though not many."

Recker smiled at her. "I'm going to pay the *Gorgadar* a visit."

"And I will see you when you return?"

"I promise."

Lera-Vel raised one arm and made a circular motion with three fingers. One of the other technicians across the bridge made the same movement, spoke something into her comms unit and then the consoles simultaneously went offline. A moment later, the ever-present drone of the propulsion dropped to silence. Recker didn't know how the Daklan had managed to accomplish the shut down since they hadn't obviously interacted with the bridge consoles, and he didn't ask. Instead, he headed over to Lieutenant Eastwood.

"I'm heading to the *Gorgadar*," he said.

"Need company?" asked Eastwood, standing from his own console.

"You're welcome along."

"What about me, sir?" asked Montero.

"Do you want to come, or do you need to see Corporal Hendrix about that eye?"

Montero glanced over her shoulder at where the other members of the squad were laughing and joking on a private channel. "I'll stick around here, if that's all right, sir?"

"Go and catch up with the squad," said Recker with a laugh. "I'll bet Drawl's invented a few more legends about himself that you haven't heard yet."

"Yes, sir."

Montero gave Recker a smile filled with warmth and then headed over toward the squad. A few seconds later, having informed Sergeants Vance and Shadar of his intentions, Recker left the bridge with Eastwood.

CHAPTER TWENTY-ONE

RECKER'S BRISK pace soon had the knots out of his muscles. The interior of the *Ixidar* was swarming with Daklan soldiers and technicians, but not so many that he couldn't stretch his legs properly.

"I'm wondering if we should stay put on the *Ixidar*," said Eastwood as they exited the internal shuttle car. A squad of Daklan soldiers were in the room outside and watchful for signs of trouble.

"The Daklan have switched everything off, Lieutenant," Recker reminded him. "Even if there's an emergency, it'll take an hour or more to bring everything back to an operational state."

"Are you expecting an emergency?" asked Eastwood.

Recker detected the suspicion in the other man's voice. "No I'm not. What gave you the impression I was?"

"It's just..." Eastwood cut himself off and tried again. "There's no need for us to leave the *Ixidar*. Usually when you decide on something that's not entirely logical, it's because you've had a feeling."

"Not this time," said Recker.

"Then why are we leaving the *Ixidar*? We've already stretched our legs."

"I don't know." Recker hadn't been expecting the question and he was stumped. "I just want to visit the *Gorgadar* – to see how the others are coping."

"Well, maybe you don't always get a feeling. Maybe you're just one of those people who does something because you get it into your head that it needs to be done, and then when you follow that instinct, suddenly end up in the right place at the right time."

Recker was about to give a flippant response. He didn't and he slowed to a halt. "I don't understand."

"I think you're a statistical anomaly," said Eastwood. "Whatever you do, you end up causing or responding to a significant event."

"The right place at the right time," Recker repeated. "Whether I want to be there or not."

"We could return to the bridge, sir."

"I don't want to do that."

"In which case, I suggest we get our asses in gear."

Recker picked up the pace, without being exactly sure why. When he arrived at the bay where the *Gorgadar*'s shuttle was still docked, the scent of burned Lavorix hung cloying in the air, and the blood of those chewed-up corpses was turned to a cracked brown layer.

The two men entered the shuttle's airlock, crossed the loading bay, and climbed the steps to the cockpit.

"Did you tell anyone we were coming?" asked Eastwood.

"Lieutenant Burner."

With a growing sense of unease, Recker activated the launch sequence for the shuttle and the huge doors on the bay lumbered open, the backup power clearly struggling with their weight. Piloting the vessel along the tunnel, Recker checked via the *Gorgadar* that he had clearance to fly across the construction yard without being shot to pieces by a ground launcher or a jumpy Daklan warship captain.

"Is something wrong, sir?" asked Burner.

Recker wondered if he'd fought so often with this same crew that they sensed when something was amiss, even when he couldn't feel it himself.

"Maybe, Lieutenant. Is there anything on the sensors?"

"No, sir. The Daklan fleet has dispersed and most of them are back on normal patrol."

"Have you heard from Fleet Admiral Telar?"

"Yes, sir, just about two minutes ago. He's agreed with Admiral Ivinstol to hold off the most destructive work on the *Ixidar* and the *Gorgadar* until it's absolutely necessary."

Even Telar feels it. Maybe Admiral Ivinstol does too. Something's about to happen.

"We'll be with you in a few minutes," said Recker.

The final door in the *Ixidar*'s armour opened and the shuttle entered the overcast light of Terrani's early morning. Travelling between planets, each with their own day lengths, in conjunction with sensors which could turn night into day, made it hard for Recker to keep track of where in the HPA's standardised twenty-four-hour day he was. Evidently, they'd arrived before the planet's dawn and only now was it becoming light.

Recker didn't dwell. He adjusted the shuttle's sensors with one hand, while the other controlled the flight.

"The Daklan are making progress," Eastwood observed. "Good progress."

A few thousand metres below, twenty lifter shuttles hovered in perfect order above a line of thick, near-black cable which had already been laid on the ground between the *Ixidar* and the *Gorgadar*. Countless ground vehicles were in evidence, and dozens of cranes adjusted the position of the cable, while bright flashes from floating, cylindrical robots indicated the places where the joins were still being made.

"It's no wonder we were losing to the Daklan," said Eastwood. "Even the teams on Lancer or Adamantine couldn't match this for efficiency."

Recker had no intention of arguing. It wasn't as if the human construction teams were lazy or inefficient, and this was a job where physical strength was irrelevant. Yet, somehow, the Daklan were better than the HPA at putting things together. Maybe one day, Fleet Admiral Telar would have the chance to send his senior officers here to learn a few lessons about construction.

"There's our docking bay," said Recker, switching his attention from the activity below.

He fed in extra power and the shuttle sped across the intervening space between the two huge vessels.

"We're coming in fast," said Eastwood.

"You told me this is an emergency situation, Lieutenant," said Recker with forced lightness.

He slowed at the last minute, rotated the shuttle and then guided it rear-first into its original docking tunnel. The transport made a gentle impact with the airlock and a blue light appeared on Recker's console.

"We're docked," he said, already two paces towards the exit.

Mentally, he retraced his route through the *Gorgadar* in preparation for a sprint to the bridge. The airlock didn't need to cycle and he dashed straight through, waving impatiently for Eastwood to keep up.

"Don't worry about me, sir. I can still beat you in a sprint."

"Let's find out," said Recker, lengthening his stride.

They hastened along gloomy corridors, stepping over the corpses of long-dead Lavorix which still littered the floors. Recker's breathing deepened, but not so much that he couldn't hear the beat of the warship's propulsion, the steadiness of which indicated the *Gorgadar* was still at Hakarul.

When he arrived at the bridge steps, Recker took them two at a time and the effort made his leg muscles burn with righteous pain. The blast door opened and he rushed inside, to find his crew at their stations, and fifteen or twenty Daklan technicians armed with diagnostic tablets. As one, they turned at his arrival.

"Don't mind them, sir," said Burner. "They're friendly when you get to know them."

"Anything to report?" asked Recker.

"Nothing you need worry about, sir," said Aston. "The ground teams have finished joining the cable and they're about to turn on the taps."

"My apologies, sir," said Eastwood. "I thought that..."

"Don't worry about it, Lieutenant," said Recker. He made his way to the command seat, which Aston was in the process of vacating. "Something doesn't feel right."

"What doesn't feel right?" said Aston.

"We're working on the assumption we have fifteen days," said Recker. "I think the Lavorix changed their plans."

"Because they realised they sent their exploration route to the *Ixidar*?"

"It could be that," said Recker. "Or it could just be that the Lavorix are slippery bastards. They've been at war for centuries and evidence suggests they're pretty good at it. I don't want to make assumptions that we've got a whole fifteen days before trouble shows up."

"There's no trouble at the moment, sir," said Larson, back at her comms station.

Now that he was at his console and everything seemed in good order, Recker wondered if he'd allowed himself to be carried along by Eastwood's claims that he was a statistical anomaly. Certainly the HPA had studied various people who could apparently beat the odds far more than the extremes of chance would dictate, but as far as Recker knew, nothing much had come from those studies.

"Captain Recker, we will begin the energy transfer."

Recker turned at the voice – it was another female Daklan. He'd been told that the males did the fighting, while the females had a greater aptitude for science, so it wasn't a surprise to find most of the techs fell into the latter category.

The technician smiled and again, Recker got the impression she was asking herself if he'd taste better off the barbecue or straight out of the frying pan. "My name is Olos-Tir," she said.

"Is there anything my crew or I can do?" he asked. "And are there any risks I should know about?"

"There are always risks, human. The time has come for us to accept them."

It was a viewpoint Recker could accept. "Please," he said. "Go ahead with the transfer."

Olos-Tir lifted her diagnostic tablet. "It has already begun."

"The Daklan don't hang around," said Eastwood with a short laugh.

Recker called up the monitoring tools for the *Gorgadar*'s Extractor batteries. The readout was at zero percent.

"Nothing yet," he said.

"Watch," said Olos-Tir.

Having fought with Shadar and the other Daklan in his squad, Recker had learned to recognize their different moods, and from that, he knew Olos-Tir was excited. He looked again at the battery readout and it had climbed to one percent.

"It's working!" he said.

"We will monitor for a time and then we will increase the flow rate," said Olos-Tir.

"How long will you monitor?" asked Recker.

"Such impatience, Captain Recker."

"You're damn right I'm impatient," he said, without irritation. "Two percent."

"I'll keep an eye on the decay pulse and the destabiliser," said Aston. "I'm sure they require power from the superstressed engines as well as the batteries." She considered it further. "Maybe they'll even deplete some tenixite from our storage bay, but I could be wrong."

"If they need all three power sources, they're going to be dangerous," said Burner. "Hopefully only for the Lavorix."

A lot was riding on those two weapons, and Recker loaded the monitoring software onto his own screen as well. The battery charge level advanced to three percent and the activation lights on the weapons remained unlit.

The Daklan lacked the HPA's obsession with safety – which was probably one of the reasons they could build warships so quickly, because they didn't spend hours filling in safety observation cards, require a full safety audit before someone climbed three rungs up a ladder, or require a safety spotter to accompany every technician who was simply off to take a leak or eat a sandwich containing potential allergens - and Recker was interested to find out how long the aliens would hold out before they turned the taps from a trickle to a flood. He didn't have to wait long for his answer.

"We will increase the flow," said Olos-Tir, five seconds after Recker had completed his internal tirade.

"Four percent!" said Recker as the readout nudged upwards. "Five!"

"The second Extractor green light came online!" said Aston. "If we put the engines into superstress, we should be able to fire it."

"It won't fire without the life energy of the people it's killed?" asked Eastwood. "That doesn't sound right."

"The *Gorgadar* is different to the other Laws of Ancidium, Lieutenant," said Aston. "The Extractor is tied in to the decay pulse and the destabiliser and I don't know the reason. Those two are still offline as well."

"Access to the Extractor is an improvement," said Recker. "Though I'd prefer it if we didn't have to switch the propulsion into superstress again." He remembered how one of the ternium modules had only reluctantly returned to its normal state and he also remembered Lieutenant Eastwood's warning about the potential for harm if a superstressed module went irretrievably critical.

"We are at the maximum flow rate supported by our cable," said Olos-Tir. "Any more and the heat build-up will have an adverse effect on the transfer."

"Six percent," said Recker.

The charge level was rising much faster now, though it wasn't exactly racing towards a hundred percent.

"Sir, I have an inbound comm from Fleet Admiral Telar," said Burner. "He says it's urgent."

"Bring him through," said Recker, preparing for the worst.

"Carl, we've had some bad news," said Telar at once. "One of our deep space probes out in Zavind-N detected the Ancidium's arrival."

"I recognize the name of the solar system, but I don't

know where it appears in the expected sequence of planets, sir."

"It's out of sequence, that's the problem. Well out of sequence."

Recker closed his eyes and swore. "The Lavorix have altered their plans," he said.

"I've had my data analysis teams examining the locations, times and distances on the plans that the Ancidium sent to the *Ixidar* and they believe the enemy have skipped forward several steps, rather than altering their plans entirely."

"How sure are the analysts?" asked Recker.

"This isn't the time to go over the data, Carl. My teams believe the discovery of Earth has moved significantly closer and in the absence of anything to contradict their findings, I have to base my decisions on their conclusions."

"How significantly closer?"

"The analysts are predicting a 68% likelihood that the Ancidium will arrive in Earth's solar system anywhere between four and twenty-four hours from now. My personnel had to make educated guesses on how long the enemy will remain at the final three destinations on their route to Earth, plus uncertainty around whether one particular transit will be done by Gateway or at an unknown lightspeed multiplier."

"What's the 95% outcome?"

"If the analysis is accurate – and I know your feelings on the matter – there's a 95% chance the Ancidium will arrive at Earth between one hour and forty-eight hours from now."

"What are your orders, sir?"

"I've agreed with Admiral Ivinstol that the *Gorgadar* should leave Terrani immediately and the *Ixidar* should follow the moment it's brought back online."

"Is Earth our destination?"

"Negative – a confrontation in our home solar system is unthinkable. We will meet the Lavorix at their expected destination one prior to Earth."

"What is the name of that place, sir?"

"The Evia system."

It was a name Recker hadn't heard before, just like a trillion others. If it was to be Evia, then that's where it would be. He moved on to the next issue. "We don't have enough personnel to crew both Laws of Ancidium at anything like maximum effectiveness."

"I know and this is where I need your opinion, Captain Recker. If the Daklan send some of their best officers onto the *Ixidar* and *Gorgadar*, will it help or be a hindrance?"

"In a few hours, I could have them trained in the basics, sir."

"We don't have a few hours to spare." Telar went quiet, thinking.

"Sir!" yelled Burner from his station. "The Terrani deep space monitors have detected an inbound particle wave. It's not the Ancidium, but it's going to be bigger than the *Gorgadar* or the *Ixidar*."

"Distance?"

"Ten million klicks from the planet, sir. The local fleet is on its way."

"Fleet Admiral, can you hear this?" asked Recker.

When Telar responded, he sounded almost like a beaten man. There again, he'd just had his fifteen days of preparation knocked down to one day, give or take. "I hear it, Carl. Do what you must and, if you make it through, speak to me again."

"Yes, sir."

Telar closed the channel and Recker's eyes moved to the *Gorgadar*'s battery readout.

"Fifteen percent," he said.

"Nothing on the decay pulse or the destabiliser, sir," said Aston. "They're both still offline."

Recker desperately wanted to wait for one or other of these weapons to become available, but he could only guess how much charge would be required in the batteries. Maybe the hardware had failed anyway, and by the time he discovered the fact, it would be too late for the billions of Daklan living on Terrani.

"Some of the Daklan ground batteries have launched, sir," said Larson. "The only thing that'll target from this range is lightspeed missiles."

"Olos-Tir – order the ground crews to sever the cable," said Recker.

"I have done, so," said the Daklan a moment later. "It will require a few seconds."

Recker scanned the console in front of him, reassuring himself that the onboard systems were ready for flight.

"Sixteen percent on the batteries," he said.

"The cable is severed," said Olos-Tir, appearing at Recker's side.

He took a deep breath and rested his hands on the controls.

"I've obtained a link to the local battle network," said Burner. "It's running through a security filter and it's a second behind."

A sprinkling of green on the tactical was joined by a single red dot. Recker knew instinctively this was the warship he'd glimpsed as the *Ixidar* escaped from the Ancidium's bay. Right now, lots of clear space separated the two sides and the Daklan fleet had no way of covering the distance without warming up their ternium drives. He doubted they'd be in a hurry to do so, in case the enemy warships went past them at mode 3 and wrecked the planet.

"That warship is called *Ruklior*, sir," said Larson. "Our battle computer is aware of it, but only by name, not capability."

"We screwed up," said Recker, his heart sinking. "They followed the *Ixidar* out of the Ancidium and kept themselves away from sensor sight until we left DEKA-L."

"And then they followed us," said Eastwood. "Through a damned Gateway."

"Terrani was on the list of 170 planets – the enemy must have linked the lightspeed tunnel to this planet and realised there was a reason for us coming here." Recker swore bitterly. "After that, the Lavorix changed their other plans and soon they'll reach Earth."

Most of this was speculation, but Recker was sure it contained more than a grain of truth. By trying to do the right thing, his actions had jeopardised the home worlds of both the HPA and the Daklan. Once, Recker would have blamed himself. Not this time. This time, he recognized that he wasn't responsible for unforeseen consequences. All he could do was handle whatever came his way.

Recker gave a smile that promised death to the Lavorix.

"Let's do this," he said.

CHAPTER TWENTY-TWO

THE *GORGADAR'S* engine note deepened and the warship lifted from the ground as if it weighed nothing. Without needing to be told, the Daklan technicians retreated to the rear bulkhead and kept quiet. Recker forgot about them at once.

Careful that waves of sonic energy didn't sweep aside the ground crews, he accelerated steadily at first, and, once the low-lying rainclouds were far below, with increased urgency. Still the propulsion gauge showed hardly any utilisation and it wasn't until the skies turned into the blackness of space that Recker requested maximum output from the engines. A howling of technology accompanied the *Gorgadar*'s overstressed rush towards this new opponent.

"The *Ruklior* took a mode 3 jump, sir," said Burner. "They went fifty million klicks from their previous position."

A glance at the tactical told Recker where the *Ruklior* had emerged from its transit, and he altered course towards it. "They're fifty-eight million klicks from here. That's a good spot, Lieutenant."

"I'd like to claim the credit, sir, but the enemy re-entered local space within the scanning arc of a Daklan monitor."

"The Lavorix travelled away from Terrani," said Aston. "Are they testing the range of the lightspeed missiles?"

"Usually the enemy just drop into high orbit and start firing their Extractor, Commander. They must be holding back because they know the *Ixidar* and the *Gorgadar* are here."

"The Lavorix wouldn't have sent the *Ruklior* if they didn't think it had a chance of success against us," said Aston.

"I've got a sensor lock on the *Ruklior*," said Larson.

The enemy warship appeared on the central bulkhead feeds and it was a fifty-thousand metre alloy colossus with a cuboid shape and a row of what appeared to be superfluous spines running along its top section. Larson enhanced the feed, but most details were swallowed up by the distance, except for the pinprick specks of plasma heat from the ground-launched lightspeed missiles.

"It's travelling at low velocity, sir, and on an erratic course," said Burner.

"That doesn't look so much like a warship as it does a transport," said Recker.

As he spoke, several smaller red dots appeared on the

tactical and, on the sensor feed, Recker saw those newly emerged warships accelerating away from the *Ruklior*.

"A warship carrier," said Eastwood. "Able to carry a fleet in its hold."

"How big a fleet?" asked Recker. "The *Ixidar* is our best tool for such an engagement and it's out of action."

"I've got Admiral Ildir-Ta-Rok on the comms, sir," said Burner. "He's in charge of the local Daklan fleet."

"Put him on open."

"Captain Recker, you command the *Gorgadar*," said Ildir-Ta-Rok. Like most of his species, his voice sounded like an unholy union between white noise and a cheese grater. "What do you know of this enemy warship?"

"It is the *Ruklior*," said Recker. "It's unloading warships."

"So we have detected. I believe the enemy arrived closer than they intended to our planet."

Recker nodded his agreement. "Had they deployed their fleet before we detected them, their position would have been much stronger."

"The *Ruklior* is within range of our lightspeed missiles, Captain Recker, yet its flight pattern and velocity are such that our warheads will enter local space outside of its shield, rather than within."

A limitation of the lightspeed missiles was their requirement to re-enter local space before detonation. Their guidance systems were programmed to activate the transition early rather than late, and that meant they'd explode against the Lavorix energy shields, rather than bypassing them and striking armour instead.

"Sir, it's possible the *Ruklior* is unaware they were detected by the outer Daklan monitor," said Burner. "That monitor remains operational."

"Is that your sensor officer?" asked Ildir-Ta-Rok.

"It is," Recker confirmed.

"I believe he might be correct. This gives us an opportunity to strike first!"

Recker's mind jumped unbidden to his early days in the military, to a lesson in warfare strategy he'd attended where the officer delivering his pearls of wisdom was a grizzled, cynical-as-hell, miserable old bastard who'd seen it all and got a shoulder full of medals to prove it.

You think a war between equals is won by the bravest or the most righteous? The side that outthinks its opponent and fights the hardest? Bullshit! The side that wins is the side that screws up the least.

That old man's viewpoint was just another amongst many – one of the myriad different ways to think about the universe and events happening within it. Taking the current situation at face value, the *Ruklior*'s crew had made an error and all Recker might have to do was activate mode 3 and fire the Extractor through the guts of that fleet carrier.

And yet, this was the warship chosen by the Lavorix to face the *Gorgadar* and the *Ixidar*. A fleet carrier was useless if it succumbed to the first attack and that, in Recker's mind, meant the *Ruklior* was going to be a tough nut.

"Admiral Ildir-Ta-Rok, I am concerned that our enemy has chosen the *Ruklior* as the best equipped for its task. It followed the *Gorgadar* and the *Ixidar* to your planet.

There is more to this warship than its size and the contents of its bay."

"What is your evaluation, Captain Recker?"

"The Ancidium was immune to every weapon except the *Gorgadar*'s particle beam. If the *Ruklior* had the same defences, the *Ixidar* would be unable to harm it."

"Several of our lightspeed missiles have successfully detonated and our monitor confirms visible damage. The enemy craft has adapted its flight pattern to limit the effectiveness of our attacks."

"So it's not immune," said Recker. "That means it has an energy shield that can withstand at least a few hits from the *Ixidar*'s destroyer cannons."

"What of this particle beam you mentioned?" asked the Daklan.

"It has a twenty-second recharge interval. The *Ruklior*'s going to require a few shots before it breaks up."

"I do not wish to wait idly by as the *Ruklior* disgorges its fleet near the planet I am charged to protect," said Ildir-Ta-Rok. "Equally, I am aware that should I instruct my fleet members to activate their lightspeed drives, the enemy will easily outmanoeuvre us."

Recker was sympathetic to the Daklan's plight – Ildir-Ta-Rok was in command of the most powerful warships his species had ever created, yet it wasn't nearly enough to combat the Lavorix. Had the *Ruklior*'s crew not been wary about the *Gorgadar* and *Ixidar*, Recker was sure that the local fleet would already be reduced to molten debris and the planet fallen to the enemy.

"I'll get back to you, Admiral," Recker said.

His eye went to the tactical, where four red dots had

become fifteen. As Recker watched, three others exited the *Ruklior*'s bay, and he tried to guess their tactics.

"Do they know the *Ixidar* is grounded?" he wondered.

"They may do, sir," said Burner. "Perhaps that's why they've started unloading their fleet, because they know the Destroyer is no immediate threat."

"The *Gorgadar* is no pushover," said Recker.

He sensed he was falling into the trap in which he would waste time attempting to nail down every single variable. It was an impossible task and sometimes it was better to just act. The mode 3 button on the control bar caught Recker's eye and his thumb brushed gently against it without providing enough pressure to activate.

"I've got thirty-two enemy warships on the sensors and counting," said Burner.

"They could potentially have another fifty battleships within their hold, sir," said Eastwood. "And we're watching them spill out."

"I know, Lieutenant. There's a lot riding on this," growled Recker.

"Why don't we target a proximity mode 3 arrival and hope the death sphere catches them unawares?" said Aston.

"Their course is too erratic to predict, and the death sphere radius is only eighty klicks." said Recker. "I'm sure we can catch their entire hull within an Extractor cone, but I've got a feeling they're immune to it."

"Even if you're right, those smaller ships aren't immune, sir," said Larson.

"They're too far spread," said Recker. A lightbulb illuminated in his head. "Except the ones in the bay! Lieutenant Burner, open that channel to Ildir-Ta-Rok."

"Yes, sir."

The Daklan Admiral entered the channel and he wasn't happy. "This lack of action is intolerable, human, and you are the only one who can break the deadlock."

"And that's exactly what I'm about to do, Admiral. We're going to mode 3 into the middle of the pack."

"What about my fleet?"

"There's nothing you can do from this range, except watch and react," said Recker.

"My two least favourite responses."

"Mine too, Admiral."

"Will the *Gorgadar*'s shield withstand the bombardment it will receive?"

"Against those ships already deployed? Definitely. It's the unknowns I'm concerned about."

"Go," said Ildir-Ta-Rok. "Delay no longer."

Recker cut the channel and turned to Aston. "We're going to fire the Extractor directly into their bay, Commander, and we're going to test our conventional armaments against the *Ruklior*. I trust you to pick your targets wisely."

"Yes, sir."

The side that wins is the side that screws up the least.

It occurred to Recker exactly how much the negativity of those words had always angered him, as if the skills and bravery of fighting men and women counted for absolutely nothing. He reached towards the tactical and chose his destination. The *Ruklior*'s velocity and course alterations were effective against lightspeed missiles, but they wouldn't take it out of Extractor range.

"Activating mode 3," he said.

The sensors went blank and Recker jammed the control bars forward, producing an exhilarating cacophony from the engines. He banked hard and then again.

"Sensors coming up!" said Burner.

"Locate the *Ruklior*!" snarled Recker.

The enemy ship might have activated its own mode 3, but he didn't think so. After all, there was nothing stopping the *Gorgadar* following again. If this was a trap laid by the Lavorix, it was about to be sprung.

"Sensors online!" yelled Larson. "Targets locked!"

Those initial targets included several Lavorix battleships and a quantity of smaller vessels, all within ten thousand kilometres of the *Gorgadar*. Recker wasn't interested in the battleships, nor the missiles they were ejecting in great quantities towards his vessel.

"Find the *Ruklior*, damnit!"

"Got it!" said Burner.

At eighteen thousand kilometres away, the enemy vessel was farther than Recker had anticipated and he saw that it was travelling at increased velocity. It was stern-facing and with its pattern of movement unchanged.

At this close distance, the features of the *Ruklior* were crisp and sharp-edged against the black canvas. Visibly, it held few surprises and its hull was mostly unmarked, suggesting it was fitted with an energy shield to rival that of the *Gorgadar*. Not that the *Ruklior* was entirely undamaged – an angry crater still burned with the heat of a lightspeed missile detonation and Recker wondered how many others had struck in the places out of his visual arc.

Altering course, he aimed to sweep around in order that he could locate the bay opening into which he intended firing the Extractor.

"Acquiring targets," said Aston. "Priority list created. Upper missile clusters one through fifteen: launched. Forward clusters one through five: launched."

Aston worked with incredible speed and Recker glanced at her priority list. The *Ruklior* was at number one, with the known battleships coming beneath. His gaze went back to the sensors in time to see the first-launched Lavorix missiles detonate against the *Gorgadar*'s shield. The reserve gauge didn't drop more than a fraction.

"They'll need to do better than that," said Eastwood.

"Second wave of enemy missiles launched," intoned Aston. "Enemy countermeasures active. *Gorgadar* missile impacts imminent. Underside clusters one through fifteen: launched. Portside clusters one through fifteen: launched. Starboard clusters, one through fifteen: launched."

The forward sixty missiles impacted with the *Ruklior*'s energy shield. On a different feed, one of the Lavorix battleships was torn apart by dozens of the *Gorgadar*'s warheads. Other feeds offered an incomplete picture of the conflict. Tracer lines swept through the darkness, while hundreds of propulsion trails from offensive and defensive missiles raced from one screen to another. Around one battleship, Recker spotted a shield of dancing lights appear, like an imperfect copy of a Meklon mesh deflector. The barrier wasn't enough to protect the

Lavorix craft and it vanished within a hundred plasma explosions.

Recker dragged his attention away and focused on the *Ruklior*. A battleship emerged from its starboard side and a second from its portside. He cursed, having hoped for a clear Extractor shot directly into a single bay. Now, it seemed likely the enemy craft had two separate bays.

Perhaps it won't matter. Perhaps the Extractor will go clean through from one side to another.

"We've received a core override, sir," said Eastwood. "The *Gorgadar*'s internal security system has isolated the code."

A second, much larger, wave of Lavorix missiles, along with a few dozen gauss slugs, crashed into the *Gorgadar*'s shield. This time the gauge fell, if not by much.

"Should I fire the particle beam, sir?" said Aston. "It'll give them something to think about."

The *Gorgadar*'s sweeping approach had brought the *Ruklior*'s portside bay into sight, though the angle wasn't enough to see what lay within. Six further lightspeed missiles had smashed into the visible side – not nearly enough to fatally wound the *Ruklior*, but enough to make the warship's crew take notice. As if sensing danger from the *Gorgadar*'s approach, the enemy craft accelerated. It wasn't able to pull away and the distance between the two vessels fell rapidly.

"Hold the particle beam, Commander," said Recker. His mind was already conjuring up thoughts of capturing this warship and adding it to the list of others stolen from the Lavorix.

A total of four spaceships exited the bay, two from each side of the *Ruklior*. Recker ignored them.

One Extractor shot into that bay and then I'll see if I can catch them in the death sphere.

The plan was straightforward and Recker bared his teeth in anticipation. Bringing the *Gorgadar* into a tighter turn, he found the angle into the bay he was looking for. At six thousand metres wide and three thousand high, the opening was immense and within, Recker saw dozens of Lavorix craft. Two sped out, side-by-side and banked opposite ways around the *Gorgadar*.

"Lieutenant Eastwood, switch the engines into superstress."

"Engines in superstress."

The corpse-sigh note of the propulsion which Recker well-remembered from the first time was somehow both dreary and thrilling - ancient and new alike, and hinting at tiers of knowledge and possibility far beyond anything humanity had attained. It made his skin tingle and imbued him with fear and longing all at once.

"Commander Aston, fire the Extractor," he said.

The Extractor shot didn't come. Recker's console software kicked him out, returning him to the top-level menu. At the same moment, the controls went unresponsive in his hands.

"Shutdown code!" yelled Eastwood.

Recker knew he'd taken the sucker punch to end all sucker punches. Maybe the *Ruklior* had a super-weapon designed to combat the *Gorgadar*, or perhaps it existed only in his head. Whatever the truth, the enemy hadn't even needed to show what they had. All they'd needed was a shutdown code, and with the *Ixidar* offline in the Hakarul construction yard, there was no allied ship to rescind it.

The side that wins is the side that screws up the least.

Cursing in fury, Recker smashed his clenched fist against his console and wondered what he could possibly do to make things right.

CHAPTER TWENTY-THREE

"WILL THEY DESTROY US?" asked Lieutenant Larson, when Recker had stopped shouting.

"I don't know," he replied through gritted teeth. "They left the *Gorgadar* untouched after the original crew were killed. It's possible they retain a hope that one day the death sphere will fade enough that they can salvage the vessel."

"We'll soon find out," said Eastwood. He cocked his head, listening. "We probably won't hear the explosions until our armour plating is gone."

Recker had a thought. "We were travelling at 3200 kilometres per second when we received the shutdown code. Our propulsion is offline, but we'll be coasting at the same velocity. I doubt anything bar the *Ruklior* itself would be able to keep up."

"The Lavorix missiles don't travel fast enough either," said Aston. "That leaves gauss slugs and the *Ruklior* as the only concerns."

"I'm not worried about gauss weapons," said Recker. "The *Gorgadar*'s armour is thick enough to withstand hundreds of shots from anything those battleships are packing. They'd need a Tri-Cannon or a Toll to destroy us."

"The *Ruklior* could match velocity and anything that came out of its bays would inherit that same velocity," said Eastwood. "And the missiles those warships fired would boost fast enough to hit us."

"That would be a scrappy kill," said Recker. "Would they bother diverting from Terrani long enough to finish us off?"

"We die now or we die later," said Eastwood, looking up from his console. "Does it matter which?"

"The local Daklan fleet and the ground launchers are capable of firing enough lightspeed missiles to give the *Ruklior* and these other warships a real headache," mused Recker. His fury was gone, replaced by a cold calculation. He *had* screwed up and he didn't think he'd be able to fix things, but that wasn't going to stop him trying. "If the *Ruklior* is concentrating on us, the Daklan might have a better chance of landing their missiles on target."

"All we can do is sit and wait," said Larson. "That's what sucks."

Minutes passed and Recker heard a distant, low sound coming from a place he couldn't pinpoint. He knew at once what it was.

"The enemy have had enough of the *Gorgadar*," he said. "They're taking us out of the picture."

The faraway explosions continued, yet became no louder.

"I reckon the *Ruklior* matched speeds, left a handful of its warships to do the job, and then returned to Terrani," said Eastwood. "But even without the shield to contend with, those warships are finding it hard to destroy something as massive as the *Gorgadar*."

Recker wasn't fooled. If the bombardment continued much longer, the damage would soon turn from superficial to catastrophic. The *Gorgadar*'s hardened alloy plates could withstand tremendous heat and punishment and the warship was clad in many layers of those plates. Once the enemy made a breach, the inner blocks of ternium were far more vulnerable to attack.

"There's got to be something we can do," said Larson.

"Nope," said Eastwood. "We can't override the shutdown code. Not from here."

Listening carefully, Recker detected that the rumbling blasts had become suddenly louder, as if a huge section of the outer armour had been torn out.

"That's not good," said Eastwood. "I wouldn't mind so much if I had access to the status monitors. It's the blindness which is hardest to cope with."

Recker turned in his seat. He'd left Itrol, Litos, Private Carrington and Private Givens behind on the *Gorgadar* when he first took the other members of the squad to the *Ixidar*. Those soldiers now huddled miserably in the far corner, keeping out of everyone's way. The guilt Recker felt was a pounding reminder of how unfair the universe could be to anyone caught on the wrong side of a decision - not that Sergeant Vance and the rest had anything more than a stay of execution.

You've had a good run, Carl. Done better than you could possibly have hoped.

It wasn't enough and the bitter taste of failure mingled with the bridge air's stench of dead Lavorix. The flavour was something unique and vile, and his hatred of it made him rage inside.

"I still have partial access to the internal monitors, sir," said Larson. "They record the sound pressure levels throughout the *Gorgadar* and the volume is definitely picking up."

"The effort is appreciated, Lieutenant," said Recker. "It won't help us, so don't waste your time."

"I feel like I have to do something, sir. In the same way Lieutenant Eastwood wants his status lights."

Recker didn't say anything more and he tapped a few buttons on his control panel, if only to keep himself occupied. His anger had already declined to a simmer, and his mind hadn't given up. In the furthest recesses, where ideas could form without the distraction of conscious thought, his brain turned over every variable, examining them for possibilities. So far, viable plans were non-existent.

"It doesn't seem as if those lightspeed missiles are going to save us," said Aston.

"No, it doesn't," Recker conceded. He cleared his throat. "When the end comes, I want you all to know I couldn't have wished for a better crew. More than that, I couldn't have wished for better people."

"It's been a good ride," said Eastwood. "But I'm damned if I'm accepting defeat. This isn't the end of the road."

"No way," said Larson.

"Write down your plans for getting us out of this and I'll draw one from a hat," said Recker.

"You could try the dead captain's finger like I asked you before, sir," offered Aston. "That's such a guaranteed way to rescind the shutdown code I don't even need to put it into the hat."

For some reason Recker couldn't stop himself from laughing. "You bite the finger off and I'll place it on the security interface."

His smile faded quickly and nobody offered a plan. Not that he'd expected anything different – this was one of those *end of the road* moments. He'd escaped from other such moments before, yet this one had a finality about it – a certainty that no amount of thinking or talking could alter.

At this, the moment of Recker's failure, he felt no despair, only a yearning to have done more. Another faraway booming of plasma warheads, louder than all the others, created a vibration in the control bars which he felt in his palms through the absorbent layers in his suit gauntlets.

I promised Lera-Vel I'd see her again.

Recker was given his chance.

The frozen menus on his command console unlocked before his eyes and his hands darted out to the control panel.

"I can access the software!" Recker said.

"Sensors coming online!" yelled Burner.

"I have a Daklan called Lera-Vel on the comms, sir," said Larson. "She tells me she brought the *Ixidar* back online and she wishes us good hunting."

"The shutdown code was rescinded by the *Ixidar*, sir!" said Eastwood. "Our propulsion is coming online and the energy shield generator should activate at any moment!"

"Battle stations!" shouted Recker. "Lieutenant Larson, pass on our thanks to Lera-Vel." He tested the controls and they responded, albeit sluggishly. A few gauges and read-outs were emerging from slumber and they hadn't yet settled.

"Shield online," said Eastwood. "It dumped its reserves during the shutdown, so it's filling from zero."

"Sensors up!" said Burner. "We have lost most of the forward arrays and some on the starboard flank. Searching for targets."

"Commander Aston – as soon as you obtain a lock light, blow the crap out of those bastards."

A grin appeared on her face to go alongside the look of disbelief. "Hell yes!" She entered a command into her console. "Missile control systems online and available."

The first target appeared on the tactical. It was a battleship, ten thousand kilometres directly ahead of the *Gorgadar* and travelling at the same velocity. Specks of white light appeared on its hull to indicate a missile launch, and those warheads detonated almost at once. This time, they struck energy shield instead of hull plating and the reserve gauge dropped straight to zero before increasing to one percent, then two.

"Forward tubes one though eight and twelve through fifteen: launched," said Aston. "Uppers one though six: launched. Failure lights on the others. Shit – and an amber light on the particle beam."

"Will it fire?"

"It might, but there's not enough power for it yet."

Recker didn't have time to consider the ramifications of the particle beam's potential hardware failure. His eyes jumped to the tactical, where three additional red dots had appeared as Burner, Larson and the warship's own battle computer identified and locked onto targets.

"Four is the total, sir," said Burner. "All of them battleships."

"Engine mode 3 will not be available for a minute or two, sir," said Eastwood. "We'll have to face these enemy ships head-on."

"With pleasure," said Recker.

Too late, the enemy crews realised the danger. The first battleship erupted into plasma flames at the same moment as Aston targeted another.

"Locked onto target #2. Range: twenty thousand klicks," she intoned. "Portside clusters one through fifteen: launched. Underside clusters one through fifteen: launched. Locked onto target #3. Range, eighteen thousand klicks. Starboard clusters one though seven and nine through twelve: launched. Undersides one through five: launched."

Had the *Gorgadar*'s shield been at maximum, the Lavorix battleships would have been distinctly lacking in penetrative firepower. As it was, their inbound salvos were enough to keep the reserve levels depleted. The energy shield flickered in and out, blocking many warheads, while others broke through and exploded against the *Gorgadar*'s hull.

"Target #2 destroyed," said Aston.

Recker didn't spare the fiery ball of plasma on the

bulkhead screen anything more than a glance. He was too busy figuring out where the launch clusters had failed, so that he could bring the already-loaded missile tubes to bear against the Lavorix.

"Shield at zero percent," said Eastwood. "Multiple gauss impacts against our nose plating – or whatever's left of it."

The shield gauge increased to one percent and was instantly returned to zero by a few dozen enemy missile detonations.

"Target #3 out of action," said Aston.

Recker's gaze went to the tactical, just as the fourth Lavorix battleship disappeared from the screen. "They activated mode 3," he said.

"Must have gone back to Terrani," said Eastwood.

The third battleship had been crippled by the *Gorgadar*'s missiles, but it wasn't destroyed. It decelerated sharply, rapidly falling behind. Unfortunately for the Lavorix, this only exposed them to the *Gorgadar*'s loaded rear missile tubes.

"Rear missile clusters one through fifteen: launched," said Aston with an unusual edge of nastiness in her voice.

Pinpricks of orange propulsions appeared on the rear feeds and then they were gone into the distance.

"Target #3 destroyed."

Recker reduced the *Gorgadar*'s velocity and banked hard, so the portside flank with its largely operational sensor arrays were aimed directly towards Terrani.

"Scan quickly!" Recker ordered. "I need a damage report! And when will mode 3 become available?"

"The energy shield has priority, sir," said Eastwood. "There'll be no mode 3 until it's at fifty percent."

"I'm scanning Terrani for the *Ruklior* and the rest of the enemy fleet," said Burner. "We should be back on the local battle network soon."

"We've lost approximately twenty-five percent of our launch clusters, sir," said Aston. "Most of them on the nose and starboard forward flank."

"What about the other weapons systems?"

"No reported errors, sir, except for the amber on the particle beam. The status report indicates it'll still fire."

"We took a pounding while we were shut down," said Eastwood. "I've got errors on several ternium blocks and our total output is down fifteen percent."

"Anything you can do to recover it?"

"I don't think it would be wise to try, sir."

"I trust your judgement, Lieutenant. Don't touch those engine blocks."

"Here's what we're facing at Terrani, sir," said Burner.

"The *Ruklior* and every warship it was carrying," said Recker, staring at the clustered grey specks on one of the feeds. Here and there, he spotted flashes of light which appeared tiny at this distance, but which he knew were nothing of the sort. The Daklan fleet had engaged with the Lavorix and, given the disparity in numbers and capabilities, Recker was shocked the fight was still ongoing.

Maybe it only just started, he thought. *Perhaps the Lavorix were delayed chasing the Gorgadar for just long enough that we've got a chance to turn this around for the Daklan.*

"I need mode 3, Lieutenant Eastwood," said Recker.

He set the *Gorgadar* on course for the planet and the warship's velocity gauge climbed strongly.

"You're slowing down the energy shield recharge and delaying the mode 3, sir," Eastwood said. "When the propulsion is at maximum, there's nothing left for elsewhere."

"If we switch into superstress again that'll speed everything up, won't it?"

"I don't know, sir." Eastwood took a noisy breath. "I wasn't going to tell you until I was sure, but do you remember how I showed you that some of the ternium blocks keep the superstressed ones from going critical?"

"I remember."

"We lost some of those stabilisers in the Lavorix attack, sir. We might not have enough remaining."

"Stabiliser and destabiliser," said Recker. "What the hell have the enemy created here?"

It was a rhetorical question and even Lieutenant Eastwood didn't speculate.

"We owe the Daklan," said Recker. "If we wait, they'll lose the planet. We might already be too late." In his mind, he imagined the effect of an Extractor attack on the billions of people living on Terrani. "Lieutenant Eastwood, switch the propulsion into superstress."

Eastwood didn't hesitate. "You got it, sir."

The thundering bass of the engine changed immediately superstress was activated and this time it no longer sounded like the respiration of a dying man. This time, it sounded deeper and infinitely more powerful.

Now it's like the breath of a sleeping god – one that can

never be roused, but with power that can be tapped and utilised.

"Sir, the stable blocks are no longer enough," said Eastwood. "The readouts are totally screwed up – I don't know what's happening."

The words made Recker fear what he might have unleashed. Having opened the gates to hell or salvation, it wasn't time to turn back and he prepared himself for what was to come.

CHAPTER TWENTY-FOUR

"THE SHIELD IS RECHARGING at about four times its previous rate, sir," said Eastwood. "The generator module wasn't designed to cope with such a high influx."

"I want to hear about the mode 3, Lieutenant."

"You'll have it available any second now, sir."

"Commander Aston, what of our weapons?"

"Two green lights on the Extractor, sir, and nothing on the decay pulse or the destabiliser."

"Set the Extractor to its widest arc. This time the *Ruklior*'s shutdown code won't stop us."

"The Lavorix might destroy the *Ixidar*, sir," said Eastwood. "If they're clever enough to realise what happened."

"Then let's hope the enemy aren't clever." Recker didn't take his eyes from the tactical. The *Gorgadar* was back on the battle network with the Daklan and that gave him an accurate picture of events at Terrani. His eyes searched for patterns amongst the duelling warships.

"Mode 3 is available, sir," said Eastwood.

"Let's test it out." Recker's hand went to the tactical and he touched a fingertip to his intended destination. "Activating mode 3," he said.

For once, Recker hardly noticed the in-out thump of transition, so focused was he on the enemy fleet. Having emerged from lightspeed, he held the *Gorgadar* stationary and readied himself for the sensors coming online.

"Sensors coming up," said Larson.

"No impacts against the energy shield," said Eastwood. "Not yet."

A rush of data threatened to flood Recker's senses. The *Gorgadar* had emerged from lightspeed on the edge of the Lavorix fleet, half a million kilometres above Terrani. A glance was enough for Recker to spot the Hakarul base, around the planet's curve, yet sharply visible. So far, the Lavorix had made no significant attack on the ground facilities.

"The lightspeed transit did not affect the propulsion state," said Eastwood. "We're still in superstress."

"I have two green lights on the Extractor, sir," said Aston.

"Choose well, Commander."

The enemy fleet was neither clustered, nor spread, and they occupied a rough sphere with an approximate diameter of sixty thousand kilometres. At the centre, the *Ruklior* travelled the same slow but erratic course that would keep it protected from lightspeed missiles. Evasive manoeuvres weren't enough to protect it from conventional warheads and plasma wreathed much of the enemy vessel's energy shield. Recker doubted the incoming fire was enough to trouble the Lavorix too much.

Fifty thousand kilometres from Terrani, the Daklan fleet showed no signs they intended to engage in a dogfight. The two sides exchanged missiles in enormous quantities and Recker saw that the planet's thousands of ground interceptor batteries were doing an effective job of pulverising the incoming Lavorix warheads. Those batteries were all that was keeping the local fleet from rapid destruction.

"We've received a shutdown code," said Eastwood. "The *Ixidar* has rescinded it."

"The *Ruklior*'s crew knows we're here," said Recker. A warning light appeared on his console and he bared his teeth at the accompanying text. "They're equipped with a Halo and they're charging it up."

The *Hexidine* – another of the Laws of Ancidium – had also been fitted with a Halo, and the weapon had been entirely effective in shutting down the *Aeklu*. Recker didn't want to lose the *Gorgadar* in the same way.

"Hit them with the Extractor," said Recker.

"Extractor activated," said Aston. "The cone of effect is overlaid on the tactical."

The weapon's arc was narrow, but it grew with distance. Recker estimated that Aston had caught thirty of the Lavorix warships in the effect cone, including the *Ruklior*.

"Activating mode 3," said Recker, selecting a new destination and pressing the button on the controls.

Another in-out transit took the *Gorgadar* to a place approximately centre of the Lavorix fleet. The sensors came online and the tactical indicated that several hundred missiles were already inbound.

"Fire the particle beam, Commander. Aim for the *Ruklior*."

Recker wasn't sure if the enemy command ship had been disabled by the Extractor and it seemed sensible to take no chances.

"Particle beam targeted. Fired," said Aston.

The thick beam of blue stabbed across the intervening thirty thousand kilometres. Ignoring the *Ruklior*'s shield, the attack skewered the enemy vessel a third of the way back from its nose and a third of the way from its topside armour.

"Hopefully, I took out the bridge," said Aston.

"Halo charging again, sir," said Eastwood.

Recker swore at the news. The particle beam required twenty seconds between shots and it wouldn't be ready before the Halo discharge. He spotted something from the corner of one eye – the *Gorgadar*'s batteries had climbed to twenty-five percent. One or more of the thirty Lavorix warships hit by the Extractor must have been packed to the ceilings with troops – either that or the *Ruklior*'s personnel had all been killed and the warship's battle computer was now running the show.

"The decay pulse," said Recker.

"It's available!" said Aston. "One green light and one amber."

"Activate the weapon," said Recker. "Quickly!"

"There's no targeting option – it must be an area weapon," said Aston. "Decay pulse activated."

The lights on the bridge dimmed, though not because their power supply was interrupted. Rather, it was as if the decay pulse itself was suppressing the illumination in a way which added to the ever-present miasma of the death sphere. Recker felt a force tugging violently at his body, as though the weapon was designed to rip his soul from his body and channel his essence into a magnification of its effectiveness.

A split second after Aston had pressed the button to fire the decay pulse, a visible ripple swept out from the *Gorgadar*, like a wave across the fabric of reality. Travelling at incredible speed, the decay pulse struck the closest Lavorix warships and continued onwards.

At the same time, a fountain of shredded armour and razor shards of much darker ternium - totalling millions and millions of tons - erupted from beneath the *Gorgadar*, about ten thousand metres back from the nose. Red lights appeared on Recker's console.

A damaged warship was nothing new to him and he dragged his attention to the other feeds. The discharge of the decay pulse was not positive for the enemy fleet. One of the closest battleships began to crumble, huge pieces of it breaking away and then bursting into powder as if the bonds between the atoms hadn't simply been severed, but savagely ruptured, using their own energy against them.

Recker's eyes shot to a different feed and on this one, a different battleship had already split into three sections, then six, then twenty. In moments it was little more than a dispersing cloud, travelling at the velocity of the vessel it had once been.

"They're breaking up, sir," said Burner, his expression one of disbelief. "All of them."

"Like the Fracture," said Aston. "Only this seems a whole lot worse."

"Some of those warships were fifty thousand kilometres away..." Recker started. He bit his tongue. "What about the *Ruklior*?"

The *Ruklior* was not gone. Either its energy shield or the strength of its design had been enough to protect it from disintegration, though the huge warship was not in a good way. Its outer plating had been unevenly stripped, changing its shape to something indistinct and revealing the ternium modules beneath.

"The Halo warning has gone, sir," said Eastwood. "Either we've interrupted the charge-up, or the weapon has failed."

"We've lost the decay pulse, sir," said Aston. She pushed buttons. "There are red lights on the monitoring tools."

"I think it blew out when we activated it," said Recker. He looked at the *Gorgadar*'s battery gauge, which was reading five percent. "That one shot used up most of our juice anyway."

The chaos of the moment was fading and, amongst the ruins of an entire fleet, Recker didn't know what he should do. One part of his mind insisted he should activate another mode 3 to put some distance between his warship and this carnage. Another part – that dark part within him that hated the Lavorix for what they had done – wanted to watch the unfolding spectacle.

One-by-one, the red target markers on the tactical vanished, while Recker kept a careful eye on the *Ruklior*. Burner and Larson hunted with the *Gorgadar*'s remaining sensor arrays, and everywhere they focused, the story was the same. Dust, debris, and death.

"One of the Daklan sensor satellites was taken out by the decay pulse, sir," said Larson. "It was 238,000 kilometres from the *Gorgadar*."

"Oh crap," said Eastwood quietly. "What cage have we opened?"

Recker's order to fire the decay pulse had resulted in this atrocity, yet he felt no guilt, nor accepted any failing in his humanity. The Lavorix deserved no hold over him and he wouldn't allow them one. Not after everything they'd done.

He turned once more to the *Ruklior*. It made no detectable attempt to charge the Halo weapon and it had commenced a laboured acceleration that caused pieces of semi-decayed ternium to break free and fall into its wake. Here and there, Daklan long-range surface-launched missiles detonated against the vessel, though it wouldn't be long until it was out of range of the conventional ground batteries.

"They're sensor and comms blind, sir," said Larson. "The decay pulse has stripped away all their hull-mounted arrays and antennae."

"They're a sitting duck," said Burner.

Recker knew what he had to do. The Lavorix fleet was gone, though some of the larger vessels had been reduced to non-functioning cores of decayed ternium and technology, which, even now, the Daklan bombarded with missiles.

"The decay pulse drained our batteries to five percent," said Recker. "Commander Aston, target the *Ruklior* and fire the Extractor. Let's see if there's anyone left alive. The Lavorix started this and we're going to show them what it feels like to lose."

"I don't think the last Extractor shot worked against them, sir," said Aston. "I think one of those other warships I hit was filled with troops."

"Whatever defence the *Ruklior* used against us, I'm sure it's not available any longer, Commander. And if it is, we'll turn them to ash with our missiles."

"Extractor targeted," said Aston. She looked at Recker, her eyes wide.

"Kill them," said Recker, without remorse.

"Extractor fired."

The Lavorix must have been crammed into the *Ruklior*, Recker decided, having seen the effect their deaths had on the *Gorgadar*'s battery levels.

"Back up to thirty-five percent," he said. His mind went to the future. The Ancidium was still out there. "And no decay pulse left to fire."

"I don't know how much we'll need in the batteries to fire the destabiliser," said Aston. "More than thirty-five percent."

"What are we doing about the *Ruklior*?" asked Eastwood. "I'm sure everyone's dead, but it's likely the battle computer has fallback orders."

"They aren't going anywhere, but let's finish that warship off," said Recker. "Lieutenant Burner, coordinate with the Daklan ground forces and tell them what happened."

Conscious of the *Gorgadar*'s accumulated damage, Recker didn't give the warship anything like full acceleration. With the conflict over, other problems sprang into his mind, gleefully reminding him he had plenty to do.

"Command Aston, for the avoidance of doubt, fire at will against the *Ruklior*," he said.

"Yes, sir."

"Lieutenant Eastwood, our propulsion is in superstress. Do we need to worry about it?"

"Anything unknown is a worry, sir. I haven't yet attempted to return our engine modules to a stable state."

"What are the downsides of failure?"

"Some of the stabilisers already went into superstress, which means it's possible some of the others might do the same. The *Gorgadar* is already packing tech that's way beyond my expertise, so I'm not confident I can offer you a meaningful conclusion about any of this, sir."

Recker didn't take his eyes off the feeds. Owing to the loss of many forward arrays, he was piloting the *Gorgadar* at an angle which allowed some of the portside arrays to compensate. The *Ruklior* wasn't far ahead and its course was straight and predictable.

"Missiles launched," said Aston. "Seventy clusters in total. 840 missiles heading for the target."

"What's the damage report from the loss of the decay pulse, Lieutenant Eastwood?" asked Recker. Hundreds of orange dots appeared on the feed and then accelerated out of sight.

"No breach into the interior, sir. The exact cause of the failure is unknown. We suffered a lot of damage from those enemy battleships while they had us shut down. I'm sure that was a major factor."

Recker had caught glimpses of that damage, though

the arrays which would have granted the clearest view were out of action. Whatever the extent, he was sure the *Gorgadar* would no longer resemble the sleek warship he and his crew had stolen not many days before.

"Impact," said Aston.

All 840 missiles struck the *Ruklior*. Under normal circumstances, the result would have been dramatic but not fatal to a vessel of such colossal size and mass. Having been weakened by the decay pulse, the *Ruklior*'s rear twenty thousand metres were obliterated, turning first into flaming pieces before fragmenting into a trillion tiny stars which dwindled and were extinguished by the dispassionate void.

"Waiting on reload," said Aston.

Recker would have preferred to hold onto the ammunition, but the *Gorgadar*'s magazines had been full at the time of its capture and it was designed to carry enough warheads for an extended campaign. He said nothing and let Aston fire a second salvo of 840 missiles after the first.

"The death of another major enemy warship," said Eastwood, after the detonations.

When the second star-bright explosion faded, nothing much remained of the *Ruklior* and the burning flecks of its destruction vanished into darkness, lost forever.

"We're done here," said Recker. "But the game's not over."

"The Ancidium," said Aston. "We have to face it."

"Just when you think you're at the top of the mountain, there's another peak behind it, twice the height and twice as steep," said Eastwood.

"The Ancidium is the last of those peaks, Lieutenant."

"We'd better hit the trail then, sir."

Recker nodded and smiled without humour. It was easy to tell himself that all roads led to this point – a confrontation with the Ancidium - yet many had been dead ends. Those were the roads down which failure would have taken him and his crew. They'd given everything to journey so far and now they deserved a shot at a real, lasting victory.

It was going to be tough, and whatever it took, Recker planned to come out on top.

CHAPTER TWENTY-FIVE

THE QUESTION CAME, like it always did.

"What's the plan, sir?" asked Burner.

Recker aimed the *Gorgadar* for Terrani and accelerated. The warship had lost part of its ternium drive, but with the balance between stable and superstressed modules broken, it seemed like it had infinite wells from which to draw.

"We're going to Evia, Lieutenant." Recker shouted over the din. The velocity gauge raced past seven thousand kilometres per second and then, unbelievably, it surged again, hitting eight thousand without apparent effort. The noise increased commensurately, yet the solidity of the *Gorgadar*'s construction meant Recker heard no indication of distress from the straining alloys, despite the punishment the exterior had suffered.

"We should stay away from Terrani, sir!" said Eastwood. "I don't want to think what might happen if one of the superstressed modules goes critical."

"Have you detected any change that indicates such an outcome is imminent, Lieutenant?"

"Probably not imminent, sir, but I just don't know."

"We can't face the Ancidium alone," said Recker. "The *Ixidar* has to come with us, else we'll lose our protection against the next shutdown code the enemy sends our way."

"If we add it to our battle network again, we can bring it with us on remote-pilot," said Aston.

"The Ancidium is carrying fleets of warships within its bays, Commander," said Recker.

Aston narrowed her eyes in his direction. "You've made up your mind, so tell us what you going to do."

"There's nobody amongst the Daklan ready to fly the *Ixidar*, so I'll do it," said Recker. "I will also request that Admiral Ildir-Ta-Rok brings his fleet with us to Evia through the Gateway we'll create."

"You should inform the Daklan if you intend bringing the *Gorgadar* any closer to their planet, sir," said Aston firmly.

"I will. First, I need to speak with Fleet Admiral Telar."

"I sent him a top-priority message when we were chasing the *Ruklior*, sir, so he has an idea of what's happened," said Burner. "I'm requesting a link."

Telar entered the channel immediately. His first words were chilling. "Captain Recker, a Lavorix *representative* arrived in Earth orbit to give us their terms."

"What terms?" asked Recker. "What kind of representative?"

"They sent a battleship – nothing our local fleet and ground launchers can't handle. Their terms are what you have likely guessed already. We are to surrender immediately or face extinction."

"They won't kill us, sir, they're lying!" said Recker. "They've figured out how to do a partial life energy drain that fills their batteries in the same way as an outright kill. It's in their interests to keep us alive for as long as possible. Our subjugation will allow them to resume their war against the Kilvar."

"It is a shame we have lacked the time for a catch-up discussion, Carl," said Telar. "Regardless, we have not yet provided an answer to our enemy. I am playing for time in the hope you can pull something out of the bag. The *Gorgadar* and the *Ixidar* are the only weapons capable of winning this fight, assuming the fight can be won at all."

"I will take the Laws of Ancidium to the Evia system, sir. I planned to speak with the local Daklan commander – his fleet's lightspeed missiles might turn the tide."

"I made those arrangements shortly before this conversation," said Telar. "Admiral Ildir-Ta-Rok will follow you through your Gateway."

"Do we have any other support?" asked Recker.

"Additional warships – both HPA and Daklan - are on route to Evia. Given the reactive nature of our response, the resources I gathered previously are not within easy range of that solar system."

"Those warships might be nothing other than cannon fodder, sir, but their sacrifice may be necessary."

"I understand this too," said Telar, his voice dropping

so that it was hard to hear his words above the propulsion. "I will not keep you any longer, Captain Recker. Make sure I am informed of developments."

"Yes, sir."

Telar closed out of the channel.

"Admiral Ildir-Ta-Rok, next, sir?" asked Burner.

"Please."

"Requesting a channel."

Ildir-Ta-Rok's voice emerged through the bridge speakers moments later. "I have spoken to your Fleet Admiral and my own superiors, Captain Recker. The Terrani local fleet is committed to the fight against the Ancidium. Should the Lavorix mothership remain operational, we will never be free of our enemies."

"I must transfer to the *Ixidar*, Admiral," said Recker. "However, the *Gorgadar*'s propulsion is potentially unstable. If it fails, the consequences for your planet will be grave."

"Do what you must," said Ildir-Ta-Rok without hesitation. "But do it quickly."

"Thank you."

"There is no need for thanks, human. The existence of our two species is at a crossroads. Without commitment, we will perish like the Meklon."

"We'll activate a short-range lightspeed transit towards your planet, Admiral. If you could issue an evacuation order for the personnel on the *Ixidar* I would appreciate it."

"I cannot issue that order," said Ildir-Ta-Rok. "Not while there is a possibility of Lavorix troops remaining onboard."

"What about the technicians?"

"I will ask them to leave."

The Daklan left the channel, leaving Recker in awe at how extreme circumstances could make the impossible happen so quickly and turn the hardest of decisions into the easiest. The single remaining forward sensor array was focused on Terrani – a home to billions – and the coming hours would determine whether those people lived in freedom or suffered a lifetime of agony at the hands of a species most of them had never seen first-hand.

"Time to get this done," said Recker. He selected the *Gorgadar*'s destination. "Activating mode 3."

Recker felt nothing from the transitions and upon the warship's re-entry to local space, he sprang from his seat. "Commander Aston, this is your time. The *Gorgadar* is yours."

"What about me, sir?" asked Eastwood. "Am I coming with you?"

"You're needed here, Lieutenant. The *Ixidar* is a killing machine and nothing else. Here on the *Gorgadar* is where your expertise will benefit us most."

"Yes, sir."

"Which leaves you and Corporal Montero to handle everything," said Aston.

"The two of us will be more effective than if we remote operate the *Ixidar* from here, Commander. It will be enough."

Aston didn't even try to smile. "It'll have to be."

"The sensors are up," said Larson. "We're right over the Hakarul base at a half-million klicks."

"Time to leave," said Recker. "Good luck to us all."

Alone, he sprinted from the bridge. His destination was the same shuttle he'd used before and he ran with his rifle clutched tightly. For a short time, the *Gorgadar*'s propulsion rose in volume and, away from the bridge, it was raw and deep enough to be felt in his bones. The journey to Hakarul wasn't long and the engine sound fell away long before Recker had arrived at the shuttle's airlock.

He entered the vessel and dashed over the storage bay and up the steps to the cockpit. Laying his gauss rifle at his feet, Recker dropped into the centre seat and connected to the *Gorgadar*'s bridge.

"I'm ready for launch," he said on the comms.

"You've got a green light, sir," said Burner.

"A blue light," said Recker.

"The Lavorix might use blue lights in place of our green lights, but to me, they'll always be green."

"A green light it is."

Ahead of the shuttle, the doors to the launch tunnel opened and Recker accelerated along the passage. The next doors opened and then the next, and the shuttle emerged into the planet's atmosphere at an altitude of a hundred kilometres.

He adjusted the sensors and focused them on the *Ixidar*, now alone on the Hakarul yard and making everything else seem tiny. The damage to the huge warship was more apparent from this distance, with its armour buckled and one of the particle beam holes partially visible. It had lost two of its destroyer cannons and Recker hoped that wouldn't reduce its effectiveness too much.

He accelerated away from the *Gorgadar* and banked the shuttle towards his target. At the same time, Recker's suit comms automatically linked to the *Ixidar*'s external antennae, which allowed him to reconnect with the squad channel.

"Corporal Montero, have you heard the good news?"

"Yes, sir. Lieutenant Burner let me know."

"You're ready for the showdown?"

"Yes, sir."

Recker was pleased at the response and even more pleased that Montero didn't add a *hopefully* or a *I'll do my best* at the end of it.

"You're going far, Corporal. I have to stop myself calling you *lieutenant* as it is."

"Thank you, sir."

The shuttle plunged though the now-patchy clouds above Hakarul. Rain was falling and a strong wind had picked up as the morning advanced. For a short time, Recker imagined himself away from here, somewhere beautiful and exposed to the purity of the same clean, cutting wind and stinging rain as he saw here on Terrani.

It wasn't to be and he piloted the shuttle lower, while his eyes searched for the docking bay. The ground crews hadn't gone anywhere, though their part in this was over.

There's the bay.

The blue light to indicate he was permitted to dock appeared and he rotated the shuttle to enter rear-first. Moments later, Recker felt the shuttle connect with the airlock coupling and another blue light appeared. He ran for the exit.

It was only a short journey to the *Ixidar*'s bridge – now Recker had learned the quickest route – and he dashed for the internal car. The same Daklan squad he'd encountered earlier hadn't gone anywhere. They made no effort to delay him or engage in conversation.

During the shuttle car journey, Recker confronted the uncomfortable thoughts he'd been ignoring in the hope they would settle and no longer trouble him. Unfortunately, those thoughts had become more turbulent rather than less and they wondered if, having come so far with his crew, he was doing the right thing by insisting they split so close to the end.

We aren't splitting. We'll fight side-by-side and against the same opponent.

He exited the shuttle car and hurried along the corridor to the bridge. The queasiness in his stomach, which had started the moment he left the *Gorgadar*, turned up a notch and yet more adrenaline rushed into his bloodstream.

Climbing the steps, Recker entered the bridge. The remains of his squad lounged against the same wall, as if they were in a competition to see who could act the most laid-back in the face of death. All the Daklan personnel were missing, apart from one.

"Captain Recker," said Lera-Vel. "You have returned."

"Like I promised."

Swallowing down his emotions, Recker took his seat. He knew suddenly this was the place he was meant to be. Without the *Ixidar*, the confrontation with the Ancidium was doomed to failure and Recker was the only man in tune with this incredible warship.

The presence of Lera-Vel only added to the weight upon his shoulders, like his own happiness was inextricably tied up with the success of the coming mission. It was a burden Recker knew he'd bear, come what may.

CHAPTER TWENTY-SIX

"CORPORAL MONTERO, open a channel to the *Gorgadar*," said Recker. He called up the command menu and began some rapid checks of the status readouts.

"Requesting channel, sir," said Montero, operating her console easily.

"Been practicing?"

She grinned at Recker. "I didn't spend the whole time you were away talking crap with the squad. Here's your channel, sir."

"We're about ready to lift off, Lieutenant Burner," said Recker into the comms. "Leave this channel open, so we can communicate without needing to open a new one."

"Yes, sir. Admiral Ildir-Ta-Rok and his fleet are in proximity to the *Gorgadar* – it's you we're waiting for."

"I'd best stop scratching my ass and get moving," said Recker dryly.

"Yes, sir." Burner paused and then continued. "This feels like a mess. Like we're charging into the unknown without a single idea what we're going to do when the shooting starts."

"That's an accurate summation, Lieutenant. I wish it were otherwise."

"Me too, sir."

Recker remembered something. "I've been busy flying to the *Ixidar* – you'd best give me a summary of what we can expect at the Evia system."

"Nothing out of the ordinary, sir. The Evia star is big and older than most. It's orbited by ten planets in the usual kind of mix - two gas giants, one clad in ice, another a molten ball of rock. A couple of hundred moons scattered amongst them, most of those around the gas giants..."

"I get the message," said Recker. "Where are you aiming the Gateway?"

"Way out on the fringe, sir. Commander Aston thought it best if we check out what's happening at a safe distance – assuming such a distance exists."

"What about the warships Fleet Admiral Telar mustered?"

"He wasn't shitting you when he said he couldn't gather as many as he wanted. We've got eight HPA warships, including only a single battleship, and an additional five from the Daklan fleet."

"Forty-eight in total," said Recker. "Plus the *Ixidar* and *Gorgadar*."

"Those additional warships are hours away, sir. We'll have thirty-seven when we arrive. Against anything else, I'd gamble on us having the upper hand even with thirty-seven," said Burner.

Recker didn't respond. He left the channel open and

turned to Montero. "*Ixidar* stuff we discuss on the bridge channel. Anything the *Gorgadar* needs to hear comes through your chin speaker."

"Yes, sir."

He gave her a thumbs up and she returned one of her own.

"Want me to request clearance to depart, sir?"

"I think the Daklan know we're leaving, Corporal."

The *Ixidar*'s instrumentation readings were exactly where Recker wanted them and he lifted the warship carefully from its trench. The underside destroyer cannon emerged cleanly from the shaft and he increased velocity, passing through the clouds and into the upper atmosphere.

"I've received a request to join the local battle network and I've accepted, sir," said Montero.

"Tactical populating," Recker confirmed. "No chance of sonic damage to the ground facilities at our current altitude. Switching engines to overstress – let's join the others."

A surge of acceleration carried the *Ixidar* into space and Recker set a course for the warships which had clustered at half a million kilometres. At seven thousand kilometres per second, the intervening distance wasn't significant and shortly, the *Ixidar* joined with the fleet. Montero focused the sensors and the approach trajectory gave Recker his best view yet of the *Gorgadar*'s exterior.

"The enemy really did a number on you," said Montero.

"That they did," said Recker.

Deep impact craters resulting from both gauss shots and missile detonations covered much of the *Gorgadar*'s visible starboard flank and five thousand metres of the nose section was unrecognizable. Torn armour plates dangled precariously, and ternium blocks showed through the openings. The heat had not yet dissipated, and a faint redness lingered in the alloy.

"There's all kinds of particulate crap spilling out," said Montero. "I guess we're not too concerned about that."

"Damn right we're not," said Recker. "Lieutenant Burner, we're coming alongside. Ready the Gateway."

"Lieutenant Eastwood was waiting for the order and he confirms the warmup has commenced, sir. Eight minutes and we'll be in the Evia system. Do we know for definite the Ancidium will be there ahead of us?"

"There's not much we have confirmation on, Lieutenant and this is one of those things. We've seen combat before – be ready for some more."

"Fan, meet shit," said Burner.

"Eloquently put," said Montero.

Recker swapped back to the bridge channel and finished positioning the *Ixidar*. When he was done, the two Laws of Ancidium were side-by-side, with little more than a thousand metres separating their nearest extremities. In the space around, Admiral Ildir-Ta-Rok and the other Daklan officers had arranged the local fleet. For a minute or two, Recker studied their warships. A few had suffered recent damage, but the overall outcome of their engagement with the Lavorix fleet was a good one, considering the disparity in numbers and capabilities.

"They didn't lose a single warship," said Recker. "The Daklan fight well. They always have." He couldn't stop himself from turning. Lera-Vel was sitting at the engine console, her head down as if she were working on a difficult problem. She didn't look up, nor even notice Recker's attention.

"Corporal Hendrix looked at my eye, sir," said Montero, her expression full of mischief.

"And what did she say?" asked Recker, going with the joke.

"It might be a recurring problem."

"Why am I not surprised at that diagnosis?" said Recker, shaking his head.

"You should go and see her, sir," said Montero, surreptitiously pointing over her shoulder.

The timer on Recker's console informed him the Gateway would activate in four minutes. He knew he shouldn't leave his station.

Screw it.

He climbed from his seat and approached Lera-Vel. This time she looked up.

Recker crouched next to her. "When this is over, I want to be with you," he said.

"You will, Captain Recker. It is destined."

He stared into her alien eyes and felt himself becoming lost. Lera-Vel's expression was less confident than her words, as if this were new to her as well.

"I'm Carl," he said.

"You will not lose, Carl. You are not accustomed to failure, though you fear it."

"It's not failure that fills me with dread, Lera-Vel. Only the future. And now not that. Not anymore."

Recker didn't want to take his eyes away, but he forced himself to stand. Giddiness swept through him and he wondered if Lera-Vel was no more than an illusion – an image of alien perfection conjured up by his mind to strengthen him against what was to come. He placed a hand on her shoulder and she was as real as everything else.

"I must return to my station," he said.

Lera-Vel smiled and indicated the control panel in front of her. "I had hoped to learn something useful from this console. Something that might help. I am too late."

Recker returned to his seat, wondering which of Corporal Montero's eyes would be affected by dust this time. It turned out her eyes were fine and she gave him another smile.

"One minute to go, sir," she said, pointing at the timer. "I love Gateway travel."

"Sarcasm doesn't suit you, Corporal."

"I learned it from Drawl, sir."

"Is there anything that Private Drawl isn't responsible for?"

"There's a simple rule to follow, sir. If it's bad, Drawl did it. If it's good, it was someone other than Drawl."

Recker laughed, though only briefly. The sound of it faded on his lips and instead he grimaced as he took the controls in an iron grip.

"One Gateway coming right up," said Montero on the squad channel. "Be ready and be steady."

A few seconds later, the timer fell to zero and the *Gorgadar* opened its Gateway. Darkness engulfed the *Ixidar* and the sensors went offline, and the effects of the transit were no better or worse than they always were.

"Get those sensors up," said Recker. It was a struggle to make his voice sound normal.

Montero uttered a couple of random curses and then acknowledged. "Sensors coming online, sir."

"We'll have dropped off the battle network during the transit. Watch for the request to re-join."

Recker held the *Ixidar* stationary. The distance between the warships would have diverged a little during the transit, but not enough that he could safely begin evasive manoeuvres.

"Sensors up, working on the adjustment," said Montero. "Battle network request received and accepted. Lieutenant Burner has requested a new open channel. Also accepted."

The first feeds were of darkness, as they usually were before the sensor operators got on top of things. Recker waited for developments, which he expected to hear about any moment now.

"Sir, the local battle network is in place," said Burner. "The eight HPA and five Daklan warships which were inbound separately will not arrive for another two and three hours, respectively."

"The ninety-five percent outcome for the Ancidium's arrival at Earth was between one and forty-eight hours, Lieutenant." Recker tried to figure out how much of that had already been taken up by the engagement with the *Ruklior*, and he wasn't sure. "We can't afford delays."

"I know, sir. I'm looking to see what I can find."

Lieutenant Eastwood's voice came through the speakers. "Sir, another of our engine modules has switched itself into superstress."

"Have you made any effort to switch it back?"

"No, sir. Like you ordered, I've left well alone. Eventually, we're going to run out of stabilisers and I don't want to imagine what'll happen then."

"Another reason to deal with the Ancidium quickly," said Recker. He swapped into the bridge channel. "Have you found anything, Corporal Montero?"

"Planet five, sir. It's called Vaan – a gas giant."

The fleet had a lot of space to scan and the distances were great. Recker's frustration climbed as the minutes passed, but gradually the combined efforts of the warships located the different planets. Since Evia was known to the HPA and had been scouted, the locations of the planets, as well as their orbital track positions, would have been available to an HPA warship. Unfortunately, those vessels hadn't arrived yet, and the Daklan charts only had data on the Evia star, rather than on anything orbiting it.

"It's not the planets I care about," said Recker. "It's the damned Ancidium. Is it here or is it not here?"

"There's a lot of space to scan, sir," said Montero. "I doubt the enemy ship is blind side of anything, but there's a chance of it."

"We've located an object close to Evia, sir," said Burner.

"We're six billion klicks out, Lieutenant!" said Recker in astonishment. "This has to be your best spot yet."

"I'm afraid I can't claim the credit," said Burner. "Not this time."

"I figured it out, sir," said Eastwood. "I scanned for lightspeed tunnels and there's an end point of one right next to Evia. I can't confirm it's the Ancidium, but whatever came through that tunnel, it's in the centre of the sun's corona – the temperatures are likely greater than a million Fahrenheit and there's only one spaceship we know that's going to be comfortable in the middle of that."

While Recker and his crew had recovered the *Gorgadar* on the edge of a different star's corona, the temperatures there hadn't been anything like so extreme as those endured by the object at Evia. Perhaps the *Gorgadar*'s energy shield could have withstood the burning heat, but he doubted it. The Ancidium was immune to most physical damage, and that's what made Recker believe it was the Lavorix mothership so close to the sun.

"What better place to hide while you scan for life?" said Montero.

"I don't think the Ancidium does much in the way of hiding," said Recker.

Or maybe it does, came the thought. *It's running from the Kilvar. Now it's found humanity and the Daklan, and we've destroyed its most powerful warships. Perhaps those bastards have learned something of fear and respect.*

At that moment, the planet Vaan, which was still on one of the bulkhead feeds, exploded.

CHAPTER TWENTY-SEVEN

RECKER HAD NEVER WITNESSED anything like this before. The Ancidium had destroyed Tokladan, though he hadn't seen it happening. Regardless, Vaan had about a hundred times the mass of the Daklan world and here it was, reduced to discrete sections of grey, liquid metallic hydrogen which were hurled away from the original core in defiance of all known science.

It happened quickly – as the compressed matter was flung apart, the forces holding it together lessened and the remains of the planet become indistinct, as if the process which had initiated the planet's demise was designed to continue until no trace was left of the original.

"We're six billion klicks from there, sir," said Montero. "I can't improve the feed any more than this."

"I'm not sure I want you to improve it, Corporal. I don't think I want to see any more than this." Recker spoke loudly through his chin speaker. "We weren't the only ones scanning the Evia system," he said.

"I can't confirm the Ancidium has located us, sir," said Burner. "We're twelve billion klicks from the star and I have yet to locate the enemy warship using our sensors."

"The Lavorix know we're here," said Recker with certainty.

"What orders, sir?" asked Commander Aston. "Admiral Ildir-Ta-Rok accepts his warships lack our capabilities and knows he must follow our lead."

"We can't go anywhere," said Recker. "If we've been detected, then there's no time to warm up the Gateway, even if I wanted us to."

"Why blow up a planet?" said Larson.

"To show that it's easy for them," said Recker.

"Planet seven – Louna - just went the same way, sir!" said Burner, his voice climbing an octave.

Louna was on another of the feeds. It was a much smaller planet than Vaan, and cased in ice. Smaller it was, but the death of Louna was no less shocking to watch, and Recker asked himself if whoever or whatever commanded the Lavorix was no more than a petulant child given control of a weapon with hideous potential.

"What are we going to do, sir?" asked Montero.

"The Ancidium is coming, Corporal and there's nothing we can do to escape. Not unless we abandon the Daklan, and that's not happening."

Recker's problems ran deeper than just the Ancidium.

"Sir, another of the *Gorgadar*'s stable modules went superstress," said Eastwood, talking quickly. "I think a tipping point has been reached – there are too few stabilisers left and they're going to switch over one by one. It's too late to stop it happening."

"How long before they're all in superstress?"

"I don't know - less than an hour. Maybe a lot less. I said before that if the *Gorgadar*'s propulsion went critical, we might be facing an event that makes the Dark Bomb look insignificant, but I really don't know what's going to happen, sir." Eastwood's exhalation between clenched teeth was audible over the speakers. "I don't want to be here to find out."

The same old mountain of crap was building the same way it always did and Recker struggled to think of the best way to stay on top of it. More than anything, he wanted a target – something tangible he could destroy.

"Where's the Ancidium?" he said. "Lieutenant Eastwood, do you have precise coordinates?"

"Yes and no, sir. The lightspeed tunnels are fuzzy and the detection tools aren't perfect. I can tell you within half a million klicks where the Ancidium emerged."

"I want precise coordinates – we can't enter million-degree heat and then start searching!"

"It might have moved anyway, sir."

"What about the sensors?" asked Recker. "Is it showing up on those?"

"The star's radiation is screwing up the readings, sir," said Larson. "We have no sensor confirmation of the Ancidium's position."

At that moment, the tactical display began filling with red as first ten, then thirty Lavorix warships dropped out of short-range lightspeed transits less than five thousand kilometres from the allied fleet. Recker acted instinctively, pushing the controls away from him and setting the *Ixidar* into a tumble. With physics-defying ease, the warship's velocity increased.

The Daklan were no slower to react, and their fleet of thirty-five accelerated from their starting positions, spilling missiles at the first of the Lavorix warships.

"The enemy are still coming, sir!" said Montero. "We have seventy confirmed targets on the tactical. Now seventy-five!"

The incoming Lavorix warships were a mixture of types, most of which Recker had encountered before in Meklon space. Even the smallest rivalled a desolator in size and mass and he knew they were dangerous and their crews experienced.

Arriving from lightspeed put the enemy at a temporary disadvantage – they were stationary and their sensors were not yet online. Missiles and gauss slugs crashed into the Lavorix warships, reducing the firstcomers to fiery debris, which spun outwards with the force of multiple explosions.

Recker found himself rapidly falling into the semi-trance he'd first experienced when piloting the *Ixidar* within the Ancidium. He targeted an enemy warship – this one an eight-thousand-metre battleship – and hit it with the facing destroyer cannon, reducing its armour plating and many of its ternium modules into powder.

Meanwhile, the *Gorgadar* pulled away from its start point, ejecting hundreds of warheads. Its particle beam stabbed into a Lavorix heavy, separating the vessel at its midsection. The heat expansion produced immense showers of torn plating which raced from the severed halves.

"Extractor fired!" said Larson. "Three enemy warships caught in the arc. Our batteries have fallen to thirty-four percent."

"These Lavorix spaceships aren't carrying enough personnel to replenish what the Extractor pulls from the life batteries," said Eastwood.

"Three of the enemy ships out of action from a single discharge," said Recker. "That's a good return whichever way you look at it. Fire the Extractor again, the moment it's ready."

"I've got a count of ninety targets on the tactical, sir," said Montero. "They're sending plenty of firepower our way."

"They're going to need it," growled Recker. He had another thought and he didn't say it out loud.

Why isn't the Ancidium joining them?

It was a question with several potential answers and Recker wasn't able to give the possibilities much consideration. The *Ixidar*'s next cannon finished charging and he fired it at another of the Lavorix battleships. A dark energy flash engulfed the enemy vessel's forward two-thirds and what remained when the blast faded wasn't going to trouble anything.

"The enemy spaceships are recovering from their transits, sir," said Montero.

Recker could see it too – the tactical became so crowded with missiles that the data became meaningless. His hand darted out and switched off one of the information layers, so that only the warships remained on the screen.

A scattering of plasma warheads exploded against the

Ixidar's energy shield and Recker took out a third Lavorix spaceship with a destroyer cannon strike. The Daklan were ruthless opponents and they were showing a remarkable coordination as they focused on the enemy craft, destroying them three at a time.

Ready for the chaos.

The moment came, as it did in every fleet battle. Countermeasures were unleashed and every warship unloaded their arsenals without restraint. Whites, oranges and pulsing reds appeared and disappeared, and dense clusters of interceptor missiles tore into the staggering waves of plasma warheads heading in both directions.

Still the Lavorix kept on coming and Recker stopped counting. The *Ixidar* had achieved a punishing velocity and it was incredibly agile. He fired the next destroyer cannon and then used the energy shield as a battering ram, knocking aside a sixty-billion-ton enemy battleship as if it were nothing.

"That impact affected our shield, sir," said Montero.

"Not enough to stop me doing the same thing again, Corporal," said Recker, smashing the *Ixidar* straight into a Lavorix heavy.

The *Gorgadar*'s particle beam cut a sharp line of blue across one of the feeds. It was a shot that broke one enemy warship in half and continued into a second a few hundred kilometres directly behind. Recker couldn't decide if the double-kill was a result of luck or if it was the most incredible demonstration of skill and timing he'd ever witnessed.

It wasn't all good news.

"The Daklan lost a desolator and three ravagers, sir,"

said Montero. "And one of their annihilators is under heavy fire."

"Focus on the *Ixidar*!" Recker yelled at his opponents.

The enemy weren't listening. While the *Ixidar*'s energy shield was subjected to a sustained bombardment, the Lavorix didn't forget about the Daklan. Outnumbered and lacking energy shields of their own, Ildir-Ta-Rok's fleet would be whittled away with inescapable certainty, and there wasn't a damned thing Recker could do to stop it.

"We've still got ninety Lavorix warships on the tactical, sir," said Montero. "But there's been nothing new for the last twenty seconds."

"What I wouldn't give for another decay pulse," shouted Recker through his chin speaker.

"I'd give double," said Aston.

"We've lost another stabiliser, sir," said Eastwood. "The rate of switchover is increasing. On the plus side, our energy shield is recharging so quickly it's nailed on one hundred percent."

"Lieutenant Eastwood, I thought I asked you to pinpoint the Ancidium."

"I'm on it, sir. The lightspeed tunnel data contains more precise coordinates, but I'm having to drill down through a lot of unfamiliar crap to find them."

Recker targeted and destroyed yet another battleship. With two of the *Ixidar*'s cannons out of action, he'd modified the charging pattern so that the failed guns were cut out of the sequence. Already he was adapting and by altering the warship's roll hardly any of its efficiency was lost, as the Lavorix were learning to their cost.

"We're dancing to our enemy's tune," said Recker. "The Ancidium either doesn't want to commit, or it doesn't see the need."

"It's got to be the destabiliser, sir," said Aston. "They're scared we've figured out what it does."

"Our batteries are at thirty-three percent, sir," said Larson. "I fired the Extractor again and the charge level dropped."

Gritting his teeth, Recker took his frustration out on the enemy fleet, reducing two of their largest vessels to powder in rapid succession. By this point, the nonstop plasma explosions against the *Ixidar*'s shield were taking their toll and the reserve gauge was falling – not rapidly, but steadily enough that it would collapse long before this fleet of Lavorix warships was finished.

For a period – Recker wasn't keeping count of the seconds or minutes – the two sides exchanged fire. The *Ixidar* and the *Gorgadar* inflicted enormous harm on the opposing forces. Each shot from a destroyer cannon reduced the enemy total by one and to Recker, piloting the *Ixidar* had become second nature. He revelled in the way it responded to the skill of the pilot and how it tore through its opponents. Truly, it deserved to be called The Destroyer.

Yet, it wasn't going to be enough. The enemy fleet still numbered sixty and they made hardly any effort to evade the *Ixidar* or the *Gorgadar* – not that it would have done them much good. Slowly, they were coming out on top.

As if to rub salt in the wound, another ten Lavorix spaceships exited lightspeed within a few thousand kilometres of the ongoing engagement. Recker wanted to take advantage of their stationary positions, but he had too many other targets on his mental radar. He disintegrated an enemy battleship that was focused on Ildir-Ta-Rok's flagship and then got a second one in his sights. The next gun wasn't charged in time and Recker chose another Lavorix warship instead.

"Down you go," he said, reducing its outer five hundred metres to powder. What remained was no threat, and Recker's eyes sought out the next target.

"We've got to change this!" he said, loudly so the crew on the *Gorgadar* would hear the words over everything else.

"How?" asked Burner. "We're outnumbered and we can't retreat without leaving the Daklan neck deep."

"Lieutenant Eastwood, I need you to locate the Ancidium!" said Recker.

"I'm doing the best I can, sir." The man sounded stressed, though that wasn't always a bad thing when it came to Eastwood.

"Why is it so important, sir?" asked Aston, her own voice fraying. "We don't have a destabiliser. The *Gorgadar*'s Extractor only worked once against the Ancidium and the only other weapon confirmed to damage the enemy ship is the particle beam. It'll take a few hundred shots from that to do any serious harm!"

Recker didn't want to give up and, even as his brain formulated a reply, he landed a destroyer cannon shot on a Lavorix heavy cruiser. He didn't watch the aftermath and switched his attention to a new target, while he counted down the recharge for the *Ixidar*'s guns.

"We can't lose this," he said.

Recognition followed immediately after he spoke. Whatever he said, this battle *was* lost and he doubted the Ancidium had dispatched any more than a fraction of the warships in its hold. Defeat hadn't happened yet, but the bitterness of it was there nonetheless.

For once, no amount of effort, skill or experience was going to be enough to turn things around. The Lavorix were on the verge of victory over the only two warships capable of inflicting any serious harm upon their fleet, and Recker either had to let it happen or abandon his allies and get the hell out of the Evia system.

Recker cursed everything for bringing him to this moment.

CHAPTER TWENTY-EIGHT

"CORPORAL MONTERO, open a channel to Admiral Ildir-Ta-Rok," said Recker. "I need to tell him this myself."

"We're getting out of here?"

"We have no choice, Corporal." Recker disintegrated a Lavorix battleship, just as six more emerged from light-speed. He glanced at the *Ixidar*'s shield reserves. "Twenty-five percent," he said.

"Sir!" yelled Eastwood. "Another two of our stabilising modules went into superstress!"

"The destabiliser is now available!" said Larson with equal excitement.

"We thought the destabiliser required energy from the life batteries and maybe it does, but the superstressed propulsion modules must be enough to activate the weapon!" said Eastwood.

"The *Ixidar*'s shield is in a bad way," said Recker. "It'll collapse soon."

"I'm analysing the last of the data for the Ancidium's inbound lightspeed tunnel, sir. I should have their location any moment."

Even as he talked, Recker never let up on the controls and the *Ixidar* continued tearing through the enemy fleet. The Daklan had lost seventeen of their ships and two of the annihilators had exhausted their lightspeed missiles. Constant reinforcements had brought the enemy fleet up to sixty-three, though Recker didn't lose his appetite for cutting them down.

"I have Admiral Ildir-Ta-Rok on the comms, sir," said Montero.

"Pass him through."

"Captain Recker, we are not outfought, yet this battle is lost," said the Daklan.

"I don't think the Lavorix are even trying, Admiral. If we came with two hundred ships, the Ancidium would have sent five hundred to meet us."

"No doubt you are correct. It is time for you to leave the Evia system. There is no need to lose the *Ixidar* and the *Gorgadar* – they will prove useful when the Ancidium arrives at your planet Earth."

This was the best of the Daklan, reminding Recker in a way he didn't need what selfless and loyal allies they were - their word truly was their bond, in letter and spirit.

"We may have to leave your warships behind, Admiral, but I assure we're not running from this encounter," said Recker. "The *Gorgadar* is carrying a weapon called the destabiliser and we're going to use it against the Ancidium, just as soon as my engine man has determined its precise location."

"Will this destabiliser bring victory?"

"I don't know, Admiral. We've had little time to study the *Gorgadar* or learn how it operates. I believe the destabiliser is what killed the original crew. I intend to test it out on its creators."

"Very well. Do as you must, Captain Recker."

Recker closed out of the channel and maintained his assault on the Lavorix fleet. The *Ixidar*'s shield was absorbing far more impacts than a few seconds ago and the reserve gauge dropped below fifteen percent.

"I think the enemy have had enough of us, sir," said Montero. "We're taking a lot more fire now."

"Lieutenant Eastwood, you may have the luxury of a fully-charged shield, but we on the *Ixidar* do not. Please find those coordinates."

"Nearly there, sir!"

A salvo of several hundred warheads detonated against the *Ixidar*'s shield and the gauge fell to nine percent.

"We're running out of time, Lieutenant Eastwood."

At that moment, the dodecahedral warship Recker had seen in the Ancidium's construction yard appeared from lightspeed, complete with the hole created by the *Gorgadar*'s particle beam. Recker didn't need to alter course to put a destroyer cannon shot into its shield. The blue sphere darkened, but didn't collapse. In a few seconds, the enemy warship's sensors would be online, its crew would be oriented and the *Ixidar* would go down in a barrage of dark energy.

"Have a particle beam," said Larson with satisfaction.

The blue shaft of energy jumping from the *Gorgadar*'s

nose made a new hole in the huge enemy warship and Recker hoped it had taken out a few critical hardware modules on the way through. His wish wasn't granted and the dodecahedron accelerated across the *Ixidar*'s path, twelve thousand kilometres distant, and the intense light from the superheated alloy around the new particle beam opening left a blur on the sensor feed.

Recker gave it a second destroyer cannon shot and again the enemy warship's shield held. He was sure it would withstand another five or six shots, while the *Ixidar*'s would not.

Suddenly, many of the sensor feeds went completely dark and a sprinkling of amber lights appeared on Recker's console. The *Ixidar*'s shield gauge flashed orange and its reading had fallen to zero. A moment later, a hundred or more inbound missiles detonated against the warship's armour. It wasn't a fatal wound, but without its shield, the *Ixidar* was doomed.

"Lieutenant Eastwood, my shield is depleted," said Recker. He reached for the tactical screen, wondering if he should take an immediate mode 3 exit.

"Hold your course, sir!" said Aston.

Recker wasn't sure what she intended, but he did as she asked. The dodecahedral warship had begun rotating and he got a sense that its crew weren't competent to control twelve guns at once. It likely didn't matter – with its shield down, the *Ixidar* was easy meat.

"Next shot and we're goners," said Montero.

From Recker's left, the *Gorgadar* swept in under maximum acceleration. At the last moment, Aston slowed sharply and then matched velocity with the *Ixidar*. It happened just as Recker detected a dark flash and recoil from one of the enemy destroyer cannons. The blast hit the *Gorgadar*'s shield, turning it deep blue and leaving the *Ixidar* intact.

"Nice block, Commander Aston," said Recker.

He watched the dodecahedron ship bank hard as it attempted to bring its guns to bear again. Aston was having none of it and she held her ship directly between the enemy vessel and the *Ixidar*. It was an incredible demonstration of intuition piloting, though given the velocities and distances involved, Recker didn't think she'd be able to keep it up for long.

Lieutenant Eastwood came up with the goods in the nick of time.

"I've extracted the Ancidium's coordinates, and I'm sending them over to you, sir," yelled Eastwood. "Oh crap – I think they're warming up for a Gateway transit! They're getting out of here."

"How certain are you?"

"The readings aren't clear from this distance, and the background radiation isn't helping. But I'm sure enough, sir."

"It's going to Earth," said Recker. "Damnit!"

"And the *Gorgadar* just lost another stabiliser. When I guessed we had an hour, I was wrong. Every stable module is going into superstress. I've got an amber light on our energy shield generator – it can't handle the flow and it's going to fail soon."

As the missiles rained down upon the *Ixidar*'s armour

and Aston did her best to protect the warship from enemy destroyer cannons, Recker shouted his order.

"Lieutenant Eastwood – create a synch code – we're going inside the Ancidium."

"Sir, I don't know if the coordinates of the lightspeed tunnel's end point coincide with one of the internal bays. If we arrive in the middle of anything solid, we'll be destroyed."

"We should mode 3 next to the Ancidium, sir!" said Aston. "That's the only way we can be sure of a destabiliser activation!"

"The *Ixidar* has no shield left to withstand the corona's heat, Commander. If you and everyone else on the *Gorgadar* are to get out of this alive, I need this ship intact to mode 3 you out of there."

"That means a shuttle trip, sir. There's no time!"

"There will be no time if you keep arguing, Commander!"

"I'd rather die with the Ancidium than survive and see it escape to Earth!"

"It's not ending this way!" shouted Recker.

"Sir!" yelled Eastwood. "I've got what you need - the coordinates to the same bay we put a particle beam hole into last time we encountered the Ancidium!"

Recker didn't question how Eastwood had derived the precise coordinates of the bay. "Create the synch code, Lieutenant Burner. That's an order!"

"Synch code created, sir."

"Corporal Montero, accept that code."

"Code accepted, sir," she confirmed.

"Commander Aston, we started this together and we're getting out of it together. Activate mode 3."

"Damnit, sir, the destabiliser might kill us anyway."

"That's a chance I'm willing to take."

Aston delayed no longer. "Activating mode 3."

The short lightspeed journey left Recker feeling like he'd been punched in the guts, kicked in the balls and had a spike hammered into his skull, right between the eyes. It was the hardest in-out he could remember and it couldn't have come at a worse time. He groaned and tensed every muscle, as if it would somehow drive out the pain.

"Shitting hell!" said Montero with feeling. "Waiting on sensors. Waiting on battle network. Waiting on everything."

"Focus, Corporal," Recker snapped.

The sensors came online a moment before his brain regained the ability to interpret the visual feeds. He saw shapes and edges, along with misshapen lumps he didn't recognize. Then, his recovery from the transitions gathered pace and he understood what he was looking at.

"We're in the construction bay," he said, remembering the place where the Lavorix had been building their new Laws of Ancidium. The enemy hadn't swept up after the *Gorgadar*'s particle beam made its passage across the bay, and the spaces in between the part-built warships were littered with debris. The only ship missing was the dodecahedron.

"Battle network request received and accepted," said Montero. "Adjusting sensors. No targets detected. The *Gorgadar* is fifty klicks from our position and at the same altitude. Accepting new comms channel request from Lieutenant Burner. Bridge channel open."

"Sir, another bunch of our propulsion stabilisers went red," said Aston. "We don't have long before they're all red. Our shield module failed when we came out of the transit."

"Commander Aston, give the order! Activate the destabiliser," said Recker.

"Yes, sir."

The dodecahedron warship appeared in the bay, directly between the *Ixidar* and the *Gorgadar*, and Recker found himself staring down one of the destroyer barrels. His eye darted to the shield reserve gauge. Six percent wasn't going to be enough.

"The destabiliser! Do it!"

"Destabiliser activated," said Larson. "Good luck to us all."

Recker wasn't about to put his entire faith in an unknown weapon, and he shot the dodecahedron warship with the *Ixidar*'s cannons. It was a direct hit, but the Lavorix shield held.

Then, the destabiliser swept through him and it hurt as much as anything he'd ever experienced. The agony of it was terrifying and he thought his mind would shut down to protect him. Unconsciousness would not come and he clenched his jaw against the pain.

It's like I'm ageing ten thousand times faster than normal.

Still, the agony did not subside and Recker wondered if it would ever end, or if this was to be his new state of being. Belatedly, he remembered the Frenziol injectors in his leg pocket and he reached for one.

As quickly as it had come, the pain switched off, leaving Recker dazed and in horror at the memory. Worst of all, was the fear that it might return unexpectedly. The thought was enough to make him jab the injector into his thigh and still, after everything he'd suffered, the needle's passage into his skin make him wince.

The Ancidium. Is it over?

He raised his head and looked at the sensor feeds. The dodecahedron warship hadn't gone anywhere, but it was stationary still, and it hadn't fired its cannons. Something else caught Recker's eye. The bay had changed – no longer was the air within it clear and dark. Now, the thickest of miasmas clung to the place, dense like lead, yet ephemeral and elusive at the same time.

A new death sphere. We did it.

The hope of victory didn't bring even a hint of joy and Recker guessed he was feeling the suppressive effects of the death sphere at their most potent. Every emotion was blunted and it took an enormous effort for him to speak.

"Commander Aston?" asked Recker. He cleared his throat and called out louder. "Commander Aston?"

"Yes, sir, I'm here."

"The Lavorix are dead. What's your status?"

"They're dead?"

"Yes, Commander. We created a death sphere and it killed the Lavorix."

"It really happened?"

Recker was as certain of this as he was about anything. "Yes, it really happened. Now tell me your status."

"Everyone's awake apart from Lieutenant Eastwood, Itrol and Litos."

"I'm here," said Eastwood. He sounded rough. "I know what you're about to ask, so I'll tell you. We've got five remaining stabilisers. When we lose the last one, there'll be nothing stopping the superstressed engines from entering a critical state."

"You'd better get out of there."

"I'll get everyone up and we'll be on our way," said Aston.

Recker owed his soldiers a debt for their service, but he felt no guilt at his first priority. He half-climbed, half-fell from his seat and stumbled across to Lera-Vel. She was face-down on the console, and, for a moment, he feared she was dead – killed like Unvak. With the greatest of care he reached out with both hands and pulled her upright. She groaned and her eyes opened enough that he could see her pupils.

"That was not..."

Her eyes closed again and then opened once more. Lera-Vel tried to smile and Recker knew she was going to recover.

"I need to check on the others," he said.

"Go."

The squad members were rousing themselves and Corporal Hendrix was dragging her medical box towards the still-unconscious Zivor.

"See to the ship, sir," said Hendrix, without looking up.

"Report when you're done, Corporal."

"Yes, sir."

Recker's strength was returning and he returned to his chair. The moment he was seated, his body demanded he sleep, while the new dose of Frenziol demanded that stay awake. It was tempting to close his eyes and find out if death sphere or Frenziol would come out on top, but Recker didn't take the risk.

Instead, he watched the sensors and waited for the emergence of the *Gorgadar*'s shuttle.

CHAPTER TWENTY-NINE

ALONG WITH HIS returning physical strength, Recker found his emotions were steadily climbing from the pit into which they'd sunk. He still didn't feel anything like normal, but now the urgency of the situation was making him take greater notice.

I've got to fight this, he told himself. Straight after came the counter-thought. *Why bother fighting the death sphere? If we get out of here, we win. Otherwise, we lose.*

"Damnit," he growled. "Corporal Montero, find out if Commander Aston and the others are patched into the *Gorgadar*'s internal comms."

"They are, sir. You need to scan for the receptor."

Recker did so and he linked to the shared channel used by the *Gorgadar*'s crew. "What's your progress?" he asked.

"We're heading for the shuttle, sir," said Aston. "Itrol died, everyone else is with us."

"Another death," said Recker. It would hit him hard

later, he knew. "How long before we lose the last stabiliser?"

Eastwood answered. "I've created a link between my suit computer and the monitoring hardware. We're down to four stabilisers. No, make that three stabilisers."

Shifting his gaze to the *Gorgadar*, Recker studied it for any indication of what was happening within its hull. He saw nothing different.

"I'm bringing the *Ixidar* closer to you," he said.

The *Ixidar*'s hardware was unaffected by the destabiliser and Recker guided it around the dodecahedron spaceship towards the *Gorgadar*. One of the sensor arrays was aimed at the far wall, and he noted that the visible vibration he'd observed last time he was on the Ancidium was no longer present. Perhaps the change was significant. He didn't know.

"We're entering the shuttle," said Aston. "I hope you left the cockpit clean and tidy."

It was the first sign that Aston was recovering and Recker smiled a little. Perhaps it was the deadening of his emotions that made him remember Corporal Hendrix's words, back when he'd first discovered she was seeing Private Enfield.

Besides, you've already got what you need, except you're too dumb to see it.

She'd been talking about Commander Aston, Recker saw that now. He didn't spend any time wondering if Hendrix was right. Deep inside, he hoped she'd misread everything. It would be easier that way.

"The shuttle is powered up and I've sent the launch command to the *Gorgadar*'s control computer," said Aston.

"We're watching out for you, Commander."

The shuttle emerged, a tiny vessel against the might of the *Gorgadar*. It accelerated directly for the *Ixidar*, and Commander Aston rotated the transport mid-flight without slowing down.

"Stop showing off," said Recker.

"All in the name of speed, sir."

"Another stabiliser went into superstress," said Eastwood. "We're down to two. I'd suggest you get us out of here the moment this shuttle enters the docking tunnel, sir."

"Acknowledged," said Recker.

The *Ixidar*'s propulsion was already in overstress. He guessed he must have switched it automatically upon their arrival into the Ancidium's bay.

"One stabiliser left," said Eastwood.

Still travelling at speed, the shuttle disappeared rear-first into the docking tunnel. Recker didn't delay - he activated a mode 3 transit, holding the button down until he felt the shuddering re-entry into local space.

"That transit wasn't so bad," said Montero, the relief in her voice echoing that in Recker's head.

"Feels like the death sphere effects have lessened," he said.

"Not gone," said Montero.

"No, not gone. I wonder how much of it we brought with us." It was a question for later. "Find out if the *Gorgadar* is showing a comms receptor."

"Sensors and comms coming online. Scanning for receptors...none found, sir."

Recker opened a channel to his bridge crew. "Lieutenant Eastwood, the *Gorgadar* is no longer showing a receptor."

"My suit link is down as well, sir. That could be caused by distance."

"You don't think so."

"No, sir. The *Gorgadar* lost its final stabiliser and something happened."

"Hurry to the bridge." Recker switched out of the channel. "Where are we, Corporal Montero?"

"I'm running area sweeps - you'll know as soon as I know, sir."

The *Ixidar* had travelled a long distance – way beyond the fringes of the Evia system. When Corporal Montero located the Ancidium, she was confronted with readings and data that she lacked the training to understand.

"You've done far better than I could have hoped, Corporal Montero," said Recker. "Lieutenant Burner and Lieutenant Larson will be here soon. This is one for them to deal with." He stared at the readouts. "Probably Lieutenant Eastwood too."

His crew entered the bridge and Corporal Montero returned to the squad. A few minutes earlier, Corporal Hendrix had reported no additional deaths, which left Itrol as the only casualty. Nobody was celebrating.

"What are we looking at?" asked Recker, once the others had taken their seats.

"I don't know," said Burner. "We're about fifty billion klicks too far away."

"I'll take us closer," said Recker. "Another mode 3. If we find any Lavorix, we'll deal with them."

"Should I contact Fleet Admiral Telar first?" asked Larson. "Does he know what's happened?"

The question caught Recker by surprise. "I haven't spoken to him. You'd best let him know, Lieutenant."

Recker's error didn't bother him much, though he was aware enough to realise that it should have done, and aware enough to worry that the destabiliser might have left him permanently dulled. He checked the shield gauge and it was at one hundred percent. "Activating mode 3."

This next transit carried the *Ixidar* to within a hundred million kilometres of the Evia star and Recker left the warship stationary where it had arrived. The hull sensors indicated it was cold outside – far colder than expected, given the proximity to the star.

On the main sensor feed, Recker saw an immense sphere of the strangest darkness, directly between the *Ixidar* and Evia.

"The Ancidium is in the exact middle, and there are many smaller warships clustered around it," said Burner. "I wonder if some or all of the fleet that was attacking us returned to the mothership when they learned we'd entered one of its bays."

"Maybe," said Recker. "Is there still no sign of Daklan survivors?"

"No, sir. I've located debris at the place of the engagement, but it'll take time to unravel which piece belongs to which ship. Ildir-Ta-Rok has had enough time to enter lightspeed and get out of here."

"Tell me about the sphere, Lieutenant."

"It's four million klicks in diameter - bigger than Evia -

and the farthest extreme of it is probably touching the star's surface."

This new death sphere let through the intense light of the star, yet at the same time muted it, as if the two were in conflict. Stranger still, it appeared as though nothing was moving, making it seem like a static image, rather than a live feed.

"Our sensors are gathering hardly any data from the sphere, sir," said Larson. "They're working fine if I focus them elsewhere."

"What happened here?" asked Recker.

"I think we're looking two spheres, not one, sir," said Eastwood. "One created by the destabiliser and the second an aftereffect of whatever happened when the super-stressed ternium went critical."

Recker had the feeling that Eastwood, Burner and Larson, all had their own ideas about this phenomenon. He didn't push them for answers and let them continue monitoring.

While that happened, Fleet Admiral Telar came on the comms and Recker gave him the details of the engagement. Admiral Ildir-Ta-Rok and a few members of the Daklan fleet had survived. Details were scant.

"You sound...dead," said Telar. "I know the price was high, but we won."

"I want to be happy, sir," said Recker. "The destabiliser has affected us. I can't feel much of anything."

"Come home, Carl," Suddenly Telar's voice cracked. "I don't want to lose you after everything you've done."

Recker felt something on his cheek and he lifted his

helmet. He touched a fingertip to his face and it came back glistening with a tear.

"Thank you, sir," he said.

Fingers brushed Recker's hair – hair grown too long during his time away. He turned and Lera-Vel was there, her own helmet removed and in her eyes he saw everything he'd ever wanted and never known.

Recker took a deep breath. "We've done it, folks." He smiled at them in turn. "Lieutenant Eastwood, set a Gateway course for Earth. Let's get the hell out of here. It's time for a rest."

OTHER SCIENCE FICTION BOOKS BY ANTHONY JAMES

Survival Wars (Seven Books) – Available in Ebook, Paperback and Audio.

1. Crimson Tempest
2. Bane of Worlds
3. Chains of Duty
4. Fires of Oblivion
5. Terminus Gate
6. Guns of the Valpian
7. Mission: Nemesis

Obsidiar Fleet (Six Books – set after the events in Survival Wars) – Available in Ebook and Paperback.

1. Negation Force
2. Inferno Sphere
3. God Ship
4. Earth's Fury

5. Suns of the Aranol
6. Mission: Eradicate

The Transcended (Seven Books – set after the events in Obsidiar Fleet) – Available in Ebook, Paperback and Audio

1. Augmented
2. Fleet Vanguard
3. Far Strike
4. Galaxy Bomb
5. Void Blade
6. Monolith
7. Mission: Destructor

Fire and Rust (Seven Books) – Available in Ebook, Paperback and Audio.

1. Iron Dogs
2. Alien Firestorm
3. Havoc Squad
4. Death Skies
5. Refuge 9
6. Nullifier
7. Scum of the Universe

Anomalies (Two Books) – Available in Ebook and Paperback.

1. Planet Wreckers
2. Assault Amplified